SCORPIONS
FOR SALE

SCORPIONS
FOR SALE

LARRY ZOLF

First published in 1989 by
Stoddart Publishing Co. Limited
34 Lesmill Road
Toronto, Canada
M3B 2T6

CANADIAN CATALOGUING IN PUBLICATION DATA

Zolf, Larry
    Scorpions for sale

ISBN 0-7737-2356-0

I. Title.

PS8599.05S36 1989   C813'.54   C89-094770-8
PR9199.3.Z6S36 1989

Typesetting: Tony Gordon Limited
Printed in Canada

To Robert Fulford,
the best of friends,
the best of editors

And to the North End of Winnipeg

And to the CBC,
for providing so many of these
stories free of charge

CONTENTS

SCORPIONS
FOR SALE

Being of Sound Mind and Body

F lying home for his mother's funeral, Daniel Shtarker, the veteran journalist, was miserable. Not only was he bereaved, but he also had to meet his sisters and his brother, always a trial. His older brother, On the Ball Saul, was flying in from Vancouver. Sweaters Shoshannah, one of Daniel's two sisters, was coming in from Wichita. Too Good Teibel, the oldest sibling, would be at the airport to greet them. The funeral was tomorrow. Sunday was the reading of the will. It would be painful, and Daniel geared himself for the ordeal.

Still, he had something going for him. As the last of the four, he'd had a special bond with his mother. Born in the summer of 1934, the worst year of the Great Depression, Daniel was not an entirely welcome arrival. When Zipporah told her husband, Menachem, that she was with child, he was taken aback. Forty-two was too old to bear children, he argued.

Menachem was thinking of Teibel, his eldest, rapidly approaching sixteen, whom he couldn't afford to send to university to meet the right class of men. Then there was Shoshannah, the clotheshorse, who had enough sweaters and skirts to clothe all the naked women of Ethiopia. As for fifteen-year-old Saul, what future awaited him in the pool halls, blind pigs, and brothels that dotted the North End of Winnipeg?

There was also money to be taken into account. Menachem's double duty as the *Jewish Street Fighter*'s chief ad salesman and

1

features writer brought a pittance. Teibel and Shoshannah were both ferocious eaters and Saul was no slouch. Menachem could barely make ends meet as it was; a fourth child (with his luck, another girl) was impossible.

Nor was there room in the shanty the Shtarkers were forced to live in. Already Menachem and Saul slept in one bedroom, Teibel and Zipporah in another. A blanket resting on a rope separated Shoshannah from her father and brother.

So, two days after the pregnancy announcement, Menachem confronted Zipporah with an ultimatum: her fetus must go! Since abortionists (or doctors of any kind) hardly abounded in the North End of Winnipeg, Menachem recommended the best-known remedy. "Take hot baths," he said. "Hot baths will do the trick. Hot baths are a Jewish woman's best friend." Since Zipporah was somewhat religious, Menachem assured her that even the Vilner Gaon, legendary giant of Orthodox Jewish scholasticism, had once noted that hot baths were particularly good for the Jewish people because they opened up the pores of the Jews to the message of God.

Zipporah was unconvinced. A fourth child, perhaps a boy, could be her companion in middle age. A second boy would balance her two daughters. True, the Shtarkers were poor, but if there was enough to feed Teibel, Saul and Shoshannah, why shouldn't there be enough for a fourth? Besides, she reasoned, God doesn't place fetuses in the wombs of pious Jewish women so they can drown them in hot baths. But Zipporah did not contradict her husband. Instead she took all steps necessary to preserve her child. Menachem had ordered hot baths; Zipporah, to be on the safe side, took no baths of any kind. The result was that Daniel Shtarker arrived in the maternity ward of St. Stanislaus the Avenger's Polish Roman Catholic Hospital as possibly the smelliest baby born in the Dominion of Canada that Depression day.

ZIPPORAH told the abortion story to Daniel when he was very young. Even then he laughed heartily at it, though he didn't quite understand it all. Sitting in the plane, strapped in, halfway through his third double Scotch, Daniel realized that from now on there would be no more stories, nobody around whose memory bank could tell him what he was like back when. With both his parents gone, Daniel felt alone and frightened.

To shake off his mood, he brought back the stories he'd shared with Zipporah. There was her marvellous tale of how her village celebrated the defeat of the Russian navy in the Russo-Japanese War of 1905. The celebration had to be secret, said Zipporah, lest the czarist authorities find out and launch a pogrom. "It was nice to see little yellow men beat the bully Russian bear at his own game," Zipporah said. She was also impressed with the demeanour of the German occupying forces in the First World War. "They wore helmets with a spike in the top of them. They always clicked their heels and removed their helmets when I walked by. They were perfect gentlemen, but they certainly thought I was kind of cute."

Daniel loved Zipporah's story of how she met Menachem. "Menachem's older brother, Mendel, had his eye on me. Mendel came calling to ask my father for permission to take me out. My father believed his daughters should be consulted in matters of this kind, so he went upstairs to get me. I didn't find Mendel attractive, so I hid under the bed and he couldn't find me." Mendel was furious and told his brothers he had been treated shabbily. They designated Menachem to go and woo Zipporah, win her heart, and then jilt her, teaching her a lesson.

Menachem then was a captain in Alexander Kerensky's revolutionary army. Looking resplendently military, he came calling on Zipporah. This time she didn't hide. She went for long walks in the woods with him. She was tall, long legged, full breasted, and a good listener. On the banks of the Dnieper, Menachem read her the personal manifesto he had given the Kerensky Army Recruitment Office:

To: The Russian Revolutionary Army
Dear Sirs:

Whereas, I, Menachem Shtarker, have hitherto refused to

shed my blood for the bloody Nikolai the Second, enemy of my people, and

Whereas the great Revolution has freed my people, and all other peoples that inhabit Mother Russia, I today present myself in payment of my holy debt of loyalty to the Fatherland.

Zipporah, many years later, said to Daniel, "How could I help falling in love with someone who could write that? And your father fell in love with me. Revenge was forgotten. But Mendel never spoke to your father again."

Daniel also remembered the many lessons in life Zipporah had passed on. As a youngster, Daniel would go with his mother to shop at Eaton's on Portage Avenue. It had elevators, stairs, and an escalator. Daniel and Zipporah always used the elevators or the stairs, never the escalator. Once Daniel asked her why.

"That's easy, my son," she said. "Do you remember Mrs. Greenberg who lived down the street?"

"Yes, Ma."

"Mrs. Greenberg," said Zipporah, "used an escalator once and never came back!"

Toward the end of the war, a newsreel at a movie theatre showed Mussolini and his mistress hanging from their heels. The theatre audience cheered, but Zipporah remained silent. As she told Daniel, "Never wish for the death of a tyrant. The next one may be worse."

ZIPPORAH'S funeral was a success. The streets were lined with people waiting to see the cortege. Hardened Ukrainians and Poles, who all knew her well, mourned her passing. Telegrams from the prime minister and the premier of Manitoba were read at the service. A Talmudic scholar, Rabbi Reuben Untermeyer, gave the eulogy. Zipporah's two sons and eight distinguished Winnipegers carried the coffin.

Later, Daniel went back to the family home for a last look. Sitting in the kitchen, he decided he needed a cup of tea. He reached for the sugar bowl and found behind it a file card on which was written, in very clear Yiddish: "I, Zipporah Shtarker, being of sound mind and body, leave all my earthly possessions, equally, to my four children, who are in order of birth: Teibel, Saul, Shoshannah, and Daniel." It was signed: "Zipporah Shtarker, Jewish wife and mother."

Daniel found a second card with the same words in the laundry chute, a third behind the furnace, a fourth, fifth, and sixth in the bedrooms upstairs, a seventh in the china set, an eighth in the refrigerator.

The bank manager phoned to have the family witness the opening of Zipporah's safe-deposit box. Inside were seventeen thousand one-dollar bills. The family lawyer later noted that with the sale of the house the estate would come to $40,000.

Riding back to the hotel where Saul, Shoshannah, and Daniel were staying, Saul said, "I don't need the ten thousand that's coming to me. Let Teibel have my share." Teibel, married to a cap maker, was the least prosperous of the four Shtarker children.

Shoshannah, who was living on precarious wealth but didn't know it, chimed in, "Give Teibel my ten thousand too."

Daniel was infuriated. "Excuse me, Mr. and Mrs. Showoff, but I didn't see either of you giving Teibel a ten-thousand-dollar scholarship for her children while Zipporah was still alive to enjoy such an act of generosity. Mother left eight copies of her will, the wording of which she no doubt got from watching soap operas, so one thing would not happen. That thing is the shaming of Teibel, her oldest daughter and best friend. I'll take my ten thousand, thank you, and spend it on my family. Teibel has survived so far. She never needed your charity before. She doesn't need it now."

Zipporah's estate was divided as she wished. The memory of Zipporah, however, could never be divided. Daniel Shtarker held it, pure and whole, for the rest of his life.

Landlords, Cats, and Rats

T he home the Shtarkers lived in from Daniel's birth to his bar mitzvah in 1947 was a two-bedroom *chaloopah*, a dump. Until Teibel's wedding, shortly before the war, Teibel and Zipporah slept in one tiny bedroom. The master bedroom contained Daniel's crib, a bed for Menachem and Saul, and the bed on which Shoshannah slept, separated by a blanket hanging on a rope. When Daniel reached the age of two, he moved into the bed with his father and his brother.

A coal furnace in the basement heated only the living room and dining room downstairs. The kitchen stove sent heat by pipe to the master bedroom, but by 4:00 a.m. the stove died. Teibel and Zipporah froze nightly in their bed. Anyone using the washroom in the middle of the night was as courageous as Scott of Antarctica and probably colder.

The basement of this fourplex was a labyrinth and a fire hazard. Thin wood partitions separated the Shtarker basement from their next-door neighbour, Mrs. Shechwitz, and she from the Rosenbergs, and the Rosenbergs from the Kleimans. Small fires occurred often, and when firemen came in to douse the flames the neighbours outside let out loud cheers. Daniel, a performer at heart, took the applause as his and bowed gracefully outside the house. When the firemen — Anglo-Saxons all, from the fire station just a few blocks away — finished their work, Daniel spoke on behalf of all the neighbourhood. "Servants of the British Empire, we salute you!" The firemen and Daniel exchanged salutes and the firemen departed.

After the fires, Daniel would go across the street to Smitnik's Groceteria. At Smitnik's the boys gathered around the potbelly stove in the middle of the store. Berl Zivtok, the anthem writer, was one of the boys. Berl had written four hundred anthems and sent copies of them all to Buckingham Palace. Finally the Palace replied with a letter, curt and minimalist, that said virtually nothing. Still, it was agreed that nothing from Buckingham Palace was something.

Aaron Globisch was another regular. Globisch was Smitnik's landlord; he also owned the Polish block, twenty suites, all unheated, just across the street from St. Stanislaus the Avenger's Polish Roman Catholic Church. For each of his Polish tenants, Globisch provided a woodshed, wood, and an axe. As landlords went, Globisch was a saint. Delays in rent payments due to drunkenness or illness were excused. Indeed, medical help was secretly provided. So were loans at no interest.

At Smitnik's, after a fire, Daniel was a big hit. He would describe each detail of the fire with such gusto that the boys began to feel sorry they had no fires in their basements. At the end of each performance, Globisch would yell, "Smitnik, give the boy a Cadbury's cream caramel on me!" Wartime regulations forbade the sale of chocolate bars, but Smitnik's always managed to come up with one for the young Jewish firefighter.

Zipporah, unfortunately, didn't share Daniel's enthusiasm for fires. To Menachem she said, "In Lithuania I lived in a fine house with four sisters and no fires. The house was brick, my father owned a foundry. I have travelled an ocean to die in a firetrap like this." Zipporah's feelings didn't improve when, two days after a fire, Daniel rushed in yelling, "I think there's something wrong with Mrs. Shechwitz!" There was. She was dead, slumped over in her rocking chair. The smell was awful. Mrs. Shechwitz, Zipporah guessed, had been dead for over a week. There was cat pee and cat shit all over the place. Rosenbergs' Cat had been there lately, Zipporah concluded.

Daniel's story of the Shechwitz death was a big hit at Smitnik's, but Zipporah was not amused. She told Menachem, "Daniel is not even six and he's already faced death. He won't reach bar mitzvah at this rate. We've got to get out of here."

The Shtarkers did, but only for a week. Mrs. Shechwitz's body had spread bedbugs and cockroaches through the fourplex, and Saul took Daniel to city hall to show the mayor Daniel's bedbug bites. The mayor, a socialist, agreed to act. The fourplex was fumigated by the city, which also paid for a seven-day Shtarker holiday at Winnipeg Beach.

Mr. Gutkeit, the landlord, was a prince, as refined as Leslie Howard. "Zipporah," he would say, "your beauty is a menace to those innocent of heart." To Menachem, Mr. Gutkeit would say, "Your editorials are pure Chekhov, pure Mark Twain." This was naturally quite easy to take. On his visits Mr. Gutkeit would always stay for tea, often for supper, and always for at least three hours. He took note of the problems in the house and sometimes fixed them. But even Mr. Gutkeit's charm didn't compensate for the fires, the bedbugs, the rats, and the mice. Zipporah was fiercely territorial about where she lived. It was her house, not the house of the bugs or the rats.

In her kitchen, beside the wash-basin, rested a large snowshoe Zipporah had bought at a yard sale. When a mouse or rat surfaced from the hole below the sink, Zipporah would take a swipe at it with her snowshoe. Oftener than not, the rodent was decapitated. Satisfied, Zipporah would drop the body in the garbage.

Daniel loved watching his mother as a killer, and the boys at Smitnik's loved hearing about it. Globisch dubbed her the Butcher of Brest-Litovsk, both Menachem and Zipporah having come from a village near Brest-Litovsk.

Menachem decided to get the Butcher some help with the rats and mice. He paid a visit to a city street cleaner who collected cats as a hobby and for profit. For one dollar, Menachem bought what was said to be a true cat, a real fighter.

The cat's first months in the house were not promising. One night a noise awoke Daniel. He went downstairs and there, in the cat's mouth, was a mouse. Excited, Daniel ran upstairs to wake Menachem and Zipporah. They both ran down to the kitchen. For exactly three seconds, they glimpsed the mouse in the cat's jaws. At the sight of the Shtarkers, the cat let the mouse go. Menachem, disgusted, barred the cat from the house for a week.

When finally it was allowed back in, Daniel finally gave it a name. The cat's favourite pastime was sitting in the kitchen sink, watching the water drip from a leaky faucet. Cats hate water, but this cat would frequently get drenched when he stuck his head under the faucet; he was too stupid to get out of the sink. Daniel named him Tippush, the Yiddish word for the slow of wit. Tippush was more cowardly lion than fighting tom. Once the legendary ninety-pound tom known as Rosenbergs' Cat burst into Zipporah's summer kitchen and seized, right from Zipporah's hands, a huge porterhouse steak. Zipporah fought like a tigress to save her steak, but to no avail. Meanwhile, Tippush brought shame to the household by cowering behind the stove.

Several weeks later, in the labyrinth that linked the basements of the fourplex, Rosenbergs' Cat caught up with Tippush and broke his neck. Once again the Butcher of Brest-Litovsk was on her own.

The assassination of Tippush intensified Zipporah's grumbling. "You can't even keep a cat alive in this dump. Nor is this neighbourhood a safe place for young Daniel. He tells me things like Elsie Chyko is a prostitute and Lemmele Fiedler is an embezzler. How does he know these things? He's only eight years old. We've got to get out of this house!"

ONE DAY Mr. Gutkeit sold the house to Sergei Styrko, a man on the move — plasterer by day, landlord and developer by night. Sergei raised the rent and also insisted his wife be Zipporah's cleaning lady. "My vife, Olga," Styrko said, "strong like bull, smart like streetcar. She clean house, it glisten like diamonds. Cost you four dollar a week. Cheap, cheap!" It wasn't cheap. Zipporah dreaded Olga's visits. Olga would complain about Zipporah's housekeeping. Olga would complain about the mice and rats, as if Zipporah had brought them. Olga was poison, Zipporah said. A plea for a new home was raised again.

Menachem was certainly giving it a lot of thought. He had a

secret project on his mind but was biding his time until the war was over and people had money in their pockets to buy jewellery, perfume, roses, and — books.

Then came the worst blow of all. Sergei, after owning the fourplex for less than six months, flipped the property for a big profit to Leibele Tveizeit, the biggest slum landlord in town, three times the subject of *Winnipeg Tribune* investigations, five times a witness at coroners' inquests following deaths in his slums. Leibele was also a landsman, from the same town as Menachem. They had come to Canada on the same boat, had been agricultural labourers together for two years, and had attended the El Mole Rachmim services every Saturday morning. "I can't live here under Leibele's domination," said Menachem to Zipporah. "That would be too big a humiliation for me! We've got to get out of this house!" But he did not tell Zipporah of his secret plan. It was to be a book, a collection of his stories and features, plus new stuff. He had discussed his idea with the executive of the Jewish Writers Union of Canada West. Dr. Redbelly promised to canvass the Jewish communists for support and financing. Gershon Grosartik said he would look into a Freedom Workers Temple–*Street Fighter* joint publishing venture. Shabsi Spilkes was full of ideas for special events to raise money and publicize the book.

The enthusiasm of his fellow writers excited Menachem. He could hear cries of Author! Author! He was already planning how he would answer the comely Jewish matrons who asked him, "Are you not Menachem Shtarker, the author?"

"Yes, Mrs. Greenberg, I am!" Menachem would say, and then ask, "Are you not the handsomest woman in the North End of the city? Can I then interest you, Mrs. Greenberg, in a book — my book — that will help make your spiritual beauty equal your physical attractiveness. Besides, Mrs. Greenberg, my book will also make you laugh!"

Menachem's book would sell. He was sure of it.

Fiction Can Kill You

Menachem Shtarker may have been no Hemingway, but he too dabbled in the black arts of fiction writing. As the chief feature writer for the *Jewish Street Fighter*, Menachem was frequently called upon to engage in works of the imagination, and it was to Yiddish writers like Sholem Aleichem and Sholem Asch that he looked for inspiration.

Still, Menachem was a pioneer, evolving magic realist techniques rarely seen in a place as small and as sensitive as Winnipeg. One thing you could say about Menachem's stories in the *Street Fighter* is that magically they were realistic. When a rumour spread rapidly through the North End that a socialist alderman had been caught fondling a small boy in the basement of his hardware store, Menachem found himself called to the bar of literature. In Menachem's story it was a Liberal politician who did the fondling; it was a little girl who was fondled; and the transgression took place not in a grimy North End basement but in the stately River Heights home of a wealthy Jewish Liberal MP. With this story, Menachem Shtarker felt he had proved three important things: socialists do not molest small children; Liberals and capitalists generally can and do; only with the coming of socialism will child molesting disappear. Menachem was therefore surprised when Abraham Bukovsky, the socialist alderman, snubbed him in the street and refused to speak to him. Other socialists averted their eyes or crossed the street when they saw Menachem approaching.

11

Menachem's literary zeal remained unabated. In another short story, he detailed the remarkable changes that occurred to one Bronstein, who had given up Zionism to join the Communist Party. Shtarker wrote: "Bronstein, who had once been a laugher, a talker, a boisterous story-teller had become quiet, secretive, furtive, and dull. Bronstein, whose appetite for female flesh had once known no bounds, now preferred party cell meetings to his marital bed. Bronstein, the communist, no longer was the life of the party; the party was his life and his life was tedious." Brodsky, Shtarker's shoemaker, who had recently switched from Zionism to communism, tried to assault Shtarker with a half-sewn boot when Menachem entered Brodsky's store for shoe repairs one day.

Menachem's passion for incisive and revealing fiction drove him into areas that threatened his very livelihood. One of the members of the board of directors of the *Jewish Street Fighter* was a famous socialist grain merchant, Vladek Cheeribim. Vladek's wife, Adelina, was easily the fattest, roundest woman in the Canadian prairies and possibly in the world. One evening, at a supper dance held in honour of Dr. Zarab, the great Yiddish cultural critic, Menachem, who had never danced in his life before, suddenly got up, approached Adelina Cheeribim, and asked her for a waltz. As he manoeuvred her around the dance floor, Menachem said, "Adelina, you are a beautiful woman, with a true radiance. You are just like Stella Dallas." Adelina slapped Menachem across the face and ran away in tears. Vladek demanded Menachem's dismissal from his job. The furor lasted a few months, and fortunately for Menachem finally died out. Now, *Stella Dallas* was a best-seller in 1936, and an Oscar-nominated picture in 1938. Stella was a slattern, a drunk, and a bit of a dummy. It's fair to say that Adelina had read and seen *Stella Dallas*. It's equally fair to say that Menachem had not.

Menachem derived some literary nourishment from this experience. For the *Street Fighter*, he wrote a fable about a handsome prince who turns into a frog. One day a fat walrus asks the frog for a dance. The frog accepts and is crushed to death. When asked about the story, Menachem pooh-poohed any connection to the Adelina affair. He argued that his story was an allegory about the crushing of Czechoslovakia by the Nazis.

Dr. Zarab, the great intellectual, got his lumps from Menachem too. A close friend of Vladek and Adelina Cheeribim, Dr. Zarab was a lecher, famous for luring Jewish matrons to his hotel chamber and then seducing them. In a story by Shtarker a famous Jewish intellectual seduces a poor widow, who in her poverty asks for some money for the sexual favours just rendered. The intellectual declines to pay but instead offers the woman a copy of his latest book, a collection of essays on Jewish culture. The woman takes the book, reads it, is inspired, finds a job at the Jewish public library, and lives happily ever after.

Shtarker barely survived this story.

He ran further risks with "The Car with No Driver," another fable. A car with no driver starts driving slowly on Portage Avenue, at the southern end of the city, and is quickly perceived as a kind of miracle; people begin to follow it. As it turns down Main Street, the crowds behind the car grow. Taverns and pool halls empty, brothels lose their customers. The miracle of a car with no driver attracts bigger and bigger crowds. Finally, at Selkirk and Main, the heart of the North End, a traffic policeman stops the car, opens the door, and finds a four-foot-six-inch driver.

In real life, the four-foot-six-inch driver, who had indeed been stopped by a policeman, was Shmuel Fartik. The proprietor of Proletariat Publishing, Fartik was a member of the board of directors of the *Jewish Street Fighter*; it was to the board that Shmuel aired his grievances about Shtarker's magic realist fiction.

Again, Shtarker survived. "I have nothing against short people," Shtarker argued. "My story is an allegory about the hopes and dreams of the little people of this world for a new and better world."

Still, Menachem's worst literary moments came with what seemed at first an innocent little story, "Oi, If She Were Only Jewish," about a storekeeper in the interior of Manitoba. He is not rich and cannot afford to send his eighteen-year-old son to university in Winnipeg to meet some nice Jewish girl. Instead, the son meets and falls in love with a blonde, blue-eyed, Icelandic girl. The girl is charming and wonderful — but she is not Jewish. The mother of the boy keeps chanting, "Oi, if she were only Jewish," but admits the girl's qualities are outstanding. In the Shtarker story there is no resolution of the dilemma and the difficult situation. He left the resolution to the imagination of his readers.

The readers loved it. Praise poured in from everywhere, and Menachem even sold the story to a New York Yiddish newspaper. One day the doorbell rang and Daniel, aged six, ran to answer. Standing in the doorway, a folded umbrella in her hand, was a stout, serious woman of about fifty. "Is your father, the writer, home?" she asked.

"Who shall I say is calling?" young Shtarker asked.

"Just tell him it's one of his readers." Daniel passed on the message and Menachem, eagerly awaiting more praise, stepped into the doorway. "Murderer! Assassin! Liar!" the woman screamed. She beat Menachem over the head with her umbrella. "You've ruined my family, my life!" She kicked him in the shins. "You're nothing but a gossip, a yellow journalist."

The angry reader was the storekeeper's wife. Her son had fallen in love with a blonde, blue-eyed Ukrainian girl, and had run off with her. They had not been seen for months. "Oi, If She Were Only Jewish" was too close to the bone for her.

It was too close to the bone for young Daniel too. Seeing his father attacked frightened him, but Menachem was reassuring. "My son," he said, "the woman is mistaken. She doesn't understand it was only a story, a piece of fiction. Any resemblance between the story and real life is purely coincidental." Then, gathering steam, Menachem noted, "My son, the writing of fiction is a dangerous profession. Fiction can kill you!

"What is fiction? Sometimes it's the truth thinly disguised, sometimes it's a tale spun out of whole cloth. But a story must be told; an untold story is like an abortion — it's a denial of life."

Daniel, six years old, listened and said nothing. He was too young to know what he wanted to be in life, but fiction writing was not high on his list.

The Book

Y ou say in your book that a Liberal politician was guilty of fondling a little girl in a River Heights mansion. But my information tells me you were really talking about a revered and highly admired socialist alderman. You have slandered a good man, have you not?" The questioner was Calman Ketz, host of "The Jewish Hour," the Voice of Jewry on Winnipeg's airwaves.

Calman Ketz, a roly-poly travel agent, radio host, and lap dog of the Establishment, was grilling Menachem Shtarker on his book, *And So Help Me, God*. "Did you not poke fun at Shmuel Fartik's height in the story called "The Car with No Driver"?" Are you not picking on the handicapped, and giving the short end of the stick to short people? Did you not also make fun of Adelina Cheerebim's weight problem? This isn't story-telling; it's all pure slander!"

Menachem's real-life subjects financed Calman's travel agency and provided sponsors for his radio show. Calman knew about the howls of outrage Menachem had generated. Now, with Shtarker in his radio studio, he was attacking.

Menachem knew all this, but he was selling his book. Air time was to be seized, no matter how treacherous the terrain.

In his replies to Ketz, Menachem was modesty itself. "These are simple stories I've written. There may be mistakes here in paragraphing, the use of journalistic terms that don't belong in fiction,

15

and perhaps the style is a bit off, but these are stories from the heart. Any resemblance to anyone living or dead in these stories is purely coincidental. As long as the tales I tell are amusing, who am I to complain?"

But Menachem did complain bitterly to Zachary Zunenu, the literary critic of the *Jewish Street Fighter*. Zachary wrote that Menachem's stories were amusing but lacked style. Enraged, Menachem confronted Zachary outside the *Street Fighter* and said, "How's your wife, Zachary, the university professor? Is she still sleeping with the dean, or is it you that's sleeping with the dean? In any event, I can't separate the three of you. You should stop being a critic and stick to your day job. But of course you don't have a day job, do you? Of course you're a critic, and how much money does that bring in? No wonder you live off your wife while she lives with the dean!"

Zachary was not moved. He stuck with his original analysis and with his wife. Why not? When you're a Yiddish writer and critic, a meal ticket is a meal ticket.

Menachem was not proud of his outburst, but his response was clever in its way. He adopted Zunenu's criticism, deftly answering Calman Ketz's charges and then making a sly pitch of his own. He acknowledged the criticism, hinted that it was misplaced, and hoped it would arouse curiosity about his book.

The letters page of the *Jewish Street Fighter* was in full sympathy with Menachem; many writers recalled that Zachary had defended the British right to seize the Jewish refugee ship, *Exodus*; others noted that he had said Mackenzie King was a great prime minister. Shtarker's media strategy worked. Soon sales for the book were good and the United Left Labour Zionist Freedom Workers Temple held a banquet in honour of Menachem. Five hundred people attended, among them Zipporah and Daniel. Four hundred books were sold that night alone. The Jewish communist paper in Montreal, *Der Arbeiter Shmeist* — the workers' whip — said Menachem's book was "must" reading. Rabbi Yacov Weisman gave a sermon on it in the Butchers' Synagogue. The General Monash Jewish Branch of the Canadian Legion put up a table in the recreation room, piled high with Menachem's books.

In the rich South End of the city, Menachem peddled his book, Jewish door to Jewish door. Many bought it to get rid of Menachem. When he left their door, they dumped his book in the wastebasket. Menachem suspected as much but he chose not to see it.

Proud of his selling skills, he took Daniel with him on visits to garment manufacturers. In one factory, they were kept waiting an hour and a half. Then Moe Matzah, of Moe's Millinery, opened the door and said, "What are you peddling? Yeshivas in Palestine? The conversion of the goyim to Judaism? A donation for your family, maybe? What in hell do you want?"

Menachem said, "I'm selling a book of Jewish stories. Humble, amusing stories, perhaps lacking in style but making up for it in substance. These stories will make you laugh, they'll make you cry, they'll make you proud to be a Jew! Now, five dollars for a book that will do all that is a sure investment in oneself and in one's people."

"Look, I'm busy," said Mr. Matzah. "Here's five dollars. Keep your book. I don't read books. I'm busy."

"I can't do that," said Menachem. "I can't take your five dollars unless you take my book. Otherwise I'm a *shnorrer*, a charity case."

"Okay, give me the book — here's your money." Moe grabbed the book, went into his office, and threw it in his wastebasket.

Menachem was hurt; Daniel was crushed. "Why doesn't he want your book, Pa?" Daniel asked. "It's a good book. I like it."

Menachem laughed. "Writing is a business, son. It's capitalism. Daniel, I can sell anything — even scorpions — as long as I believe in what I'm selling. I've just made a sale. A sale is a sale. Of course I want people to read my book. But once they've paid me and taken my book, they can do with it what they want. It's a free country!"

Daniel thought *capitalism* an interesting word and decided to find out what it meant. Daniel and Menachem had lunch and went on further sales forays for the rest of the afternoon.

SOONER THAN he had expected, Menachem saturated the Winnipeg market. The Jewish communities of western Canada then became his target. Menachem hit the road.

From everywhere, he wrote back to Zipporah, telling of his discovery of Jews. One letter said: "I'm in Brandon. The place is quiet like a tomb. Everybody is Anglo-Saxon except for the owners of the two Chinese restaurants. I went there for information about Jews in Brandon. Their English was so bad I couldn't understand them. A truck driver pointed out for me an old synagogue on the outskirts of town. I reached the Brandon Jewish community, all fifty of them. I sold twenty-five books." A letter from Edmonton was despondent. "I am standing on Jasper Avenue looking at the faces of the people going by me. None has a fleshy nose and thick lips. None is Jewish. I despair of Edmonton. I'm heading for Calgary."

In Calgary, something wondrous happened to Menachem. He wandered into an office building, took the elevator to the offices of Citadel Gas and Oil, and sat down. There were three other people ahead of him. When Menachem's turn came, a secretary asked his name and ushered him into an office. He was stunned by the vastness of the room and the geological maps, framed in glass, hanging on the walls. There was also a picture on the wall of the man behind the desk holding the Grey Cup football trophy.

The man behind the desk looked no more Jewish than the people on Jasper Avenue who had so depressed Menachem. The man in the big office asked, "What can I do for you?"

Menachem made the sales pitch of his life. "I'm a British North American Jew," he said in broken English. "I deplore the Americanization of Canada. I deplore the American melting pot and I love Canada because it lets people be themselves, without having to march and salute flags. I've written a book about Jewish life in Winnipeg. That Jewish life is the same as Jewish life in Calgary and all over the West. Granted my book is in Yiddish; granted it may be a bit clumsy, but even Hemingway isn't perfect. I tell stories, simple stories from the heart. Some of these stories will make you laugh, some will make you cry. But all the stories will make you want to know, like, and work with Jewish people. Now, five dollars for my book can do all that for you; it's a very good investment in good race relations. I realize you can't read Yiddish, but I can arrange for someone to read the stories to you in English."

The tycoon roared with laughter. Rising from his desk, he approached Menachem and shook his hand. "I'm a Gentile and I can't read a word of Yiddish," he said. "But I have many Jewish friends in Calgary and I'm sure they can interpret your book for me. Otherwise I'll hire an interpreter. I can afford it and you're worth it. You're a true Canadian patriot and the best salesman I've had in this office in twenty years. Let me take you around the building and make some more sales for you."

He was Frank McMahon, a founder of Alberta's oil wealth. That afternoon, McMahon sold his fellow oil capitalists in the Petroleum Building a hundred of Menachem's books. The story of that sales exploit entered Alberta folklore. In Calgary, Shtarker was a best-seller.

The western trip was a success. An eastern trip was equally successful. Menachem had by his own hand and deed sold five thousand copies. The drummer could beat his drum. "Zipporah, we have the money," Menachem said. "Our *chaloopah* days are over. I found a new house. No more cats and rats. I'm a free man!"

Daniel, too, was overjoyed. He had learned that capitalism meant selling things. Menachem, the Kerensky soldier, Zionist, and socialist, was now a capitalist. Capitalism was fun and pretty neat. He went out to collect five dollars for Menachem from a deadbeat who had taken Menachem's book and not yet paid him.

The Great Debate

*I*N THE LATE SPRING of 1939, no United Empire Loyalist could match the affection Menachem Shtarker lavished on Anglo-Saxons and their institutions. Much of it was gratitude for being allowed into British North America, but part of it was admiration for the way Anglo-Saxons kept their distance from North End Jewry. Menachem compared this favourably to the situation in the United States. "America," he would say, "never leaves you alone. Into the melting pot goes everybody. Midgets, Mexicans, Apaches — they're all grist for the American Dream. But here in Canada a Jew is on his own. No pot to melt in, no identity to absorb, no flag to salute."

Menachem, however, joined in the pursuit of the Canadian identity. "When the German loses his colonies," Menacham noted, "he blames the Jews. When the Russian loses his crop gambling, he says it's the Jews who stack the deck. But when a Canadian loses, which is often, he only blames himself. Canadian self-loathing is a full-time business. They have no time to hate Jews!"

To someone so fiercely British North American and so Jewish at the same time, it came as a shock to hear that a group calling itself the British Israelites had invaded the public platform in Stella Park, North Winnipeg's bastion of free speech. There they proclaimed a heresy that simultaneously struck at Britophilia and Jewish pride, the twin pillars supporting Menachem's political philosophy.

The British Israelites, led by one Valiant McHaggis, insisted that Menachem and his 20,000 fellow Jews in Winnipeg were not truly Jews at all. Shtarker and company, according to the McHaggis gospel, were really Asiatics, perverted and demented offspring of a remote Tatar kingdom in the Ural Mountains. These so-called Jews, said McHaggis, were really Khazars; the Anglo-Saxons, on the other hand, were the Ten Lost Tribes and the only true Israelites.

It was Gershon Grosartick, his regular features and exquisite English enabling him to blend beautifully into a gathering of McHaggis supporters, who first told of this menace at a meeting of the Jewish Writers Union of Canada West. "McHaggis is crazy," Grosartick informed his fellow writers. "McHaggis has this Jews-kill-kings-for-profit routine. He says there's a direct link between regicide and Jewish advancement. He claims Cromwell chopped off King Charles's head and then allowed the Jews back into England. In France, King Louis lost his head — and the Jews got citizenship. In Russia, the czar was shot and the Jews took over. What's worse, McHaggis ends every meeting by telling his people the Jews may kill King George."

To Menachem, British Israelites were Nazis in the making. He rose quickly to the occasion. Rallying the Jewish Writers Union of Canada West, he issued a challenge to debate Valiant McHaggis in Stella Park. There would be decided the true racial origins of the Hebrew and the Anglo-Saxon.

A bilingual ad, Yiddish and English, was inserted in the *Jewish Street Fighter*, asking whether McHaggis had the courage to tangle with the master of inspired invective, Menachem Shtarker, British patriot and Jew. A letter to the editor of the *Winnipeg Free Press* reiterated the challenge.

Valiant McHaggis did not hesitate. Shtarker's challenge was quickly accepted. Soon telephone poles all over the city were festooned with posters demanding to know: "Is the True Jew You? Come and find out this Sunday afternoon at Stella Park at 2:00 to 5:00." Handbills appeared in the banks, libraries, delicatessens, synagogues, bookstores, chess clubs, and steam baths.

On Sunday Stella Park was a teeming, huddled mass of curious

Winnipeg humanity. From all corners of the city they poured in. Bully Boy Bulba, the Ukrainian Enforcer, brought all the weight lifters and musclemen from Smetana Sam's Gymnasium. Tea Leaf Tanya, proprietress of the Titanic Tea Room, set up shop at the outskirts of the crowd, offering predictions about the winner. Peter Paskuniak, the Ukrainian underworld czar, packed the crowd with his scoundrels and low-lifes. Stash-It Stosh, the Polish fence, sent his pickpockets to work the crowd. Lazy Leon, the Lubavitcher-Leninist, by day a socialist radical, by night a pious Chassid, brought his renowned ambivalence to the great event. Hot-dog vendors were busy satisfying rapacious appetites. Peter Paskuniak's bootleggers were freely dispensing poisonous home-brew. Policemen, on horse and on foot, lent the proper note of civility and turned a collective blind eye — on the entire proceedings.

The debate was worth waiting for. Valiant McHaggis was resplendent in Scottish kilt and red flannel tam, the insignia of the British Israelite movement adorning his chest. His badge asked the eternal question, "Would God Choose the Jews?" And his arguments impressed the crowd. Once again, McHaggis established the direct line that flowed from the Ten Lost Tribes of Israel to the Anglo-Saxon peoples of the earth. "Jesus and the Apostles, as anyone who cares to take a look at any painting can confirm, did not have long, bulbous, crooked Jewish noses, fleshy ears, and rotten teeth. Jesus and the Apostles were blonde and blue-eyed, cheerful and pleasant, like you and me. So-called Jews are really Oriental, and a danger to the Canadian way of life." As far as Valiant was concerned, Khazar Jews were Orientals fit only for domicile in Asia or Africa, Madagascar perhaps. "Or indeed why not Palestine for the Khazar Hebrews? With their noses they can blend in with the camels."

Menachem's response was swift, deflating, and above all patriotic. His voice rising ever higher, he recited the triumphant and glorious relationship of the Jewish people and the British Empire. Did not Lord Rothschild, Menacham asked, stand alone in the litter, the din, and confusion of the London Stock Exchange in total chaos, buying, buying, and buying, while the British capitalists were selling, selling? Did Rothschild not do this simply to maintain confidence in the British government until Wellington had finished God's work at Waterloo? How could anyone doubt the accuracy of the story, especially after seeing George Arliss, as Rothschild, do precisely that in the movie? "If not for Rothschild," Menachem declared, "England would have fallen, France would have ruled Europe, and Confederation would never have seen the light of day!"

Without Disraeli's shrewdness, Menachem asserted, the Suez Canal would have been another ditch, in French hands. Without Disraeli and the Jews, "the British monarchy today would be an empty shell, devoid of empire, Britain a tiny island in a sea of Frenchmen."

The audience was spellbound by Menachem's indomitable logic. Even Paskuniak and Bully Boy Bulba were startled into submissive silence. Oratory such as Shtarker's was not a daily occurrence even in North Winnipeg. Turning to McHaggis, Shtarker fired a dagger into his central argument. "If the British Israelites are right, and the Anglo-Saxons are the real Jews, why is Hitler not after them instead of us?"

This won the day for Menachem. Even McHaggis had to concede the brilliance of the counterattack.

The debate was over, the clear winner Menachem. In that late spring of 1939, North End Jewry had known the fight against fascism for the first time. Beaming, Menachem and Daniel headed home.

As they passed the Dybbuk Stops Here Delicatessen, Menachem saw Valiant McHaggis and three of his supporters eating smoked meat sandwiches. Menachem sighed. "It's a crazy world, son. McHaggis is convinced Jewish capitalists and Jewish socialists are in conspiracy to poison the world's food supply. McHaggis knows we wouldn't spoil our own food, so for safety's sake he eats kosher. Jewish food is keeping that fascist alive."

The Truth Peddlers

*E*very year Menachem and Daniel went to the Bank of Montreal building at Portage and Main to visit the lavish offices of L&L Properties. The owners, Lufthartz and Lebidig, were pillars of the German-Jewish community. Montague Lufthartz and Ludvig Lebidig had, years earlier, planted the L&L pennant firmly in the muddy flatlands that soon constituted the city's main streets. On Portage Avenue, from Petula's Porterhouse Steak House on the far west to Child's Restaurant at Portage and Main, most of the city's better enterprises paid monthly tribute to L&L. On Main Street, north and south, tithes to L&L flowed from Johnny's Polka Palace, the Revived Faith Temple, Bountiful Billiards, the union locals, and even the offices of the *Jewish Street Fighter*. L&L held mortgages on synagogues, churches, fruit stores, and slums. But Lufthartz and Lebidig were also philanthropists. Ludvig Lebidig chaired the board of a foundation for Jewish alcoholics. Montague Lufthartz was the spark behind the Hebrew Awareness Temple, a settlement house that taught deportment to recent arrivals from Galicia. Once a year Ludvig Lebidig took the kids from the Jewish orphanage for a ride on the Assiniboine in his motor cruiser.

And once a year L&L Properties bought an ad in the *Jewish Street Fighter*, in English only. (Yiddish they considered too vulgar a medium for a business message.) The ad, placed during the ten days of Jewish reckoning between Rosh Hashonah and Yom

Kippur, always said, "L&L Properties wishes its commercial, industrial, and residential tenants who are of the Hebraic Persuasion the best of the New Year season." It always included a financial statement listing L&L's assets and liabilities, the company's debentures, the preferred shares it had floated, and the many directorships in leading financial establishments held by either Lufthartz or Lebidig or both.

This implicitly reminded Winnipeg's harassed North End that some Jews did have their place in the sun, and it seemed to suggest that it was a privilege to be a tenant in L&L's dilapidated and intensely overcrowded apartment blocks. Such a privilege, the ad hinted, demanded prompt and unhesitating payment of rents on collection days, twice monthly, second and fourth Mondays.

Menachem Shtarker was aware of the advantages the L&L ad offered the *Street Fighter*, but it irked him that L&L refused to advertise in the mother tongue of the Jewish proletariat. Twice before he had tried to pitch L&L on the need to communicate to its tenants in Yiddish, but to no avail. His 1941 visit with young Daniel, following on the Nazi invasion of Russia, seemed to Menachem the perfect occasion to renew his request.

The war memorial in front of the Bank of Montreal building always inspired Menachem and enthralled Daniel. The bronze figure of the heroic Canadian Tommy, his fixed bayonet and rifle pointed in readiness, his solid iron jaw protruding from the straps of his all-metal helmet, inevitably aroused in Menachem a respectful and reverent response. "These Canadian boys died like flies in the Great War," Menachem would tell Daniel. "Wave after wave fell from the poison gas, the machine-gun fire, the shrapnel. These boys died to make the Empire safe for decent people, so we could live here. Someday, Daniel, you too may have to fight to keep Canada free."

Daniel enjoyed this annual ritual. In his mind's eye, he saw himself sweeping the German trenches clean, being lifted onto the shoulders of his comrades, publicly cheered on the main streets of French towns and villages, smothered by gentle embraces of French maidens. He could hardly wait to take his place among Canada's fighting men.

He also liked the Greco-Roman facade of the bank, its columns proclaiming that this was the temple of Canadian prudence and foresight. Inside, the glistening tellers' cages and the awesome marble pillars exuded confidence. The bank's coat of arms — the motto, In Perfect Security We Trust Perfectly, inscribed underneath — on the centre wall was impressive enough to reassure the most timid depositor. And Daniel loved the bank's elevator and the respectful dignity of the uniformed operator. Riding up, fighting off the sinking feeling as the elevator rested at each floor, gave Daniel the sensation that he was on an automatic stairway to financial security.

That reverie, of course, disappeared when Menachem and Daniel came face-to-face with the intimidatingly officious Miss Penelope Justice, confidential secretary to Messrs Lufthartz and Lebidig. "You are?" Miss Justice asked, showing Menachem and son no recognition of any kind and staring haughtily at Menachem.

"Menachem Shtarker, representative of the *Jewish Street Fighter*. I'm also the *Street Fighter*'s top feature writer. I'm at your service, ma'am. You remember us, of course. We were here last year on this very day."

Menachem's proffered hand was studiously declined. Tireless, Menachem remained unperturbed. "Say, a smart businesswoman like yourself," Menachem hinted broadly, "must have heard of the delightful piece of writing called 'She's Blonde and Beautiful But Is She Jewish?' I wrote that! I tell you, it was a sensation!" Menachem then whispered softly in Miss Justice's pin-shaped left ear, "If you don't believe me, ask the well-known counsels to the King — Rubinstein and Rubinstein, K.C. and K.C.! They said I was that short of libel—" Menachem pointed to the tip of the index finger on his right hand.

"An interesting and attractive woman like you," Menachem went on, "should find that piece of mine quite handy. I mean, just in case you should meet a tall, dark, handsome Hebrew who could sweep you off your feet!"

"I don't think that's likely," Miss Justice replied.

"Well, anyway, we've come on our annual visit. Is Mr. Lebidig or Mr. Lufthartz available to receive us?"

"Mr. Lebidig is in Europe. Mr. Lufthartz is here but he's busy. I'll see if he'll see you."

In Yiddish Manachem loudly whispered to Daniel, "A hideousness from hideous land." Daniel giggled furtively.

Miss Justice's ignorance of Yiddish and annoyance at Daniel's giggling did not improve her disposition. Mr. Lufthartz's request that the Shtarkers be ushered in at once came, as always, as a bit of a shock to Miss Justice.

"What can I do for you?" Montague Lufthartz inquired. Lufthartz, it seemed, always enjoyed the annual visit from the Shtarkers. A thin, ascetic man, short and dapper, he was a Hebrew of the British persuasion. His suit was Saville Row and his ascot would have made a Boodles man wince with envy. Above his massive mahogany desk hung a life-size portrait of Baron Nathan Rothschild; flanking the desk were two huge Union Jacks. On it, beside the pipe rack, was a map of Winnipeg on which the L&L properties were marked in orange, Mrs. Lufthartz's favourite colour. The North End of the city was a sea of orange.

"There's nothing you can do for me, Herr Lufthartz," Menachem insisted. "Selling and writing for a wonderful enterprise like the *Street Fighter* is more than a mere immigrant like me can ask for!"

"I'm glad you're happy, Herr Shtarker," the tycoon replied thoughtfully. "L&L Properties is a bit overjoyed itself. You know our motto, When the World Sells, L&L Buys. The world's been selling, Herr Shtarker! The whole universe is up for sale and for nickels and dimes only."

Rising majestically from his desk, Lufthartz gave his massive globe a playful spin. "In Canada, Mexico, Africa, L&L Properties has dealt itself a good hand, Herr Shtarker. Does the *Street Fighter*, Herr Shtarker, reach these markets? Does the peon in Mexico, the Zulu in Africa really care what's going on in your nickel-and-dime newspaper?"

"Nickels and dimes are all we're asking for," Menachem said wistfully. "A few more ads, perhaps some even in Yiddish, would certainly not frighten away the peons in Mexico, Herr Lufthartz.

In any case, perhaps in a Yiddish ad or two you can apologize to your Jewish tenants in Winnipeg, who may soon be freezing in their L&L apartments, as they froze last winter!"

Lufthartz's frigid silence simply encouraged Menachem. "In the Antarctica Apartments last winter, Herr Lufthartz, the heat was on so rarely and so low that Captain Scott of Antarctica could not have survived. The bedbugs in your Baltic Apartments are so big the children climb on their backs for rides. The rats in the Mediterranean Apartments are so big that Mrs. Goldberg's son, Avrom, the medical student, uses them for anatomy experiments. The other tenants trap them for furs and skins."

"You jest, Herr Shtarker, as always," Lufthartz acknowledged, a tight smile spreading slowly across his lips. "Too much heat is bad for Jewish blood. It only reminds Jews of the paradise they've lost in Palestine. Too much heat makes Jewish blood boil."

"I'm glad you mentioned Palestine, Herr Lufthartz," Menachem countered politely. "So many of your tenants have frozen that many of them have gone to the sands of Palestine instead. If this exodus keeps up, you may soon run out of tenants."

"Well, Herr Shtarker, Yiddish ads in the *Jewish Street Fighter* will not make me richer. If my tenants don't like my apartments, an ad in your newspaper will not make them love L&L. If they don't like L&L, let them move to Palestine." Pushing a buzzer at the side of his desk, Lufthartz summoned Miss Justice to show the Shtarkers out.

On this occasion, alas, the ritual of Shtarker's solicitations and Lufthartz's denials did not go according to form. Daniel thought Miss Justice was pushing Menachem along a bit too forcefully, and he was annoyed by Miss Justice's refusal to recognize the existence of Menachem and son. Certainly their talents deserved more than a heave-ho. Daniel eyed Miss Justice's thin, prim figure warily, looking hungrily for obvious weak spots. His growing sense of injustice transformed Miss Justice from a mechanical woman into a devil in need of exorcism. Falling slyly to all fours, he sank his teeth into her bony ankle. Miss Justice's cry of outrage, Lufthartz's hurling of his rack of pipes in anger at Menachem, the shouts for the security guards and the police — all these events convinced

Menachem and Daniel that their 1941 sales foray had not been successful. Grabbing Daniel by the collar of his shirt, Menachem dashed with efficiency and dispatch out of the L&L office doors. Down the stairway the Shtarkers fled, three floors to freedom.

"I don't know what it is about these rich Jewish magnates," Menachem confided to Daniel. "They don't have a taste for how the other Jewish half lives. But you, my son, have the appetite of a real *fresser*, a real glutton!"

Hangouts

S elkirk Avenue was the main street of North Winnipeg. On Selkirk you could buy bagels, egg loaf, chocolate cake, and tortes from Gunn's Bakery. You could sit and chat with the Jewish war veterans at the General Monash Branch of the Canadian Legion. The Dybbuk Stops Here Delicatessen served delicious corned beef sandwiches, and in the back room Canada's only chess master played regularly. St. Stanislaus the Avenger's Polish Roman Catholic Church provided interesting religious processions on Selkirk Avenue, Polish power at its most intimidating. Dr. Redbelly, the communist doctor, who treated his patients free and lectured them on Marxism, was on Selkirk. Dr. Redbelly had his office on the third floor of the Royal Bank building at Salter and Selkirk.

Zipporah often took Daniel with her on Selkirk Avenue shopping trips to Dain's Dainty Clothing, the shoe store Gladstone & Carr, and of course Oretski's, the only department store in North Winnipeg. Zipporah loved to bargain, in her own way. At Oretski's, once, Zipporah asked for a pair of Sisman Scampers fit for a little Jewish boy of eight. She waited quietly while the salesman examined Daniel's feet under the X-ray machine the store had just acquired. The shoes fitted Daniel and he was pleased. Stone-faced, Zipporah showed no emotion. When the clerk said the price of the shoes was ten dollars, Zipporah's face went from stoicism to granite determination. Her silence so upset the clerk that he went to fetch the store owner. "Good afternoon, Mrs. Shtarker," said Mr. Oretski. I see you've found a pair of shoes for Daniel. They grow so fast these days, it's hard to find shoes that can fit for three or four years. This makes a nine-dollar expenditure on Scampers worthwhile."

Zipporah nodded her head but said nothing. Without knowing it, she was using the John L. Lewis method of silent negotiation. Like the great American union leader, Zipporah was doing well. "Eight dollars should be a fair price," said Mr. Oretski. "They're Sisman Scampers. They should last for two years at least." This time Zipporah didn't even nod. She simply went deeper than ever into silence. "Well," said Mr. Oretski, "Passover is only a few weeks away and we'll have specials on everything. Why not start with these shoes, Mrs. Shtarker? Seven dollars is the price."

Zipporah reached into her purse, gave Mr. Oretski a five and a two, waited until the shoes were wrapped, and left without saying a word.

Daniel was so proud of Zipporah that he was beside himself. His mother was a real consumer, a real fighter for a fair price. Someday, Daniel thought, he would marry someone like Zipporah — tall, strong, and above all silent. Daniel would talk and his bride would listen, the way Menachem talked and Zipporah listened.

ACROSS THE STREET from Oretski's was another hangout, the State Theatre. Every Sunday afternoon, Zipporah took Daniel there to see Yiddish movies imported from New York. Fred Fife was the usher, the projectionist, and the manager of the State Theatre. From knowing so many Jews so long, Fife, a Scotsman, could almost speak Yiddish. North End Jews speculated that if he kept hanging around Jews and seeing so many Yiddish movies, he'd forget how to speak English. Fife was always courteous to Zipporah and Daniel. He steered them to the best seats and tipped them off about good movies to come.

Daniel wondered if there was really such a thing as a good Yiddish movie. The ones he saw all began with a festive Sabbath dinner. Gathered for the feast were great-grandparents, grandparents, many uncles and aunts, nephews and nieces, dozens of cousins, and a few odd friends. There were usually about fifty-eight people, somewhere in Poland. Zipporah and Daniel knew that by the end of the movie, fifty-seven of the original fifty-eight would die or disappear — some killed by typhus or in the Great War, some by tuberculosis, others from heart attacks, pneumonia or scarlet fever, still others in pogroms.

One day, Daniel asked Zipporah, "Why do so many Jews die in Jewish movies?"

Zipporah smiled lovingly. "The answer is simple. Jews die a great deal in real life. Why shouldn't they die in the movies!

"But we're here to live, Daniel, to thrive. Those movies are terribly overacted, but they remind me of home. Bad as it was — the anti-Semitism, the fascism — back home is still home. I miss it. If you don't want to come with me next Sunday, I'll go alone."

"I wouldn't think of it, Ma," said Daniel. He squeezed Zipporah's hand and thought about making his own Yiddish movie. In Daniel's movie there would be fifty-eight Jews at the banquet in the opening shot. Daniel's movie would close with a shot of sixty-eight Jews at a festive banquet — the first fifty-eight shot plus ten more. It would be up to the audience to figure out where the extra ten Jews came from.

Sticks and Stones Will Break My Bones

R abbi Yakov Weisman, scholar and Chassid, was a butchers' rabbi . . . to some butchers a saint, to others a scab, or an anarchist, or a troublemaker. Rabbi Weisman had been brought from Poland to Winnipeg in September 1939 on the last boat to escape Hitler. His sponsors were Jewish butchers who believed that the Kehila, the council of Orthodox rabbis, charged too much for certifying that meat was kosher. The butchers believed that Rabbi Yakov would offer his services on a much cheaper basis. This, in particular, was the sentiment of one Fred Kugelman, the proprietor of Kugelman's Kosher Sausage and the spiritual and financial leader of the dissident butchers. It was Kugelman who arranged for Rabbi Weisman's passage to Canada, helped to found the Beth Israel synagogue, bought the house on Derby Street for him to live in, and welcomed Rabbi Yakov on his arrival at Union Station.

Needless to say, the other Orthodox rabbis, led by the chief rabbi of Winnipeg, Rabbi Meir Abramson himself, resented the newcomer as a plaything of that ignoramus Kugelman. And when butchers put signs up in their windows announcing, "This meat made kosher by authority of Rabbi Yakov Weisman, Beth Israel Synagogue," the Kehila rabbis moved from passive resistance to active warfare.

On a certain Thursday in October, a week before the High Holidays, there assembled in the Tailors' Synagogue on Elm

33

Street: Reb Meir Abramson, his nine sons and seventeen disciples; Reb Shloime Kluger, his eight sons (the eldest, Aaron, an *eilu*, a real wizard) plus fourteen disciples; Reb Benjamin Akshen with twelve sons and twelve disciples; and, last and least, Reb Menasha Weinek, a mere junior in both wisdom and fecundity, with only six sons and four disciples.

The situation was self-evident, the remedy equally so. After Rabbi Meir quoted an appropriate passage from the Talmud and Reb Benjamin countered with an equally appropriate passage from the Mishne and Reb Shloime added a wise word from the Proverbs of our Fathers and Reb Menasha agreed with all that had been said, adding that what had been said was so perfect, so right, so wise and far-seeing that literally nothing else remained to be said, Reb Meir brought the meeting to a close with a last reminder to the assemblage that the Lord and Master Up Above, facing a similar rebellious situation, had told Moses, his disciple, to put to rout the iniquitous sons of Amalek.

The next morning at seven, thirty-six sons and disciples of the Kehila divided themselves into two picket lines, front and back of Kugelman's Kosher Sausage factory. Other sons and disciples took up picket duty front and back of the nine butcher stores of the sons of Amalek.

The Kehila pickets were well-behaved and smartly dressed. Their curly forelocks were combed, their caftans were neat and pressed, and on their heads they wore elegant, fur-lined *streimels*. Their picket signs were of good design and purest lucidity, reading (on the one side Yiddish, the other English):

ONLY KEHILA-ENDORSED MEAT IS KOSHER.
KUGELMAN'S KOSHER SAUSAGE IS NOT
KEHILA ENDORSED.
NEITHER IS THE MEAT
BEING SOLD AT
THIS BUTCHER STORE.
NEITHER IS RABBI YAKOV WEISMAN.

The Kehila picketed Kugelman's Kosher Sausage in three shifts, twenty-four hours a day, six days a week (excluding, of course, the Sabbath, since on this point the Talmud was very clear, the Gaon Elijah of Vilna himself having pronounced picketing to be an act of forceful exertion and therefore in violation of the Sabbath). The butcher stores were picketed mornings nine to twelve, afternoons two to four, evenings six to eight, and all day Friday.

Nor was this all. The pickets knew that a good picket line was one thing but divine help was something else again. If picket lines couldn't move a mountain like Kugelman, surely prayers would. With thirty-six pickets at Kugelman's, there were already enough for three congregations. So three times daily, back and front of Kugelman's factory, divine assistance was sought. Morning prayers, afternoon prayers, and evening prayers sent the names of Fred Kugelman and Yakov Weisman winding their way through Winnipeg skies toward the ears of the Almighty.

On the first morning of the Kosher War, at Kugelman's, Biff Elliott, an Irish truck driver, father of seven and a union steward, said, "Christ, I'll be damned if that don't beat all." He refused to drive his truck aross the picket line. Twenty minutes later, half that day's shift of sausage stuffers — twenty-two Ukrainian peasant girls — refused to cross the Pious picket lines. On first sight of the chanting sons and disciples of the Kehila, they crossed themselves. In their view, the bearded pickets were Wonder Workers capable of inflicting bad spells, the Evil Eye, and other hazards on simple folk who dared to oppose them. Kugelman's pleas and threats were to no avail. The girls remained outside, and that morning, only sixteen hard-headed Poles crossed the line.

At rebel butcher stores, the Kehila victory was total. After all, Reb Meir Abramson was the chief rabbi of Winnipeg, a patriarch, eighty years of age or more, six feet four inches tall, with a flowing white beard and angry grey eyes that commanded respect, if not affection. Besides, twenty years before, he had written a learned treatise on cancer in the small intestines of unkosher chickens. If this were not enough to persuade self-respecting Jewish matrons, there was the tradition of the neighbourhood. The North End had fought in a general strike, a classic socialist struggle, the memories of which were still alive. Besides, who likes to be called "scab, fink, rat" when going into a butcher shop.

On the following Tuesday, the *Jewish Street Fighter* carried a front-page editorial signed by Isaac Dvorkin, the editor, headed "A Picket Line Is a Picket Line." It pointed out that while many readers did not keep kosher, many still did, and it went on to insist that those who did, being good socialists, should not buy at the rebel butchers' stores because a good Jewish socialist, no matter what, never crosses a picket line. The editorial reminded readers of Jewish blood shed on picket lines before. In Russia czarism was toppled, and in America the union shop became standard in the garment industry. "The kosher law may be sacred to some but the picket line must be sacred to all," the editor concluded.

Two days later, *Jewish Solidarity*, a Bolshevik tabloid in Montreal, pointed out that Kugelman's was a nonunion shop, that six weeks before Kugelman had refused entry to Melvin Goldberg, an organizer for the International Brotherhood of Sausage Stuffers, and that Kugelman and three goons, using six-month-old salamis as clubs, had almost beaten Goldberg to death. Such a situation, the Bolshevik tabloid added, was a disgrace not only for the Jewish community in Winnipeg, but for the working class the world over. The paper hastened to point out that in the Soviet Union, there was no need for the martyrdom of a Melvin Goldberg, there were no fascist toadies like Kugelman, and kosher salami factories belonged to the workers.

By the end of the first week, not a single matron had crossed the Kehila picket lines. At the Chess Club in the back of the Dybbuk Stops Here Delicatessen, the players refused to eat pastrami sandwiches made from scab meat. The pool players at One Eye Louie's and the gamblers at the Valhalla Club ceased to eat Kugelman's red hots for fear they might be hexed by the Bearded Ones and bring bad luck. At the Labour Council meeting, a delegate from the International Brotherhood of Sausage Stuffers moved a successful motion from the floor: "Whereas the sons and disciples of the Kehila, while not themselves members of an affiliate organization of the Trades and Labour Congress, are in essence doing the work and carrying out the wishes of the Trades and Labour Congress, therefore be it resolved that the Trades and

Labour Council of Winnipeg go on record as endorsing the boycott of Kugelman's Kosher Sausage."

At the end of that week, Shatsky, the bookkeeper, a nervous little man with fluttering hands and watery eyes, screwed up his courage and confronted Kugelman in his office. In spurts of run-on sentences and staccato, haphazard phrases, Shatsky told Kugelman the bad news. His salesmen were being turned down flat by most of the Jewish grocers. The Dybbuk Stops Here Delicatessen was now importing salamis and corned beef from Star Kosher, a union shop in Minneapolis. Though pastrami sandwiches had necessarily gone up five cents in price, the chess players were eating them happily. As they put it to Shatsky, himself a chess player, the new sandwiches were the by-product of good union labour. Because of the Labour Council resolution, Shatsky dolefully reported, the working people of the world were avoiding the stadium and hockey rink vendors selling Kugelman's Red Hots. And there were rumours that the sons and disciples of the Kehila had moved their operations into the supermarkets in the better part of town. The Pious Ones were hiding cases of Kugelman's Kosher Canned Chicken behind boxes of All-Bran. They were discussing publicly a ptomaine case three years ago, reportedly involving a box of Kugelman's Kosher Knishes. They were even sticking skull-and-crossbones poison labels on jars of Kugelman's Kosher Gefilte Fish.

Dolefully, Shatsky concluded that sales of Kugelman products had shrunk to nearly zero. The accounts receivable, he added, were strictly from hunger; the accounts payable, don't ask. Kugelman, a rash man, asked. Shatsky, a scared man, replied, and was rewarded with a swift kick in the pants and instant dismissal from the office.

THE SHTARKER FAMILY'S response to the Kosher War was varied. For eight days, the boycott was honoured by Zipporah, the Shtarker most affected. On the ninth day, taking young Daniel with her by the hand, she went to Bassovsky's butcher shop.

At Bassovsky's, one of the Pious approached Zipporah. "You are a good and religious woman, Mrs. Shtarker," he said. "This butcher shop does not sell kosher meat."

Zipporah remained silent for a while and then said, "Mr. Bassovsky is a good and religious man. His wife, Clara, is a good woman and my friend. They would not sell me false goods."

Zipporah thus became the first person in the North End to cross the line. The Pious Ones were aghast. Yelling "scab" and "ratfink" at a woman of Zipporah's reputation and age didn't seem a good idea. They waited until she made her purchases and warned her again that the meat was unkosher. "Then God will punish me," she said. "A picket line can do me no harm."

Proudly sensing her place in history, Zipporah walked straight home. Later that day, she told Menachem of her adventure.

His response was outrage. The Pious Ones' intimidation of Zipporah infuriated Menachem. Besides, Menachem already found the *Jewish Street Fighter* role in the Kosher War erroneous. His argument was simple: the *Jewish Street Fighter* was working the same side of the street as the communists, and that could be fatal in terms of future circulation and future ads. Since the Hitler-Stalin pact, communists had been as popular in the North End as bedbugs at a slumber party.

Shtarker pointed that out to Dvorkin, the editor, and received permission to write a signed editorial of his own. "The so-called Kosher War," Menachem pronounced, "is a hoax, a fraud, a trick.

The Kehila, the Council of Orthodox Rabbis, is not some waif tossed out of a job, some factory worker beaten by a goon because he wants a union. The Kehila is a kosher monopoly, a kosher cartel, a kosher tycoonery that arbitrarily and sneakily forces up the prices of kosher goods. The Kehila defiles Rabbi Yakov Weisman. Rabbi Weisman is a graduate of the world-famous rabbinical seminary in Brest-Litovsk, a seminary I myself attended for four years. I can attest to its excellence. Rabbi Yakov Weisman has every possible qualification for pronouncing the meat kosher. The Kehila's meat is kosher, Rabbi Yakov Weisman's meat is also kosher. The only difference is that Rabbi Weisman's meat is cheaper. As the true and only spokesman for the Jewish proletariat of Winnipeg, we have a duty to tell our readers of a new and cheaper source of meat. It is common sense, and good socialism, to buy the kosher meat and salamis and all the other products Rabbi Yakov Weisman says are kosher.

The editorial had its desired effect. Business at the scab butcher shops picked up sharply; at the Dybbuk Stops Here Delicatessen and One Eye Louie's Poolroom, the boys began buying Kugelman products again. Still, two bricks flew through the front window of the Shtarker home. Constable McTavish now kept an eye out for the Shtarkers. Menachem and a Pious One almost came to blows, and the chief rabbi crossed the street when he saw Shtarker coming.

Shtarker counterattacked with the Red Menace:

Does anyone lately, this fall of 1939, find it funny that Hitler's best friends, the communists, are seen strolling down Winnipeg streets holding hands and cooing with the Pious Ones? Has Jewish Orthodoxy suddenly fallen in love with communism? Maybe the communists are teaching the rabbis how to use a hammer and sickle to cut open a chicken or pound some veal into shape. Our people should not be in bed with Hitler's friends.

Even Dr. Redbelly, the Bolshevik, Menachem Shtarker's best friend, found this great fun. But in the Montreal offices of Samuel Bronfman, president of Seagram's and of the Canadian Jewish Congress, it was disturbing. "That fucking Shtarker fellow in Winnipeg is right," said Mr. Sam. "It's obscene for our fucking rabbis to be in fucking bed with the fucking commies. And it's all over a few fucking cents a pound of meat. Jesus fucking Christ, it's got to stop!!"

"Get me Goldenberg!" Bronfman shouted to one of his flunkies. Soon H. Carl Goldenberg, who had just settled a bloody Winnipeg civic workers' strike, was on his way to Winnipeg with authority from the Canadian Jewish Congress to mediate. Goldenberg, who was on his way to a legendary career, brilliantly settled the matter.

Rabbi Weisman agreed to raise his prices a bit, the Kehila shaved their prices a bit, Rabbi Weisman was admitted to the Kehila, the Pious Ones lifted their pickets, and life in Winnipeg returned to normal.

THE RELATIONSHIP between Menachem and Rabbi Yakov Weisman did not end there. Menachem was still fully immersed in poverty. Rabbi Weisman, however, was doing much better. The commissions for keeping products kosher were small, but the volume was impressive. Soon the rabbi's caftans were of the best gabardine, his boots of the best leather, his hats lined with the finest fur. Pieces of property were quietly purchased in the rabbi's name or those of his disciples. Diamonds were bought.

The rabbi had three sons and two daughters. One son, Pinchus, had been sent at the age of eight to a theological seminary in Chicago. The rabbi's wife, Reisel, had of course had her hair shaved as Orthodox ritual required, but she wore a fancy *sheitel*, a colourful kerchief of good quality, and her dress and shoes were of the best quality.

The rabbi was doing so well that inevitably rumours spread. Many blamed him for a fire that killed six children in one of his slum properties. Toward the end of the war, in 1945, people said he was speculating in currency, in violation of wartime regulations. Still others claimed that he had a secret peephole at the ritual bath, where he could peek in and see the naked women.

Menachem heard all these rumours and dismissed them. There was nothing in Jewish law that forbade shrewd investment. Trade, money, finance made the democratic world go round, Menachem now argued.

The simple fact was that after the Holocaust, Menachem Shtarker changed his view of life. Not one of his friends or relatives survived. The village he had grown up in had been wiped out. Somehow it was all his fault — or so he imagined, Menachem the socialist had given his two sons no bar mitzvahs. Menachem the socialist had only attended the synagogue for the drinking, the singing, the nostalgia. Menachem had spurned the message of God for the false god of socialism. Socialism didn't stop Hitler, didn't stop the Holocaust, didn't stop anything.

Menachem was determined to make amends. Reaching deep into the Bible, he improvised his own version of the sacrifice of Abraham. Daniel would go to Rabbi Weisman for Talmud lessons; Daniel would then go to a theological seminary; Daniel would become a rabbi; from Daniel's pulpit, wisdom would pour in a torrent, washing away Menachem's sins. The Shtarker family would be cleansed. Atonement and fulfillment, through his son.

DANIEL WAS UNAWARE of the destiny Menachem was preparing for him. Fourteen years of age in 1948, fluent in Yiddish and fully comprehensive of the Ancient Hebrew, Daniel knew nothing of the Pious Ones. He looked forward, in fact, to a career as a basketball player. If not that, then defending the poor as a trial lawyer would be okay. So would dashing around in a felt hat with a marker saying Press in the headband. Daniel had seen these professions depicted in the movies and they all looked good. In no movie that Daniel could remember did anyone go from a fun-loving fourteen-year-old to an Orthodox rabbi. The closest was *The Jazz Singer*, where a cantor became Al Jolson.

The news that Daniel would be going to Rabbi Weisman's for lessons, Monday to Thursday, seven to eleven each night, came as a shock. The news that he would also go to the rabbi every Friday night for a *freilach*, a Chassidic festive Sabbath occasion, promised to put a dent in Daniel's social life. On Fridays, Daniel usually hung out at One Eye Louie's Poolroom and watched Coke Lavish and Boozy Roth fleece the suckers.

But Daniel loved Menachem; he knew that Menachem had nothing but the best in mind for him. Isaac-Daniel accepted his sacrifice. Now Rabbi Yakov Weisman had a fourth disciple. The first was his youngest son, Yechiel. Another, Jeremiah, an orphan, came mainly because of the cookies and jam, the appetizers, the Friday night meal, and all the other food a starving boy could not afford to turn down. The third pupil, Mendel, was an interesting case. His father was a Bolshevik, interned for a while in the war. While he was away his wife, Hinde, met a Chassid and fell in love. Rabbi Yakov granted Hinde a divorce, and the soul of Mendel was the payment. The rabbi regarded Daniel as another rescue mission. Since the strike the rabbi had moved to a mansion on St. John's Avenue, an affluent street. There Menachem often voiced his doubts about socialism and its role in the Holocaust. Rabbi Yakov was always comforting. After all, Shtarker's wife and Shtarker's editorial had turned the tide in the butchers' strike. Naturally, he supported the rabbinate for Daniel.

As a disciple, Daniel lacked some basic skills. He had a good mind and was sharp in Mishne and Talmud class. He understood the meaning of every word in the prayer book, but he did not know how to flip effortlessly from one section to another, as the other boys did. This caused considerable embarrassment during afternoon and evening prayers. Daniel also found the little boxes — the phylacteries — silly; now he had to learn to put them on.

One day Rabbi Yakov asked, "A woman faints on the Sabbath. She is two thousand paces from sanctuary. On the Sabbath one can only walk fourteen hundred paces. A step farther is a violation of the Sabbath. Daniel, what do you do?"

Daniel sucked in his breath and said, "Pick the woman up and take her to sanctuary."

Rabbi Yakov, enraged, slapped Daniel across the face. "That is not a proper answer. That is not Talmud. That is street *meshugass*, maybe a little of your Good Samaritan Christian socialism. The answer is simple. Rabbi Shmuel of Korneyev put it aptly. 'The highest law is the law of life.' A woman who has fainted on the Sabbath falls under the law of life. A higher law than the law of the Sabbath allows you to take that woman to sanctuary. When my son Pinchus returns from Chicago, he'll show you no-goodniks what Talmudic dialectics really are."

Daniel had been slapped in the face before. At the United Left Labour Zionist Freedom Workers Temple there were many face slappers. But somehow the rabbi's slap bothered him. Daniel was also bugged by the way the rabbi ordered the women of the house around, as if he were the master and they were his slaves. If the rabbi tried that with Zipporah, she'd show him, thought Daniel.

The lessons continued through the fall of 1948 and the winter of 1949. As spring approached, the policemen stopped wearing their two-foot-high fur hats and buffalo coats, and pretty girls by the dozens started crowding Portage and Main. Doors opened and windows were lifted. Winnipeg began to emerge from its winter doldrums.

At a Friday night spring *freilach*, after the singing and dancing, the roast chicken, the giblets, the potato pie, the gravy, the rhubarb dessert, the tea with lemon and honey, Rabbi Yakov Weisman announced two things. Rabbi Meir Abramson, the chief rabbi, was dying and he, Rabbi Yakov Weisman, the butchers' rabbi, the rebel rabbi, would become chief rabbi of Winnipeg. To this news, Mendel yelled, "Three cheers for Rabbi Yakov!"

And Jeremiah said, "May your name be a sword of vengeance in a desert of ignorance."

Yechiel, the rabbi's youngest son, said, "Gee, Pop, that's great!" Daniel said nothing. But the second announcement caught his attention. Pinchus, age fourteen, was coming home from Chicago. Soon, said Rabbi Yakov, Pinchus would show us, the ignoramuses, his wizardry.

On Monday night Daniel arrived to see Pinchus sitting on a chair next to Rabbi Yakov. The rabbi wasted no time. A page of the Talmud was to be dissected. As usual, Jeremiah missed the point of the exercise, but his piety was so great that the rabbi forgave him. Mendel, trained in communist dialectics, sailed through the page as always. Yechiel, a virtual baby, did not shame his father. Isaac-Daniel Shtarker, Mr. Legalese, gave legitimacy to Menachem's wildest dreams for him.

Then it was time for Pinchus to read. He read badly, his Hebrew was terrible, and his dialectics were nonexistent. Pinchus seemed as ignorant of the subtleties of Jewish Halacha and Talmud as the Poles and the Ukrainians on the street. Rabbi Yakov's wrath rose like a blast furnace. It was clear that for the past four or five years Pinchus had not been attending the yeshiva in Chicago; perhaps Pinchus preferred the pool halls, taverns, and brothels of Chicago instead. Rabbi Yakov did that detective work in his head quickly. Screaming, "Thief! Murderer! Assassin!" he smashed his two fists into Pinchus's face. Blood spurted freely. Then Rabbi Yakov broke four of Pinchus's ribs and punched him in the testicles.

Pinchus did not cry or complain. He simply chanted, "Sticks and stones will break my bones but names will never hurt me. Sticks and stones will break my bones but names will never hurt me." He chanted it as if it were something religious that could save his life.

Rabbi Yakov's pupils fled. Outside in the street, Daniel threw up his supper and then ran. He ran past Cathedral and Bannerman, past Aberdeen and Burroughs, past Magnus, then Manitoba and Aikens. And home.

Inside the house, Menachem was in the kitchen reading. He was startled by the look of terror on Daniel's face. He could hardly get from the boy what had happened. Menachem tried to comfort him: "Rabbis are under great pressure. They have to solve thousands of problems. Sometimes they lose their tempers. They're only human."

"They're monsters," said Daniel. "I hate rabbis. I hate Rabbi Yakov. Their stuff is voodoo, garbage. It has no meaning for me. I want my own life. I don't want to be a rabbi. I'd rather be dead."

Daniel's outburst infuriated Menachem. In anger, he clobbered Daniel with a salami hanging from the kitchen wall. Daniel's response was to chant Pinchus's mantra: "Sticks and stones will break my bones but names will never hurt me."

On the Ball Saul, now in his second year of chartered accountancy, was watching. He was the oldest son, and had a right to speak. "Pa," he said, "there will be no rabbis in this house. A chartered accountant, yes, but God knows what's in store for Daniel. Daniel doesn't want to be a rabbi and from now on, he shall never attend Rabbi Yakov's classes or any other rabbi's. Daniel will have a normal life, Pa, if it kills me — or for that matter, if it kills you. Go to bed, Daniel!"

Daniel went to bed. He didn't sleep well. He had hurt his father but at last he was free. He owed Saul more than he could ever give. But would Daniel and Menachem ever be as close again? Daniel wasn't sure.

Certainly Pinchus was an interesting guy. Daniel would have to get to know him, if Pinchus survived his father's blows.

THE BEATING was hushed up, even though Pinchus spent a week in Winnipeg General. He went on to become Canada's most famous tinman, a salesman of aluminum siding. Yechiel, his youngest brother, became a social worker in Seattle. Mendel joined the New Left, went to jail three times, and now runs his own brokerage business in Manhattan. Jeremiah became a rabbi, and even had some disciples, but produced no learned works. Daniel became — well, we know what he became. Alas, it was not in time to give Menachem what he so desperately needed.

Rabbi Yakov became the chief rabbi of Winnipeg. Dark rumours about him persisted. Later he and Pinchus became good friends, and when Pinchus fell into trouble, he found his two best friends were Daniel Shtarker and Yakov Weisman, the scab rabbi.

When Babkes Came Bouncing Home Again

War arrived in Winnipeg quietly, on a late summer day. Flowers were in bloom, the hobos were taking the sun on the banks of the Red River, yachts were set to sail the Assiniboine. At the People's Press, among the printers who put the *Jewish Street Fighter* to bed, there was the usual curiosity about Menachem Shtarker's first war editorial. "It'll be a lulu," said Gedalia Gevaldik, the paper's chief typographer.

"It'll fry Mackenzie King's ass," said Leibel Checik, the compositor. The printers loved Shtarker's ruthlessness. Shtarker couldn't win the war all by himself, but he'd put all the slackers, the pacifists, and the cowards in their place. On this first day, when Britain had already declared war on Germany, Canada was technically at peace. In the name of Canadian independence, Mackenzie King was waiting seven days to move. Menachem Shtarker was ready now.

The editorial opened bluntly:

Canada's at war. Mackenzie King must go. The little fat man cannot wage war. He can only drown people in chicken fat and baloney. The only man in King's Cabinet fit to be prime minister is C. D. Howe. Howe has the business experience and the toughness to make things work.

Neville Chamberlain will soon be driven from office. That great warrior and thinker Winston Churchill, May All Blessings

Fall on His Head, will lead the British Empire to victory against the Nazi beast.

This was was a shot of adrenalin for the neighbourhood. At the Fort Osborne barracks and the MacGregor barracks in the North End, the Canadian Army was already accepting volunteers and the Jewish boys were signing up. The rich, university-educated South End Jewish boys quickly went for officers' training. The poor of North Winnipeg were enrolled in the ranks.

Volunteering on the very first day of the war were On the Ball Saul and his best friend, Babkes Buchalter. Both had been placed in the dummies class at Lord Mount Stephen High School, Babkes because he wasn't too bright, Saul because through rheumatic fever he lost a year at school. Together they had pursued Icelandic girls in the West End of the city, rich WASP girls in the exclusive suburb of Tuxedo, Polish and Ukrainian girls in the North End — females anywhere they could find them.

After girls came gambling. Babkes, Spinning Eddy, Merv the Curve, and Bananas Belinsky played what young Daniel Shtarker always thought was a very strange game. They played cards for matchsticks. At the end of the game, he who had the most matchsticks was happy.

That was usually On the Ball Saul. Babkes never had a match to his name. Yet it was Babkes whom Too Good Teibel blamed for this disguised form of gambling. Too Good Teibel considered Babkes solely responsible for bad influences on Saul and frequently chased him out of the house. But Too Good Teibel was no squealer and never told their father about Saul's games, Menachem being a violent, foaming-at-the-mouth opponent of all gambling. For five cents, young Daniel played watchman outside the house. As soon as Daniel spotted Menachem, he would rush into the house and warn the players. Cards and matches would disappear.

On the first possible day, Babkes and Saul underwent the army physical. Babkes, who had never beaten Saul at any game, won this one hands down. The Canadian Army quickly swore him in, but Saul's rheumatic fever had left him with a heart murmur. The army gave Saul an impressive lapel pin that indicated that he was an honourable volunteer but a rejectee.

He came home sad and weary. Bursting into tears, Saul told his story. Menachem comforted him. "You're a strong man, Saul. You'll work in a munitions factory. You'll make bombs we can drop on the Nazi rats. You'll soon be proud of your work." Saul was not completely consoled, but he wore his button on his pyjamas, his swimming trunks, his sweat shirts, his zoot suit, and his prayer shawl in the synagogue. He wanted to go to war, but Canada would not let him. On the Ball Saul was Canada's first casualty of war — or so Merv the Curve put it to Bananas Belinsky, as they both left on the troop train for basic training at Camp Shilo.

AT THE UNITED LEFT LABOUR Zionist Freedom Workers Temple day school, involvement in the war effort was total. Every morning at nine sharp, the students in the school auditorium sang "God Save the King," followed by a silent prayer for the preservation of Britain and her Empire, then a lusty rendition of "O Canada," followed by a heart-rending "Hativkah," the Zionist anthem. Next, of course, a spirited recital of the "Internationale," the song of workers the world over. Later they added the "Partisan Hymn," the hymn of the hunted Jews of Poland and Lithuania who had fled to the hills to fight the Nazis with little but their bare hands. Finally there was the chanting of the school's slogans: "No, no, our people will not be vanquished; The People of Israel shall live; he who does not give his child a Jewish education throws himself into a sea of assimilation."

Just surviving the morning exercises was no mean feat. Benny Latkes often fainted by the time they reached the "Internationale." The "Partisan Hymn" always left David Dezon dizzy with fatigue. Both boys came from poor homes that fed them meagre breakfasts.

Daniel loved every second of the opening ceremonies and loved just about everything the school had to offer. He discovered Jewish girls at the school, and he was reprimanded for peeking over the transom that divided the girls' washroom from the boys'. Bubbles Burnstein and Chiclets Chaykovsky became his bosom companions. For a nickel, Bubbles and Chiclets let Daniel see their bare flat bosoms; they even let Daniel rest his head on their chests. In return, Daniel told Bubbles and Chiclets everything he knew, which as always was a great deal.

One day he was given his chance to sock Hitler in the snoot. Velvel Keller, chairman of the board of the United Left Labour Zionist Freedom Workers Temple and of the *Jewish Street Fighter*, underwent a sudden vicious spasm that brought him to his knees. Gasping for breath, trying to fight off the pain, Velvel uttered the words "Victory Bonds" and keeled over dead.

Those knowing Keller's wishes decided that the funeral oration would be delivered from the stage in the Workers Temple Auditorium. Afterward, Victory Bonds salesmen would circulate in the crowd. If the funeral oration went well, thousands could be raised and Velvel could rest in peace.

It was decided that a child should lead them, and Daniel was the designated child. When told of the magnitude of his job, he developed stage fright but was calmed by Falek Zolf, the legendary teacher at the temple. Zolf appealed to Daniel's pride. "This funeral oration," he said, "will trigger war bond sales by the dozens. With the money, we can pay for weapons to put Hitler on the run. Velvel Keller may be our first casualty of the war, but the funeral service is a godsend. You'll be fine, Daniel. Quote a few lines from Bialik's *Slaughter City* and say these words I've written for you."

Daniel Shtarker didn't understand how both Saul and Velvel Keller could be the first Jewish casualties of the war. On stage, however, he forgot such matters and the performer in him took over. In front of him was the coffin of Velvel Keller. The auditorium was packed. Wasil Wrykow, the Yiddish-speaking Polish janitor, had run out of coat hangers and coat racks. Loudspeakers were provided so the men and women workers of Globe Bedding, given the afternoon off to pay their last respects to the employer who had never paid them much, could stand outside and hear the funeral oration.

In a thin, quavering voice, Daniel warmed up the audience by quoting from Chaim Nachman Bialik, Jewry's national poet:

A suckling child
Asleep,
A dead and cloven breast between its lips,
And of another child they tore in two,
And many many more such
Fearful stories.

Then Daniel read the words his teacher had prepared for him. "Velvel Keller was a simple man," said Daniel. "He came here an immigrant boy of eleven. He asked no one for help. Yet this man built factories that put people to work even in the Great Depression. This man kept our schools, our newspapers, our culture alive. Velvel Keller has always fought the Nazi scourge. His last words were 'Victory Bonds.' Soon we will get a chance to buy them. Let's all do so. This is our first attack on the Nazis."

By this time, Daniel, frightened by the dead man in the coffin, was almost in tears. That only improved his delivery. Everyone else in the auditorium was crying. The janitor was in tears. Outside, the Polish and Ukrainian workers, who had unsuccessfully struck Keller for union recognition just six months before, wept openly in sympathy.

The funeral oration over, the war bond salesmen moved with dispatch and $3,600 was raised. Velvel Keller's last wish had been fulfilled.

DANIEL'S SECOND war duty was helping On the Ball Saul with his girlfriends. Saul was a handsome fellow and, with all the competition off to the Armed Forces, much in demand. He persuaded Daniel that since he was a munitions worker, keeping him happy was a major step in making munitions. Daniel believed that, and enjoyed his war work.

The problem was that Saul would get double-booked or even triple-booked. He would send Daniel to apologize and keep the women happy and ready for action on another day. The wondrous and sensuous Eve Guilline was often a rejectee, and Daniel could never figure out why. He would meet her at Tanya's Tearoom to give the bad news. Saul was sick. Saul had been sent off to a theological seminary to become a rabbi. Saul was at Radio Operators School and the classes were in the evening. That didn't deter Eve, whose affection for Daniel sometimes seemed to equal her desire for Saul. "You're my little man," she would say, "my precious little man. Could you tell Sylvanus" — that was, she thought, Gentile for Saul — "that this time we must meet at the Royal Alex side door — eight-thirty sharp."

Daniel sometimes went to see Ingrid, the mental midget fresh off the milk wagon from Steinbach. Ingrid wore her hair in braids and looked exquisite in her lederhosen outfit, a costume that was a bit daring in wartime Winnipeg. They met at Child's Restaurant. Over tea, Ingrid became philosophical: "You know, *liebchen*, I don't really like Jews! All they do is cheat, lie, and rape you. Our *Fuehrer* promises liberation from the Jews, but your brother, Siegfried, that fiendish teaser, is different!" Daniel told Ingrid she would have to wait.

At the Dybbuk Stops Here Delicatessen, Daniel talked to Olga, who resented Daniel's delivery of Saul's regrets. The Jews, Olga insisted, "couldn't farm a shit and are scared shitless of swords, umbrellas, and gunpowder. When you pull their beards, their balls fall off. The Jews only bet on horses and never ride them. At football, all Jews can play is quarterback; at boxing others get hit while they manage. But once in a long, long while, along comes a somebody like Stanislaus" — her Ukrainian name for Saul — "a handsome devil. A goddamn Jew, but a *he-man*."

Daniel truly loved his older brother. He shined Saul's shoes, pressed his pants, took his laundry to the cleaners. He screened Saul's phone calls and took messages discreetly. In return Saul took Daniel to the movies, to the pool room, and the delicatessen. He didn't even mind having Daniel around at the Fairyland Dance Hall or the Aragon Ballroom when Saul took his dates dancing. Daniel and Saul were now a team, much as Babkes and Saul had been before. Daniel did all in his power to make Saul happy so Saul could make munitions. Saul was training Daniel to take over Saul's women, and no one was prouder than Saul when Daniel was named one of the top ten oils and fats collectors in the city. Daniel even received a certificate from a Mrs. Phyllis Turner from

Ottawa — the Oils and Fats Queen, *Maclean's* called her. Mrs. Turner pressed the scroll in Daniel's hand personally and Menachem had it framed. At the United Left Labour Zionist Freedom Workers Temple, teacher Zolf gave an excellent little speech on how young Canada — the Daniel Shtarkers of the world — would someday bring peace and happiness to a troubled world.

BABKES, NOW STATIONED in England, stayed in touch. He sent postcards from Devon, Cornwall, Shropshire, Surrey, and other places with mysterious names. He was in the Second Division.

The postcards were heavily censored. On the first one, all that Daniel and Saul could read were two words, "Big tits." They concluded Babkes had found a woman to his taste in England. Saul sent a letter back and another heavily censored postcard arrived. The only words decipherable were "Nice legs."

Months passed, and no news came. Then, in one of the great fiascos of the war, the Second Division stormed Dieppe. The casualties were appallingly high, among them many Winnipegers, but there was one piece of good news for the North End: Babkes was mentioned in dispatches. "Baruch Buchalter," as the dispatch called him, was cited for bravery under fire and gallantry in the face of death. He was a hero, the North End's first. Gunn's Bakery responded with a Babkes Caramel Cake. At the Dybbuk Stops Here Delicatessen the special became the Babkes — matzoh ball soup, corned beef sandwich, cream soda, rhubarb dessert. A framed picture of Babkes appeared on the wall at the General Monash Jewish Canadian Legion Branch. In class, Zolf compared Buchalter with Judah Maccabee, Bar Kochba, General Monash, Hank Greenberg, and Max Baer. Only the cynics told stories of bad Jewish athletes or bad Jewish people, he said. These people were themselves bad and should be interned.

ONE DAY in 1944 Daniel, up first, heard "Extra! Extra!" being shouted by newsboys in the streets. It was 5:00 a.m. The headline read, "Allies Land in Normandy."

Zipporah wept, Shoshannah put on a new sweater and skirt,

Teibel and her husband rushed over to the house, and Menachem Shtarker put on his grey serge suit with the watch chain dropping from the watch pocket. On the Ball Saul had to be awakened, the previous evening having been heavy.

As the war news poured in, Baruch Buchalter was mentioned in dispatches for the second time. Again the words "gallantry," and "personal courage under fire." This time the Jewish community acted with more restraint. Gunn's Bakery did its cake trick again and the Dybbuk Stops Here renewed the Babkes special, but on the whole the neighbourhood now took the courage of Babkes for granted. He had simply proven what Jews had always known — that they were tough little bastards when they wanted to be.

Later, in the Battle of Caen, Babkes rose to new heights and his heroism was described in detail by a British war correspondent whose London *Telegraph* story also ran in the *Winnipeg Free Press*.

It was not until early afternoon that the Second Canadian Division went forward to the attack. With them went Private Baruch Buchalter of Winnipeg, age 23, from the South Saskatchewan Regiment. The German armoured counterattack hit the South Saskatchewan Regiment and hurled them back down the slope. The last step was to evacuate the wounded and the carriers, before the rifle companies caved in.

There was no one left to give orders. His company commander was dead, his platoon officer wounded, his section leader dead. Buchalter stayed, rounded up the wounded, and gave them arms to fight. For four hours, he was cut off from his own lines. Buchalter rounded up a Bren gun, two Sten guns and two rifles from his dead comrades. Some Germans were advancing. Buchalter shot at them with the Bren gun and saw them fall. A German tank moved up and Buchalter put it out of commission. Four hours later, Buchalter was relieved by an Ontario regiment.

This time Babkes won the Military Medal, next to the Victoria Cross the most important medal the British Empire gives for gallantry. That impressed even Samuel Bronfman of Montreal, head of the Canadian Jewish Congress. "This guy Buchalter is fucking something," said Bronfman. "We'll give the kid a fucking welcome at the station, a fucking big parade and a fucking big banquet."

MACKENZIE KING had Babkes plucked from the South Saskatchewan Regiment. He wanted Babkes sent home to sell Victory Bonds, give the Jews a hero, and help King hold the Jewish vote.

When Babkes Buchalter came bouncing home again, the platform at the CPR Station in the North End was jammed with well-wishers. The mayor and the premier were there, and so was Samuel Bronfman. Menachem Shtarker was in the crowd with Daniel. On the Ball Saul was at work in the munitions factory.

In the parade, platoons from the Cameron Highlanders, the Manitoba Dragoons, the Winnipeg Light Infantry were assembled. There were four Highland military bands and a big drum major waving a stick with fur on each end. The parade passed the old Bell Hotel, the Titanic Tearoom, and the Starland Theatre. When it reached Portage and Main, the country's prettiest girls waved, cheered and lifted their skirts just a little bit. Down Portage, crowds on both sides of the avenue waved little Union Jacks and cheered Babkes to the skies. At the Cenotaph on Memorial Boulevard, Babkes laid a wreath in memory of his fallen comrades. "Taps" was played, tears were shed. Babkes now joined the pantheon of heros. That night, a banquet would add the final touches.

MENACHEM SHTARKER was at home with Daniel in the evening. He had not been invited to the banquet. It was a Bronfman enterprise and Menachem was no friend of Bronfman's. Saul had not been invited either. Instead he was out with Melba Maugham, a lithe five-foot-nine-inch beauty from the rich end of town. Sweaters Shoshannah was entertaining her best friend, Bubbles Betcherman, in the kitchen.

Menachem was glad that Babkes was getting the royal treatment. The Jews would need all the heroes they could get.

Menachem knew the Allies would win the war, but then the battle for Palestine would begin. "What do you think of Babkes, Daniel?" Menachem suddenly asked his son.

"He's a hero, Pop. He's a Jewish hero! What's to ask?" said Daniel.

"Well, before the war Babkes was a bum. Today he wears ribbons and medals."

At that moment, the doorbell rang. Standing there, obviously tipsy, was Babkes Buchalter, asking for Saul. Menachem did not know where Saul was, but Daniel explained that he was at his radio operators course.

Menachem asked the warrior into the house. Babkes was dishevelled and looked the worse for wear, but the thought of his heroism was a bit too much for Menachem. Overcome, he said, "Thank you, Babkes, for all the Nazis you have killed." He offered a drink and Babkes gladly accepted. Menachem went to get some of Bronfman's best, in the bedroom upstairs. Daniel was asking himself: what was Babkes doing here instead of at the banquet in his honour?

While Menachem was upstairs, Babkes wandered into the kitchen. He was not there long before sharp female screams were heard. Menachem and Daniel rushed into the kitchen. Shoshannah was in tears, her blouse ripped. Her friend Bubbles had also been mauled.

Menachem's rage knew no bounds. "War hero, my ass! A bum is a bum! Get out of my house. I'll make sure no decent Jewish woman comes within twenty paces of you." Menachem fetched his First World War pistol.

Babkes left quietly and Shoshannah and Bubbles calmed down. Something had died in the process — hero worship. Never again would Daniel Shtarker entirely trust a Jewish hero — no, not even Sandy Koufax.

WHY BABKES was at the Shtarker home was soon explained. He had gotten drunk at the banquet and made a pass at an attractive Winnipeg matron who was also Sam Bronfman's cousin. Bronfman and Babkes came to blows, Bronfman delivered an uppercut, and Babkes fell into his soup.

When he revived he teetered out of the hotel and took a cab to the Shtarker home.

The fiasco ended his career as a Victory Bond salesman. He returned to his regiment and continued to kill Nazis. Demobilized in 1945, he headed for Calgary. Babkes was never seen in Winnipeg again, and not much heard of until his obituaries in the 1970s saluted Canada's most decorated Jewish hero of the Second World War.

King of the Jews

I n the late fall of 1941, Menachem Shtarker was no fan of
Samuel Bronfman, president of Seagram's, president of the
Canadian Jewish Congress, and self-styled King of the Jews.
But Menachem certainly did not quarrel with the quality of
Bronfman's products. Though a socialist, Menachem would take
Daniel to the El Mole Rachmim Synagogue for Saturday morning
services. There, after services, a little lunchtime spread was pro-
vided: some cream cheese, some lox, a little herring, lots of onions,
good rye bread, and bottles of Seagram's Golden Wedding Rye.

Bronfman's whiskey made Menacham happy. He would dance
Cossack dances, do Chassidic twirls, relive his youth. He would
even say a kind word about Sam Bronfman, punctuating a compliment by a request for another shot of Golden Wedding.
Menachem would get tipsy but never drunk, and Daniel was
always there to help him home. Zipporah would suggest a quiet
nap. Menachem loved the Pious Ones and their Bronfman whiskey.

But one day in late 1941, Menachem had to admit that Sam
Bronfman might have other possibilities as well. Menachem was
now a sort of elder in the neighbourhood, often consulted about
ideological problems or marriage prospects. One advice seeker
was Zelig Zeidman, the janitor at the Baltic Apartments near the
Shtarkers' home. A cantankerous man, he had one joy in his life.
Zeidman had a son, but oh, such a son! Frank Zeidman was tall

and handsome, and had a Ph.D. In something unheard of before: nuclear physics. Frank was working in a secret place in Ontario, his mail home heavily censored. That, everyone knew, meant Frank was important. Some in the neighbourhood said Frank was a friend of Einstein's. They also said he might build a weapon that would blow up only Nazis.

Zelig was proud of Frank and wanted the best for him. That's why he consulted Menachem. "You see, Menachem, I think I have this offer. I'm not sure, but someone close to those still closer to those closest to Sam Bronfman wants to pass a message on to me. Bronfman has a daughter who will be of marriageable age in a few years. I think the message bearers want to arrange a wedding — my Frank and Bronfman's daughter. What do I do? What do I say? Is it even in my hands?"

Menachem thought carefully. "If Bronfman's daughter is beautiful with an inner Jewish soul, a sense of humour, an awareness of what's going on," he said, "then the offer must not be capriciously spurned. Frank could live in the lap of luxury; Frank would have the Bronfman millions to back up his scientific research. That is nothing to sneeze at. Bronfman would also make sure you, Zelig, don't spend your old age chasing kids out of apartment blocks.

"But," he continued, "arranged marriages went out of fashion twenty years ago. Frank is handsome and intelligent. Frank will make his own choice." Frank did exactly that, but Menachem always felt his advice in this episode proved his capacity to be fair about Sam Bronfman. It was in that spirit of nonpartisanship, objectivity, and fairmindedness that Menachem Shtarker would say, "Bronfman calls himself King of the Jews. That's an insult to the Jewish people and to all Christians who regard Jesus as the King of the Jews. Now the Christians may be wrong, but Jesus to me is a far more presentable, intelligent, and sensitive King of the Jews than Samuel Bronfman!"

That quip reverberated around the neighbourhood and added to the legend of Menachem. After he had a chance meeting with Zane Zenith, the investigative reporter of the *Winnipeg Free Press*, Menachem's outrage at Bronfman grew even more intense. Zane told Menachem of a book on Bronfman he had written, which was somehow mysteriously suppressed; of cars running illegal Bronfman booze into North Dakota; of the notorious anti-Semite Ambassador Joseph P. Kennedy being in cahoots with the Bronfmans; of Bronfman's trying to buy himself a senatorship.

These stories alarmed Menachem. In the *Jewish Street Fighter*, he wrote a diatribe.

> The community has heard interesting rumours that a tycoon, one Samuel Bronfman, wants a Senate seat. Does Bronfman really need the $4,000 a year to add to his millions? The answer is no. If anyone should get a Senate seat, it's that great Canadian socialist, J. S. Woodsworth, who has worked for the poor and the immigrants all his life. The fact that Mr. Woodsworth stands for the abolition of the Senate makes such an appointment all the more appropriate.

Menachem's campaign against Bronfman caught on, at least enough to encourage him to offer himself as a delegate to the convention of the Canadian Jewish Congress being held in Montreal. North Winnipeg was entitled to fifty delegates out of the three hundred from across Canada. It was a three-day convention; expenses for all delegates were to be paid by Bronfman.

Bronfman's people in Winnipeg, who had studiously ignored Shtarker and his attacks, now sprung into action. They eyed his slate of supporters with relish. It contained all his friends: Dr. Redbelly the communist, Leibel Vladek the communist, Isadore Zeicherkeit the Trotskyite, and Sholom Schweiger the Bundist. The rest were more communists, some Labour Zionists, six of the Pious Ones from the synagogue, three Yiddish playwrights, four Yiddish novelists, six Yiddish poets, and two Yiddish set designers.

The Bronfman forces branded this mélange the Red Menace, the International Conspiracy, and the Enemy Within. The Shtarker forces counterattacked. The El Mole Rachmim Synagogue endorsed Menachem's slate. So did the butchers' rabbi, all the teachers at the Talmud Torah, and the United Left Labour Zionist

Freedom Workers Temple. The Dybbuk Stops Here Delicatessen put a sign in the window: "For a day that's not darker, vote for Menachem Shtarker." The habitués of the Jewish Chess Club promised their support. A Shtarker sign graced the entrance of the General Monash Canadian Legion Jewish War Veterans Branch. Shtarker bunting and signs were all over the Baltic, Arctic, Pacific, and Atlantic Apartment blocks. The Fur and Leather Workers Union sent money all the way from Toronto to the campaign. Four organizers from the International Ladies Garment Workers Union quietly went to work.

Menachem ran a dignified campaign. He never mentioned Bronfman's past and instead maintained that Bronfman had no influence in Ottawa and that Jews escaping Europe had not been allowed into Canada. While all this was not Bronfman's fault, it was time for new blood.

The red-baiting of the Bronfman forces failed. Menachem Shtarker's fifty chosen street fighters were all elected delegates. North Winnipeg Jewry had sent a message to the Eastern Jewish big shots in Montreal. At the victory celebration Menachem got more tipsy than usual on Bronfman rye, and Zipporah had to take him home. Daniel stayed behind to hear the hosannahs for his father, the fearless Bronfman fighter.

AT THE TRAIN PLATFORM, Menachem was beside himself with joy: "I'm going to Montreal — and Bronfman is paying for it. I'm staying at the Mount Royal Hotel — and Bronfman is paying for it! And I'm going to make him pay for it on the convention floor!"

Still, 250 delegates were handpicked by the Bronfman organization. Seventy-seven resolutions were passed at the convention; seventy-six were passed by margins of 250 to fifty. But one resolution passed unanimously. Moved by Menachem and seconded by Dr. Redbelly, the Canadian Jewish Congress went on record "pledging solidarity to the British Empire, standing with her Dominions — Canada, Australia, New Zealand, Newfoundland, and South Africa — alone against the Nazi beast. May God's righteousness triumph and the British way of life prevail." On the face of it the resolution was harmless enough, but it was a victory for Menachem. Bronfman, a Liberal, was an Americanizer and not wild about the British connection; still, Bronfman was certainly not prepared to make those sentiments public. His forces had to go along with Shtarker's resolution.

When Menachem and his band returned from Montreal they reported having a good time, and they seemed to have accepted with equanimity Bronfman's control of the Canadian Jewish community. It wasn't a matter of timorousness on their part; they all had their lives to lead and a war to fight; they all knew, after all, that while Bronfman might think he was King of the Jews, they had just proven that Bronfman was not their Lord and Master.

The Temptation of
Menachem Shtarker

September 22, 1945, was declared Bess Myerson Day by the
Canadian Jewish Congress president, Samuel Bronfman,
the chief of Seagram's Distillery of Montreal and Globe
Bedding of Winnipeg.

Bess Myerson Day was celebrated in Winnipeg in the auditorium of the United Left Labour Zionist Freedom Workers Temple.
Bess Myerson was the first Jew ever crowned Miss America. That
so soon after the Holocaust a Jewish woman should be declared
the number-one beauty of America, and therefore the world, was
regarded by Canadian and American Jewry as a miracle. The two
speakers at the Temple were Menachem Shtarker and Bella
Zunenu. Bella was Zachary Zunenu's hard-to-pin-down wife.
Their union, which everyone knew to be troubled, was like a
marriage between Peter Pan and Delilah. Zachary's tepid review
of Menachem's *And So Help Me, God* had of course led to one of
North Winnipeg's classic feuds. Bella had a Ph.D. in English and
taught at the University of Manitoba. Bella and Zachary lived in
River Heights, the rich end of the city, in a third-floor flat in the
mansion of a grain broker on hard times.

The Left Labour Hall was beautifully decorated. On the podium
were three flags in pot holders — the Union Jack, the flag of Israel,
and the Stars and Stripes. Beside the flags was a huge photograph
of a beautiful young woman, a crown on her head, a sceptre in her
right hand, her ermine cape parting to reveal a modest bathing

suit and the loveliest legs the world had seen. As on all such occasions, the walls were festooned with slogans. "The Jewish woman is number one; from the Jewish woman comes the Jewish child. The Jewish child will soon be number one!" "Beauty is in the eye of the beholder; Jewish beauty is in the eyes of Texas, New York, Mississippi, Manitoba, California, Vermont, Prince Edward Island." That sign went on to list the rest of the American states and Canada's nine provinces. Another proclaimed: "The Jewish Woman lives: Israel will prevail." A final slogan was a bit ambiguous, Menachem thought: "Up the Jewish woman!" "Take a Jewish woman home today" was another sign that perhaps needed a second hard look.

Menachem's speech was classic. "Bess Myerson, Miss America, is today the most beautiful woman in the world," said Menachem. "Bess Myerson joins, of course, the roll call of great Jewish beauties. I mention only Lauren Bacall, Sylvia Sidney, and Ruth Roman, to show you how easily the roll call of Jewish beauty can trip from the lips. But Bess Myerson is special. Her beauty is a vindication of the Jewish people and a beacon of light in the darkness ahead. I see Bess Myerson in the tradition of Judith, who tempted the Syrian and in his tent castrated and dispatched that enemy of the Jewish people. I see Bess Myerson in the tradition of Hannah Senesh, who parachuted behind Nazi lines and was caught and murdered by the Hun.

"Bess Myerson is the most beautiful woman in the world. The rest of Jewish womanhood can easily follow. The beauty and intelligence of Jewish women will be a major weapon in the battle for our homeland, in tiny Palestine, now the only refuge for our Holocaust survivors. I toast and salute Bess Myerson and Jewish beauty. And lest anyone think Bess Myerson is our only beauty, let me disabuse you of that notion by introducing to you now our next speaker, the beautiful and charming Bella Zunenu, professor of English at the University of Manitoba."

Bella Zunenu strode purposefully to the dais. She was not a true beauty, but she had an arresting face and striking figure. The face was pocked by acne, but only on her left cheek; it gave her a challenging look, like the duelling scars of the Prussian nobility.

She had large oval eyes, perhaps too large — but again there was a sharpness, a playfulness, a tough intelligence that added to Bella's mystery. She also had long, flowing hair.

As always, Bella was immaculately dressed. She had a pillbox hat on her head, with a net that fell discreetly over her face. Over her neck was draped an elegant dead fox, tail and teeth showing. Chen U lipstick made Bella's lips shine and glisten; the aroma of Evening in Paris surrounded her. She wore a tweed suit, the skirt just a tantalizing millimetre above her knee. Her style was magnificent; her speech was pure logic: "As a feminist, I must say that I do not approve of beauty contests. Beauty contests reek of the harem, the concubine, the slave girl, and all the other stereotypes. I believe, as the good Emma Goldman believed, and here I paraphrase: 'Man thinks he does; woman does, does, does.' Perhaps Emma got that aphorism from another great Jewish woman, Gertrude Stein. A rose is a rose is a rose, and the Jewish woman does, does, does; does the cleaning, does the cooking, does the laundry and everything else that keeps the Jewish home alive. But this, I suppose, is not the time to air our grievances as women. Let us honour Bess Myerson on this basis — that she proves that a Jewish woman is beautiful, not some mindless princess. I think Menachem Shtarker hit the right note. The Jewish women he stresses in his speech are the right models for our sons and daughters. So I salute you, Menachem Shtarker and Bess Myerson both. Today, Bess Myerson Day, is a good day for the Jewish people!"

Menachem was pleased. He had always found her bright and interesting, and certainly preferred her to her kvetchy husband. But he was surprised when Bella approached him after the speeches and suggested they both go for coffee.

Over coffee, Bella told Menachem how much she liked his book. Taking a wad of gum out of her mouth and sticking it under the cafeteria table, Bella said, "I really admire your stories. They're like primitive art, folkloric. Simple, yet complex." She smiled a strange smile. "I particularly like your sexy stories. You fit in well with Yiddish writing. Your characters are archetypal and your prose is imagist."

Archetypal. Imagist. Heady words. Menachem wasn't sure what they meant, but they didn't sound like a putdown. Menachem was beginning to take a shine to Bella Zunenu — nothing lewd, just respect for a truly good Winnipeg literary critic at last — and a real Jewish beauty. Real Jewish beauties, Menachem concluded, could be the salvation of the race.

At Bella's suggestion they went for a walk. Fall was about to envelop the city. The leaves were turning red, the caragana bushes needed trimming, winter was in the air, and so was the challenge of survival. The conversation with Bella roamed fast and freely. They arrived at the Dybbuk Stops Here Delicatessen.

Over coffee and smoked meat sandwiches, Bella opened up in quick and startling ways. "What do you think of the Jewish penis?" she asked.

Menachem, caught completely off guard, lamely replied, "I only think of my penis when I pee."

"Well, what do you think of it?" asked Bella.

"I don't know," said Menachem. "My penis has managed to serve me in good stead."

"I prefer the Gentile penis," said Bella. "The foreskin enclosure seems to give me more for my money, so to speak. It's an extra edge that the circumcized penis doesn't have. I mean the difference between Donald's and Zachary's penises is the difference between getting laid by Dumbo the Elephant and Jiminy Cricket."

Menachem, recognizing Donald as the first name of Donald Woodruff, the dean of arts at the university, said nothing.

Bella went on to tell of her long affair with Donald. She became so excited that she reached into her crocodile handbag, pulled out another stick of gum, and chewed profusely. Pulling out a compact, emitting clouds of powder, Bella remade her face, touching up the acne pockets with an extra flourish of attention. Bella took Menachem with her on a shopping tour. She was a ruthless, fast, and logical shopper, questioning the price of goods with amazing skill. It was Menachem's first experience of what we now call consumerism, and he was agog. Before he knew it, Menachem was standing in the lingerie department of Holt Renfrew, where Bella had decided to consult Menachem on her purchase of lingerie.

She first tried on a nightgown and a peignoir outfit and paraded before Menachem. "Do you like it?" asked Bella, chewing her gum ferociously.

Menachem, who had never seen peignoirs before, simply said, "You look lovely, Bella."

Bella disappeared for a moment; when she came back, she was wearing a push-up brassiere and powder-blue lace-trimmed panties. A garter belt was dangling from the upper parts of Bella's legs. On Bella's feet were mules with pompons on the front.

The effect on Menachem was hard to gauge. Bella was certainly not like the Jewish women he knew. Yet she was the woman of the future — Menachem felt that in his bones. He liked the effortless way Bella shared the intimacies of her life. Bella was Bella and Menachem liked her.

THEY TRAVELLED together to the Canadian Jewish Congress convention in Toronto. Sitting in the coach of the CPR train, facing Dr. Redbelly and teacher Zolf, Bella and Menachem passed the time as best they could. Menachem started telling Bella horror stories about Samuel Bronfman, Menachem's sworn enemy. Bella said, "Menachem, you're too hard on Bronfman. Bronfman worked hard to get Jewish refugees from the Nazis into Canada. It's not his fault that Mackenzie King is an asshole and the Frogs are anti-Semites. Besides, I know Bronfman better than you, Menachem. I *know* him, if you know what I mean." Bella and Sam Bronfman! Menachem couldn't believe it. Bronfman's wife, Saidye, a Winnipeg girl, was very beautiful and a first-class lady and their love for each other was legendary. Menachem wondered, Is Bella lying to me?

Bella was a delegate from South Winnipeg. Menachem was the impresario behind the anti-Bronfman slate of delegates from North Winnipeg. Menachem made his rounds, denouncing Bronfman to every delegate he could lay his hands on; but, as usual, Bronfman controlled the convention. Menachem got nowhere.

Menachem was therefore floored to hear Bella, in her speech to the plenary session, denounce Bronfman and the Canadian Jewish Congress for chauvinism, nepotism, idiocy, and incompetence.

Menachem's joy knew no bounds when Bella, in control of at least half the South Winnipeg delegation, voted with Menachem on the main motion of nonconfidence in Sam Bronfman as president. Her support raised the anti-Bronfman vote to its highest level ever.

Menachem was so proud of Bella that he gave her a big hug and a kiss, and told her he would buy her a drink at the Royal York Hotel, where they were both staying.

At the bar, Menachem couldn't stop bubbling over his minitriumph. "Look, I'd like to change," said Bella. "Come up to my room in about ten minutes and we'll have a drink there."

Ten minutes later, Menachem knocked on the door of Room 1215. "Come in, it's open." Menachem stepped in. Bella was in the washroom, but there was a drink for Menachem resting on the radio console opposite Bella's bed. Menachem sipped his drink, and, glass in hand, walked around the hotel room looking at the pictures on the wall.

Menachem suddenly developed an urge to pass water. "Bella, is it okay if I come in?"

"Sure," said Bella. As he entered the bathroom, a lovely, voluptuous Bella stepped out, dressed only in half-slip and push-up bra.

Menachem stood over the toilet. He was thinking, Five minutes from now, I'll get my revenge on Zachary Zunenu. I'll be making love to his wife, Bella. I'll be penetrating her treasure trove. But who's been there before me? The Don Cossack Choir? The Happy Gang, Hank Greenberg, and the Detroit Tigers? Scenes of mass penetration of Bella, male after male squirming in her arms, danced in Menachem's head.

When he stepped out of the bathroom, Bella was sitting on the bed, her lovely legs gleaming in the early evening light. "Thinking of servicing me, Menachem?" Bella asked. Her throaty laugh bounced off the walls of the room.

Servicing me? My God, thought Menachem, what is she, an automobile?

"You should serve me, Menachem, or I'll tell people we both know that you were unable to perform."

"You mean get it up, don't you, Bella?"

"Yes, get it up."

"You mean can't get it up, Bella, like your husband can't get it up."

"Yes, like my husband."

"Well, I've got news for you, Bella. Zachary is probably getting it up, as we speak, for the benefit of Feivush the Fagele, the fashion editor of the *Street Fighter*."

"I know," said Bella.

"You know?" Menachem was annoyed that he couldn't spring this gossip on Bella.

"Yes, I know," said Bella. "We have an open marriage. Zachary does what he wants. I do what I want."

"An open marriage? It sounds like an open sewer!" said Menachem. They both laughed. Then Menachem said, "I like you, Bella, you're fun but I'm not . . . I have my family and I want to keep them. Okay? Solidarity Forever, Bella!"

"Right," said Bella, laughing as she escorted Menachem to the door.

Back in his own hotel room, Menachem gradually drifted off to sleep. In his dream, Bella appeared, wearing still another nifty outfit. She was the same except for a tail that dangled underneath her skirt and horns that had appeared on each side of her head. Menachem awoke, sweat covering his face. He thought, Today I survived Bella, tomorrow I'll survive the world!

The Gallant Eve

S plat, splat was what the noise sounded like. Pebbles being thrown against a window. The noise woke Daniel. It was 5:00 a.m. He looked through the solidly frozen window of the bedroom he shared with On the Ball Saul. It was the winter of 1950; the war was over, so it couldn't be the Nazis coming. Now sixteen, Daniel was getting sharper every day.

Daniel went downstairs to the front door. Standing in the yard in a pile of snow was Saul. That was strange enough, but stranger still was the way Saul's hands covered his cheeks. Daniel drew Saul into the house. He understood that Saul was frightened and upset. This worried Daniel terribly. Saul was his hero, his surrogate father, the key to his future sex life, an insider Daniel could rely on to survive on the street outside. He was more than Daniel's brother; he was Daniel's friend, redeemer, and deliverer.

Saul lifted his hands from his face. Someone had gouged two chunks of flesh out of each of Saul's cheeks.

"What the fuck happened?!!"

Saul said, "It was Eve. I was playing pool at One Eye Louie's. Eve came and said we should go dancing. I was tired, I had a good run going in the game, and I told her to fuck off. She got more demanding. I pushed her, she screamed, and then rip!"

Daniel was surprised. Eve was a pretty young woman of modest physical proportions. She was from St. Boniface, a Franco-Manitoban with *joie de vivre*. She loved to dance. Once, when they

69

had gone dancing and taken Daniel along, Saul lost interest and Eve danced with Daniel till 2:00 a.m. She was a secretary at the cordite plant where Saul had once worked. The exuberant Eve, the fun-loving Eve, was a nice balance to Saul's sometimes sober and withdrawn nature. During the war the relationship flourished, but as Saul moved up in the world it soured. Saul wanted Eve to disappear, but Eve was a fighter. The gouging demonstrated how far she would go.

Daniel called a cab and took Saul to the emergency ward at Winnipeg General Hospital. The wounds were cleansed, and stitches applied, but Saul still looked as if he had been attacked by the Cat Women of the B-movies. The wounds needed time to heal.

Saul's life lately had been on an up curve. Menachem had lifted him from a dead-end job in the film-exchange business to a course in chartered accountancy. Accountancy and Saul's natural mercantile instincts were a perfect wedding. He was now in second year, near the top of his class. Tax avoidance was his specialty, a craft he intended to hone to perfection.

By now, Menachem Shtarker, annoyed by his own income taxes, found Saul's skills a delight. More important, Saul had officially stopped chasing the shiksas. He was dating rich Jewish girls in the South End, girls whose last names were invariably romantic. Some evoked great financial capitals (London, Berlin, Paris, Frankfurt), some the romantic duchies (Luxembourg, Lichtenstein, Breslau). A few surnames rang with the splendour of great deeds in the past — Gladstone, Lincoln, or Sherman. Their first names suggested great poets, great minds, and great places: Elizabeth, Victoria, Regina, Savannah, Laura, Florence. Their faces somehow seemed to have absorbed, almost by osmosis, the ambience of the Anglo-Saxon upper classes. Their clothes were Victorian tweeds, Byronic velvet pantaloons, Punjabi polo shirts, and Holt Renfrew cashmeres. Their shoes were Oxford, flat and comfortable, their necklaces pearl. More often than not, their noses were heavily bobbed; their taut little tushies were encased in Jantzen swimsuits, or Spalding tennis shorts. Their armpits were always Arrid. Modess, and not the plebian Kotex, covered their inner secrets. Bars of Lux bobbed in their sunken bathtubs. Ipana made their white capped teeth sparkle. Their breath was Sen-Sen pleasant. They chewed no gum.

High-class Jewish girls would look askance at a man with a face apparently decorated by Jack the Ripper. And Saul was already dating one Gladstone and one Savannah. Daniel preferred Saul's shiksas to the high-class Jewish girls, and he liked Eve because she seemed to like him. But now she was a menace.

"Saul," said Daniel, "Menachem must never see you in the state you're in. He's a heavy sleeper. I'll set the alarm for six every day. You'll get dressed and sneak out of the house. I'll tell Menachem you're taking two extra courses. He'll love that. If you need anything, just call me and I'll deliver it. This will take a month and then nobody will ever know you were Scarface of the North."

Saul did exactly what Daniel told him. Daniel loved Saul because Saul was always good to him, no matter who was up or down. Daniel, at the moment, was down. He had been placed in the dummies class, as Saul had once been. Things looked bleak for him, and Menachem — who had once pinned all his hopes on Daniel — was now betting on Saul. A chartered accountant, a rich wife, a big wedding — it was all in the cards.

Now, Daniel knew, it was all in danger. Eve would strike again.

DANIEL BEGAN his detective work. He interviewed the spectators at the gouging. One Eye Louie was particularly helpful. Louie said Eve screamed, "You lousy cocksucker! I'll ruin your career. I'll put you behind bars. I love you. Please come back!" Saul turned away, and in a minute Eve sank her talons in his cheeks.

At the Salisbury House, with Daniel's encouragement, the boys began to talk freely about Eve. Goose Ginsberg said, "That Eve's great! She's the only woman in town to suck off the entire Winnipeg Blue Bomber football team. If Winnipeg ever gets the Olympics, she'll suck off the world!"

Leibel Lamp Shade said Eve was a real nut case: "Eve's a nympho. Yet she can love one guy with a violent passion. I'd hate to have that broad on my back!" Merv the Curve noted Eve had a record, and was quick to fly off the handle. Daniel took his research home and brooded. He decided not to worry Saul for the moment. When Saul was healed, steps could be taken.

In a month, Saul was healed and the stitches were out. Then the calls began. Daniel, as usual, answered the phone. Menachem and Zipporah, never strong in English, were leery of Alexander Graham Bell's invention, Shoshannah was either out on dates or primping upstairs, and Saul knew a call meant trouble. Daniel could work the phone beautifully, and did.

"Hi," the familiar voice said, "is Saul there?"

"Sorry, Eve, he's gone to Banff for the Institute of Chartered Accountants Convention." Saul, listening from the sofa, smiled.

"When will he be back?"

"Well, Eve, that's hard to say. Saul's a specialist now in international debentures and the world liquidity market, and he's been asked to do an eight-week tour of Asia for the UN." Saul rolled on the floor laughing. Finally, Eve hung up.

"She'll be back," said Daniel. "She'll do you damage!"

"Relax, kid. You worry too much."

Returning from school around suppertime one day, Daniel saw two police cruisers parked in front of his home. He entered warily. His heart skipped as he saw the terror on his mother's face. Menachem looked angry and confused. Both were incapable of dealing with the police.

Daniel, by now, was quite capable. He asked the policeman what the trouble was. Sergeant McCallum replied, "Eve Guilline of 1410 Poplar Road says one Saul Shtarker stole a cigarette case and a wristwatch that belonged to her. She has also said he has been making improper advances to her."

Sergeant McCallum's cold, formal tone terrified Zipporah and unnerved Menachem. Not Daniel. Steeped in the traditions of British justice by many hours at the Odeon, he stepped in forcefully.

"Sergeant, Miss Guilline is a very sick woman. The proof of the falsity of her charges is easy. Wait one moment." He ran upstairs and found the watch and cigarette case Eve had given Saul. He was back in a moment, evidence in hand.

"Sergeant McCallum, theft is a serious charge. For there to be theft, there has to be *mens rea*, a guilty intention. Look at the watch.

On the back it says: 'Saul, Love and Kisses as Always, Eve.' The cigarette case is inscribed: 'Saul, I Love You Madly, Eve.'

"Now, Sergeant McCallum, Saul is very handsome. Saul doesn't pursue women. They pursue him. Five weeks ago, Miss Guilline gouged Saul's cheeks. Just check at One Eye Louie's Poolroom. Miss Guilline also has a special relationship with the Winnipeg Blue Bombers. Ask their trainers.

"We are the Shtarker family, Sergeant. We don't steal, and we don't beset women. We are British North Americans and proud of it. I'll see you to the door."

Daniel had been brilliant, but appreciation was scarce. All that Menachem had heard and seen had shocked him. He sat glumly in the living room. Zipporah's thoughts, Daniel could see, were turning to the old days in Europe.

Two hours later, Saul bounced into the house with his exam results; he was third in his class. Menachem's spirits rose visibly with joy. There was tea with lemon, fruits and juices. A blessed forgetfulness settled that night over the Shtarker home.

Soon Eve called again, and then again. Daniel was always brilliantly evasive, but her last call was different. "I want to speak to Saul, please. Just once. I know he's there. If you don't let me talk to him, I'll kill myself."

Daniel was used to this ploy, having heard it from earlier Saul castoffs. His riposte was ready: "You're so beautiful, Eve, you have everything to live for. I'm only sixteen, but in two years time I'll be eighteen and I'll be coming after you. I can hardly wait. As for Saul, he's in Kirkland Lake, auditing the books of Lakeshore Gold Mines."

Eve hung up. The last Eve phone call wasn't from her but from Sergeant McCallum: "Mr. Shtarker, tell your brother that last night Eve Guilline set herself and her house on fire with gasoline. Saul will have to come to the inquest. We think she may have mailed Saul a note. Saul can read it, but afterward it has to come to us."

The note arrived two days later. "I love you, Saul, the way your body moves in bed, the way you laugh, the way you listen, and the way you talk. Without you life is shit, so fuck it. See you upstairs. Eve."

Saul took the suicide well, with a mixture of relief and guilt. Menachem Shtarker brooded. But Saul was now a good son, so why spoil it? As for Daniel, he had learned a lesson — a street-smart kid, he had called the shots all wrong on Eve. Could Daniel possibly be wrong on other things?

Tutti-frutti, Punch
and Judy

D aniel Shtarker, thirteen years old in the spring of 1947, was a socialist and a Zionist. That this was in large part because of his father could not be denied. In Russia Menachem Shtarker had fought for socialism — first for the Jews, then for everybody else. Zarubovl, the founder of Mapam, the party of Labour Zionism, was a close friend. A powerfully built man and a former blacksmith, Zarubovl was said to be able to lift a horse over his head, a trick designed to lure the faint-hearted into the cause. Certainly on his visits to Winnipeg and to the Shtarker home, Zarubovl always lifted Daniel easily with one hand, twirling him around over his head like a toy.

Of course, the Shtarkers lived in the North End. Here the massive Winnipeg General Strike that terrified the whole world in 1919 was fought and lost. Here lay the cradle of Canadian socialism. A strike leader, A. A. Heaps, had been the Member of Parliament for years. The provincial member was M. A. Gray, another socialist. Daniel happily joined in the Gray victory chant: "Stick and stay, make it pay, give a *geshrai* for M. A. Gray, MLA, hip hip hooray." *Geshrai* meant "yell"; "MLA" meant "member of the legislative assembly."

But while as a socialist Daniel loved all mankind and as a Zionist loved the arid wastes of Palestine, the truth was that at thirteen he loved all things British even more. The downtown Odeon showed nothing but British films, and Daniel admired the

75

stately homes, the private schools, the stiff upper lips, the sexually unconsummated romances, and the splendour of the Raj. In his affection for the British he had his father's wholehearted support. Menachem the immigrant was grateful to British North America. He revered the monarchy and tolerated no criticism of it. He told anyone who cared to listen that Winston Churchill was a Zionist and that Churchill's first campaign manager was Harold Laski's father.

Sometimes Daniel's passion was tested. Once Captain Wickedwood, Daniel's home-room teacher, banged Izzy Shmutzik's and Beindel Ligner's heads together and shouted, "You fucking Jews come into my classroom leaving little clumps of Jew shit behind you and you expect me to come with a fucking pail and clean it up!" But everyone agreed Captain Wickedwood had killed his fair share of Nazis. He was entitled to his eccentrities, no doubt triggered by shell shock.

So Daniel endured mixed feelings when he was sent for the summer to Habonim Camp Kvutza, a Labour Zionist training camp for future Palestine freedom fighters. He arrived with a tiny suitcase and a bag that contained two corned beef sandwiches on rye, wrapped in waxed paper by Zipporah. Daniel saw that one of his fellow campers was Velvel Narish, a notorious slob. Velvel's parents kept live chickens in their living room, and Velvel ate bizarre foods that, combined with his deadly body odour, made him hard to like. Daniel also noted that Velvel was carrying a bag that was soaked through. The bag contained soggy tomato sandwiches that Velvel's mom had prepared.

The campers were ushered into a large main hall, where they were greeted by Machpaleh Meiskeit, an extremely ugly woman in shorts and halter. As camp director she welcomed them to the war against the British in Palestine. "We are all socialists here," she said, "and we practice *kupa* — Hebrew for cooperation, socialism. Some of you campers are well off, others are poor. We will meld you all into one equal team. We will begin now. All of you have brought sandwiches from home. Turn them in at once. The sandwiches will be mixed up. The sandwiches of the rich may wind up in the hands of the poor, but that is socialism." Daniel turned his sandwiches in. So did Velvel Narish and the other boys. The wheel of fortune spun. Daniel got Velvel's tomato sandwiches and Velvel got Daniel's corned beef sandwiches. Technically speaking, this was Daniel's first experience of pure socialism.

Other Camp Kvutza rituals did little to restore his faith. Having to clean out the latrine was a painful duty, having to walk through a swamp to the swimming area was unpleasant. Some things, like guarding the water tower (water being in short supply in Palestine, all Jewish freedom fighters had to guard it), were plain silly. As Daniel pointed out to Heather Zieskeit, a camp leader who had a good sense of humour but was nevertheless a fanatic Zionist, "Why guard the water tower? There's all of Lake Winnipeg out there!" Heather enjoyed arguing with Daniel. Though the British Labour government had turned on the Zionists, Daniel kept faith with the British and defended them stoutly. "Wasn't Disraeli, the greatest British prime minister, a Jew?" Daniel asked.

"Disraeli was born a Christian," Heather replied. Heather said the British were imperialist exploiters of the workers, like all empires before them.

Daniel stumped her with another question: "How can you be truly Jewish and not admire Noël Coward in *In Which We Serve*?"

One day Heather and some other leaders entered Daniel's cabin and announced that they were going to have a military exercise. Certain boys would be designated illegal Jewish refugees. At some point Heather and her team, playing British army officers, would burst in. It was the duty of the boys in the cabin to protect, with their lives if necessary, the identity of the refugees.

Velvel Narish was one of those so designated.

The raid came at three in the morning. Heather, in British khaki, announced through a bullhorn, "We are the British authorities. Do you have any illegal Jewish refugees here?"

There was a momentary silence in the cabin and then, all his revulsion with socialism and Brit-bashing welling up from his soul, Daniel yelled, "Yeah, Velvel Narish is a Jewish illegal!"

Heather and her team arrested Velvel and took him away.

Daniel's friends, the mavericks and troublemakers of the camp, thought Daniel was terrific. The Zionist zealots saw in Daniel only a traitor.

On the final day of camp, the campers sat around the fire, watching Machpaleh Meiskeit (who wore no panties under her shorts, thereby exposing massive tufts of pubic hair) and singing the camp songs, "Tutti-frutti, Punch and Judy, Habonim will do its duty" and "Goodbye America, goodbye forever, we are going to Palestine because we are so clever."

Heather sat beside Daniel and gave him frequent hugs. "You make a lousy socialist and a worse Zionist," she said. "But if you're going to turn someone in, Velvel Narish is the one. That's the best raid we ever had."

Those were soothing words, and Daniel had to admit he was getting to like Camp Kvutza and the leaders who were willing to fight and die for his people. But Daniel still liked the British. As for socialism, he could hardly wait to get home, where he, not Velvel Narish, would get his mother's corned beef sandwiches.

The Torch Song of
Sweaters Shoshannah

*A*lmost from birth, Daniel Shtarker was familiar with the intricacies of sexual charisma. Three days after he was born, in the *Jewish Street Fighter's* Most Beautiful Jewish Baby of the Year Contest, he won third place. When he was four he was included in a cute little montage of exuberant ethnic children in a special feature of the *Winnipeg Free Press*, "The Grace of the Ghetto." Daniel's picture was flanked by Teddy Wyrko, his first friend and later a lifer at Stony Mountain Penitentiary, and Klaus Kindersfeld, whose father was soon to be interned as a Nazi in wartime.

Daniel hit charismatic stardom at age five, at Too Good Teibel's wedding. He loved Teibel, his eldest sister — a blonde, blue-eyed, svelte, and attractive woman, who acted as a second mother to him. Teibel was called Too Good because of her many kindnesses and innate good nature, though what Daniel liked about her was her toughness in the face of what she thought wrong. There was a streak of Menachem in Teibel and a natural beauty that came only from the One Above. But the star of Teibel's wedding was not the bride but the sexy, charismatic ring bearer. Daniel did his job well, marching straight as an arrow down the auditorium floor of the United Left Labour Zionist Freedom Workers Temple. In his right hand, Daniel held a small purple pillow on which rested the wedding ring. All eyes were on Daniel. The socialist matrons beamed and clucked, the men smiled and nodded approval.

Daniel was the future of world Jewry; they had all seen it now and knew it would work.

Daniel's relationship with Sweaters Shoshannah was trickier. She had for many years been the baby, the favourite in the family, and the arrival of Daniel had ended all that. Nor was Shoshannah particularly impressed by Daniel's social ability.

When she held a sweet sixteen party, Menachem and Zipporah went off to a cultural evening, leaving Daniel, then eight, in the care of Sweaters Shoshannah. For most of the evening, he wandered around, watching Shosannah's friends necking and petting and eating a good deal of smoked meat sandwiches washed down by prodigious amounts of Coke. Perhaps it was the food that warmed Daniel's disposition and made him decide to take a more active part in the activities. Spotting a blonde, blue-eyed young man sitting on the sofa, looking through the high school yearbook, Daniel said, "You're not Jewish. What are you?"

The Adonis laughed and said, "Guess."

"Ukrainian?"

"No!"

"Polish?"

"No."

"German?"

"God, no."

"Lithuanian?"

"No."

"I give up. What are you?"

The Adonis told Daniel he was Danish. "The Danes are wonderful people," said Daniel. "The Danes saved their Jews. My father says the Danes are saints." This exercise in Christian-Jewish relations was interrupted by Shoshannah. She was not amused by Daniel's anthropological curiosity.

"You spoiled little brat!" she shouted. "You stuck your nose in where you're not wanted. I'm going to tell Papa what you did!"

At breakfast Shoshannah was as good as her word. She told Menachem about Daniel's appalling lack of social graces. Menachem, turning to Daniel, said, "Did you say those things about the Danes saving the Jews?"

"Yes, Papa."

"And you asked him what his nationality was?"

"Yes, Papa."

"Good for you. We must know who our friends are and enemies are, and you can only do that by asking questions."

Then Menachem turned and slapped Shoshannah. "What were Gentile boys doing in this house anyway? Are there not enough Jews in Winnipeg for you?"

On another occasion, when Shoshannah was angered by one of Daniel's indiscretions, she launched into an angry attack. Daniel, witless and in the heat of the moment, yelled, "Fuck you, Shoshannah; shove a salami up your cunt!" Indignant, Shoshannah rushed to tell Menachem what Daniel had said, word for word. The problem was that Menachem did not understand the English words. When Shoshannah explained them in graphic Yiddish, he was infuriated to learn that his sixteen-year-old daughter was familiar with such matters. Menachem at once cut off Shoshannah's dates and kept her housebound for a month. He said nothing to Daniel.

But whatever their conflicts, Daniel had to admit that Shoshannah Shtarker was a bit of a dish. Jet-black hair, sparkling hazel eyes, cameo face and a luscious body living right in one's own home was not such a bad thing after all, Daniel concluded. Finally, peace between them was imposed by Daniel's secret weapon. Shoshannah was dependent on the phone for dates, but she was always upstairs grooming herself. The phone was downstairs. Daniel was always downstairs. Daniel always answered the phone. When they were at peace, Daniel would inform Shoshannah there was a man on the phone for her. If they were at war, Daniel would say, "Shoshannah? She's gone to Africa, you know, where all the tropical diseases are. I hope she'll survive them. They could be catchy. Anyway, she'll be gone for six months! Goodbye!" Shoshannah could never be sure when Daniel would unleash his weapon. Shoshannah made peace; they became friends and later confidants.

SHOSHANNAH did not go on to the university, where she could

meet the Jewish doctors, lawyers, and accountants of Menachem's dreams. Instead, she went to work as a secretary-model in the garment centre. There she met the lewd, the crude, the rude of Jewish life. Menachem was not pleased and saw trouble ahead.

And Shoshannah's dates did become a bit bizarre. When Daniel was ten, he discovered that his sister was dating a Jewish hockey player. His real name was Shmuel Yarmolinsky but he had changed it to Sam Yale for professional reasons. Sam always wore his New York Rangers jacket when he came to pick up Shoshannah; he gave miniature pucks and hockey sticks advertising the Rangers to young Daniel. Daniel worshipped Sam, though he knew there was no record of Sam's scoring a goal or making an assist in the NHL.

Sam worried Menachem, who had no one to talk to about it except Daniel. "He's a grown man and he chases a piece of rubber for a living. Why isn't he in uniform fighting the Nazis, like all the other Jewish boys in the neighbourhood? I think they're paying him *babkes* there in New York. Sam could wind up a beggar and I certainly can't afford to keep him. I think Shoshannah should drop him."

Sam Yale, after playing only five games with the Rangers — no goals, no assists, four minutes in the penalty box — dropped into the minor leagues and vanished from Shoshannah's life. Soon Daniel became aware of two of her secret romances. One was a handsome Gentile who eventually went off to fight in Europe. Daniel, while looking out a streetcar window one day, saw him embracing Shoshannah but did not squeal to Menachem. Then there was Shoshannah's passionate romance with Oliver Crane, formerly Yankel Kranker, a notorious underworld character. Crane's other women and his heavy drinking finally scared Shoshannah away from that forbidden adventure.

Then there appeared in Shoshannah's life the handsome, the rich, the sophisticated Perry Prance, formerly Pinchus Pomerantz, owner of a shirt factory. The first time Daniel set eyes on Perry Prance was in the doorway of the Shtarker home in the summer of 1950. By now sixteen years old, Daniel was impressed by the yachting cap, blue blazer, light flannels, and white shoes.

"Is your sister home?" Perry asked.

"Whom shall I say is calling?"

"Tell her it's the Prince of Pleasure. She'll know."

"It's the Prince of Pleasure calling for you, Shoshannah." She was at the door in seconds.

That day, Perry took Shoshannah for a trip in his boat down the Red River. Later, dances, barbecues, shopping sprees in Minneapolis, and visits to museums followed. Shoshannah told On the Ball Saul and Daniel, "Perry is a perfect gentlemen. Total fun. Perry never lays a hand on me; he's so polite." Daniel found that reassuring; Saul did not. Saul was not happy, even though Menachem was overjoyed that at last Shoshannah had found a nice, rich, Jewish boy. Saul let his doubts rest, but soon the issue was abruptly resolved. An item in the *Winnipeg Tribune* said that Perry had run off with an underage office boy from his factory. The RCMP, the Winnipeg police, and the FBI were all involved in the matter.

Shoshannah, the last to hear the bad news, wept copiously. Saul tried to comfort her. "You have to understand, Shoshannah, Perry never laid a hand on you because he doesn't like women." Shoshannah wept even harder. "Some say the bride is too beautiful. I say Perry is too beautiful to be a real man." Shoshannah still did not get the point.

Exasperated, Saul stood up and said, "Look, Shoshannah, Perry doesn't want your body, he wants mine."

Shoshannah's tears continued to pour.

The Revolt of the Dummies Class

T he conversation in principal Andrew McBride's office in Lord Mount Stephen High School in the fall of 1950 was really a monologue — one-sided, mechanical, and legalistic. "If I let you in," said Principal McBride, "to a normal accelerated grade 11 class with a 59.6 average when the rules say you need a 60 average, then it follows that I have to let in someone with a 59.5 average. If I let in someone with a 59.5 average, I'll have to let in someone with a 59.4 average." Daniel, listening, thought to himself, What a fatuous asshole. McBride was in fact a legend in the neighbourhood. He had been principal of the school since it was built in 1911. He knew the founder of Canadian socialism, J. S. Woodsworth. He ran for alderman on a socialist ticket and the Jewish community rallied to his cause. Mrs. Greenberg said her daughter, Faigele, swore up and down and on the Bible that McBride was a saint. Mrs. Dvorkin said McBride loved Jews and wept openly when he read Shylock's soliloquy; McBride was so overcome with emotion, said Mrs. Dvorkin, that he wouldn't eat animal flesh of any kind for weeks thereafter. McBride *loved* Jews, said Mrs. Polson. McBride's idea of a good time, she said, was to go to Stella Park and listen to Jews talk.

Daniel had heard all these stories but had never had occasion to test them out — until now.

In grade 10, Daniel had received some discouraging marks — 22 in math, 24 in French, 14 in physical education, 50 in English,

51 in history. He had hidden them from Menachem, but one Saturday afternoon Menachem had caught him playing cards in a neighbour's basement. He dragged Daniel home, demanded to see his report card, and confined him to the house for the rest of the year.

The marks did not get much better, but with August supplementals his average finally reached 59.6. Daniel had seen the error of his ways and desperately wanted to avoid his father's ferocious wrath. He pleaded with the principal for admission to a normal grade 11. He promised to work weekends, to stay after school, study in the detention room every day.

It was like talking to a squirrel. If socialism was the rule of order and discipline, McBride was the perfect socialist. Daniel Shtarker's problems would be solved by putting him in non-accelerated grade 11A — the dummies class, as everyone but McBride called it. Daniel's classmates would go on to normal grade 11, then grade 12, then university. Daniel would be taking 11A, then 11B, then 12A, then 12B.

MENACHEM'S RESPONSE was not positive. He felt personally betrayed, and he felt Daniel had let the Jewish people down. Daniel was his second son in the dummies class, but in Saul's case rheumatic fever caused the problem; in Daniel's case laziness, sinfulness, and hooliganism were the reasons.

Menachem put Daniel in quarantine. He would not talk to Daniel, or sit at the same table with him. He would not introduce Daniel to newcomers who visited the Shtarkers. If people asked about his family, Menachem would say he had one chartered accountant and two married daughters. Daniel was badly hurt by this, but he settled down to surviving the dummies class. On his first day he was delighted to meet Klaus Kindersfeld, his friend since childhood. As a little boy, Daniel had sometimes gone to Klaus's house for supper. Daniel would eat pork and sauerbraten and look with curiosity at the picture of Adolf Hitler on the dining room wall. Klaus's father, Fritz, though a Nazi, liked little Daniel. "The Jews took over the world," Fritz would say. "We Nazis are giving the world back to the people. The Jews are the enemy of the world, but you're a good boy, Daniel, and a good influence on my son, Klaus."

Naturally, Klaus and Daniel were together learning all the dirty tricks of the street, and when Fritz was interned during the war as a Nazi, Klaus and Daniel became inseparable. Then Klaus and his mother moved to another neighbourhood. At the end of the war, when Fritz returned from the internment camp, Klaus decided not to let his father back into the house. Klaus's mother, Frieda, had a job, and Klaus worked after school every day and on weekends. Eventually they moved back into the North End.

That day in the dummies class Daniel also met a future Tory senator, a future judge of the Manitoba Court of Appeal, a future labour lawyer, and the future aluminum-siding king of Canada. Also on hand was Skip Tregebov, the son of the Bolshevik teacher at the People's Jewish Temple, the headquarters of the Winnipeg Jewish Communists. He had a clubfoot but managed his handicap with such agility that he was nicknamed Skip. He ended up as a divorce lawyer.

The class teacher was a two-hundred-pound woman, six foot four. An excellent teacher, Miss Dixon was bothered by the fact that so many bright students were in a slow learners' class. To her it wasn't the system that was at fault; the students themselves were lazy, vain, arrogant, rude, crude, self-centred, and vicious. Daniel sometimes fought bitterly with Miss Dixon, which helped get rid of his anger and frustration. He couldn't fight with Menachem at home, nor could he afford fights with his friends at school. Daniel's frustration was simple: he felt he had an A mind, but he had to live through the school day in a B world. Daniel resented that bitterly. Anything he could do to help the B world beat the A world, he would do.

The opportunity came sooner than he expected, with the October election for the student president. At first there was only one candidate, Sam Wexler, son of Wexler's Automotive Parts. Sam was everything Daniel hated — Sam was from the A class, and he had an A average. Sam's girlfriend, Malka, had one too. They were both active at the YMHA. Sam wore glasses and played no sports, but he did play chess and he was a counsellor at the B'nai B'rith

Camp. Sam, his parents, and Malka knew the world revolved around Sam. Daniel was determined to give that world a different spin.

The idea, Daniel's, was simplicity itself. He would run Klaus — six foot one, 190 pounds, the fullback on the football team, and the dream of every normal girl in the school. Klaus had perfect teeth, curly red hair, a great body. What more did Lord Mount Stephen High need?

Klaus was easily persuaded to run, with Daniel as campaign manager. Daniel wrote a slogan: "Vote Klaus Kindersfeld — he's no patsy. His father used to be a Nazi." A bit clumsy, but there was a reason for it. Klaus's father's politics would be used by the Wexler forces. Daniel would get it into the open right away and diffuse the issue.

Naturally, Daniel wrote a speech for Klaus. If he were president, Klaus promised, an official student defender would hear complaints about teachers. Klaus promised an end to arbitrary afterschool detentions, and no teacher intervention in student council affairs or in the yearbook. Klaus also promised a free and liberated Poland and Ukraine, and a school levy to be sent in aid of the poor Israelis beleaguered by a sea of hostile Arabs. Finally, Klaus promised that short skirts would not be banned in the school.

Daniel assessed the politics of the school. Klaus would win the dummies class and the Ukrainian, Polish, and German girls in Commercial. The Ukrainians, Poles and Germans in Industrial Arts would be with him all the way. The goody-goody class would of course be Wexler's, and so would a great deal of grade 12. The key was the freshman class, new to the school. On them, Daniel first tried seduction. The beauties in the dummies class, June Kozak and Bunny Senesh and their friends, started to talk to, lean on, and rub against startled boys in their first weeks of high school. This technique worked, and Bunny and June reported that some of the boys were real cute. Then Daniel sent in the class shrewdies to argue Klaus's case with the freshmen. That, too, worked. Still, not enough of the freshmen were coming onside. Daniel, who had seen every political movie ever made, decided to turn on the juice.

Threats, intimidation, shoving around, pushing against the wash-room walls — all were introduced as new elements to the campaign.

That did bring the desired result. Daniel predicted victory by fifty or more votes, but Klaus won by sixty-five. The revolt of the dummies class was over. Bunny, June, Daniel, and Klaus went to a bootlegger's to celebrate. Daniel got drunk and told June he loved her; June got drunk and told Daniel she loved Klaus; Klaus got drunk and said he loved Daniel, and everybody laughed and hollered.

Except Miss Dixon. The next morning, she addressed the class: "Are you happy now, Mr. Shtarker? You defeated an A student and elected a football player. You used seduction, intimidation, and dirty tricks to elect your president. You've made a mockery of democracy, Mr. Shtarker. I hope you're satisfied. Someday that streak of larceny in you will catch up to you and finish you."

Daniel Shtarker rose to speak: "In this class, we're all finished anyway, Miss Dixon. This is the dummies class, isn't it? Well, dummies are the salt of the earth, the little people who just keep coming. You know, like in *The Grapes of Wrath*? We dummies need a president who's a dummy. One dummy understands the other dummies. You think we're smart but lazy. The system thinks we're dumb and the system will kill us if given half a chance. Klaus's victory is a victory over the system. Beating the system is the dummy's way of life."

Miss Dixon, this time, admitted that Daniel had presented a case. Then she returned the essays she had marked. Daniel had an A.

BEING IN the dummies class represented no insurmountable problem to Daniel, apart from the hostility he faced at home. Growing more religious by the day, Menachem would say, "If I were Abraham, asked to make a sacrifice, and you were my son, a bum, I'd slit your throat so quick . . . ." On another occasion, he noted wistfully, "If I were Jepthah and I'd made a promise to sacrifice the first of my family that I saw on my return from victory, I'd make damn sure it was you, the bane of my existence."

As the impact of the Holocaust on his family and friends in

Europe sank in, and as the grim and gaunt Holocaust survivors drifted into Winnipeg, Menachem began to feel that Daniel's waywardness was a betrayal of all that the survivors stood for. Just seeing Daniel was enough to put Menachem into a fit of rage. To calm himself, he would focus his mind on the greenhorns, the newcomers. The survivors of the Holocaust simply had to do something to prove that Jews were not mere lambs to be led to slaughter. The redemption of the Jewish people was in their hands. The greenhorns would be helped to win Palestine for the Jews.

Churchill, Menachem knew, was on the side of the Jews, but the British Labour government was not. Now Menachem began to loathe socialism with a fervour. Hating socialism and earning his living on a socialist paper was of course tricky. He now began to lead a double life: a socialist by day, an Orthodox Jew by night.

Daniel was too preoccupied with his own problems to worry about the dilemma Menachem was wrestling with. One problem in particular was major. Six feet tall, Daniel had not experienced puberty, and the sight of his tiny, hairless weenie was depressing. At the Y, Daniel would study the penises of other players after basketball. All were hairy and roughly six inches in size. One greenhorn, Wankers Wolinsky, had a veritable salami between his legs. Daniel dreamt of having such a sausage of his own, but in the meantime he avoided showering with his fellow players. Daniel used every imaginable excuse. "Water causes acne." "Too much cleanliness is too close to godliness." "I showered when you guys were out."

The others suspected a hairless weenie but said nothing. Daniel, after all, was king of the dummies class, he was the best basketball strategist in the Y, and he would certainly grow out of it. They were right. One day, Daniel began to sprout pubic hairs. Two weeks later, he ejaculated. Six weeks later, he was the proud possessor of a penis just short of six inches in length. The shortfall Daniel blamed on Menachem for having an Orthodox *mohel* do his circumcision. "The old blind bastard, Baruch Moishe, took off too much," Daniel claimed. "It's lucky they don't let Baruch Moishe do heart surgery!"

His manly status encouraged Daniel to sprout in new directions. He soon became heavily involved with the greenhorns, the survivors his own age. Daniel loved the greenhorns. He could speak Yiddish, their language, and at the YMHA Daniel often translated for them. He loved the street smarts of the greenhorns; in the death camps, they had learned every trick of survival. When the boys taught the greenhorns how to shoot pool and play poker, they took to both games like a drunk to doubles.

In the dummies class the first greenhorn Daniel encountered was Yakov Mondovitz, very heavy and clumsy but enthusiastic and likable. Yakov caused Mr. Passit, the gym teacher, his first greenhorn problem. All the students were lined up to do a front roll in tumbling class. The procedure was to run thirty yards, then put your hands on the mat and flip over. Daniel would always run thirty yards, come to a complete stop, and then put his hands down on the mat and flip over. Yakov Mondovitz refused to do his front roll. In Yiddish, Yakov told Daniel, who translated, "I will not do the front roll. It is undignified. I cut my way through barbed wire and escaped from a concentration camp. The Nazis looked for me for days. I hid in a cave without food or water for weeks. To get out of Europe, I did many things. I even jumped out of a plane in a parachute. Still, I will not do a front roll. It is undignified."

Mr. Passit refused to accept Yakov's story. Mr. Passit tried to force Yakov to do a front roll. Yakov simply fled the room. Daniel, infuriated, organized counterinsurgency tactics. In Daniel's opinion, Mr. Passit had gone too far. WASP Canada needed to be put in its place once again. When the next physical education class was held, Yakov was absent on Daniel's instructions. When the class lined up and Mr. Passit asked for the singing out of the names of the class in order of height, all forty students in the class simultaneously farted. During a basketball game, four basketballs were thrown out of the window. Tumbling mats were slashed by knives, the jumping horses wrecked. Three of the class strongmen picked Mr. Passit up and hung him from a gym door. Finally, Mr. Passit got the point, and Yakov didn't have to do front rolls.

You're Frozen, Mr. Shtarker

O n a Saturday afternoon in the late spring of 1954, Duck Davidov was standing at the counter of the Bountiful Billiards pool hall, reading the *Free Press*. The owner of the poolroom, Leo Séguin, was reading his *La Presse* from Montreal. All the tables were occupied. Coke Lavish and Boozy Roth were there.

"Jesus Christ, look at this," said Duck. "That fuckin' Shtarker's got his name in the paper here about eighteen times — winner of the Isbister, the Marcus Hyman, the A. A. Baird, the Principal Sparling .... Hey, Coke, we've got a genius on our hands. Where is he? He's usually here by now."

Daniel was there, but lurking in the corner. He was proud of his achievements but unsure how his peers would take them. The boys might feel he was now a wimp. Reluctantly he stepped out of the shadows. Duck ran over and gave him a big hug. The boys, as one, put down their pool cues and applauded their new champion. Even Leo put *La Presse* down and sent a free Coke for Daniel's enjoyment.

Coke Lavish, however, spoke for everybody. Though a pool player and a gambler by profession, Coke was a widely read man, with a famous communist cousin in New York. Coke's words were pure poetry: "We frequenters of poolrooms and gambling clubs have little to brag of. Ours is a precarious life dependent on the roll of the dice, the turn-up of the cards, the steady eye on the ball, and the unshaking hand on the cue. We live on the fringe of society and maybe we don't count. But when one of our own, a Daniel Shtarker, gets listed eighteen times for academic achievement, every one of us at Bountiful Billiards stands six inches taller."

Daniel was so overcome with emotion that he burst into tears. The pool hall applauded that too. Daniel thanked Coke and the boys for their faith in him. "I'll never let you down," he declared.

ONLY MONTHS before, Daniel Shtarker had been facing the biggest hurdle of his life, his first Christmas exams at university. This was Daniel's last chance. Menachem had made it clear. Failure at Christmas would mean instant immersion in the garment factory world of Prince Albert Leather, or worse. Daniel had studied hard, and he was nervous about the stakes in the game. For the first exam, English, he took along a collection of what he considered good luck charms. Two packages of Life Savers (the very name a good omen) had been given to him by Zipporah, plus two chocolate bars for instant energy. On the desk in the exam room he put a bottle of ink and a straight pen with nib, in case his ballpoint failed. He brought two packages of blotters left over from his last high school exam, and two packages of Kleenex, also left over. For extra luck, he had the coupon showing his mark on his last high school exam, an 80 in math, a subject Daniel had always hated.

His totems in order, he picked up his pen to face the exam paper that had just been placed before him. He lifted his pen to answer. Panic gripped Daniel, something far worse than an anxiety attack. He was paralyzed, literally frozen by terror. His pen stopped in midair. There seemed to be no sign of life in his eyes.

After fifteen minutes Daniel attracted the attention of one of the proctors, a professor of psychology named Dr. Phillip Persey. Dr. Persey approached Daniel warily and began an exquisite exercise in reverse psychology. "Mr. Shtarker," Dr. Persey said, "you're frozen. Terror has gripped your very soul. You think the world has come to an end. And you're right! For you, the world has come to an end. Your worst nightmare has come true. You will fail this exam. But why chicken out now? Try the exam. You have nothing to lose. You may get a twenty, maybe a thirty. But stop worrying. The worst has already happened. Now try your best."

For Daniel, the master obfuscator, this exercise in false logic was a tonic. He lowered his pen to the page and began to write. He was still writing at the end of the three hours. The proctors, at Dr. Persey's suggestion, allowed Daniel an extra fifteen minutes to compensate for the freeze.

Daniel was now determined to go down with dignity. The second exam was philosophy, based entirely on the rules of logic, and when it was over Daniel was dismayed to find his answers differed from those of the three intellectual gurus in his class. So, thought Daniel, he had flunked at least one exam. Still, if he got four out of five, Menachem could live with it. Bravely, Daniel faced his remaining three exams, summoning up all the equanimity he could muster.

STANDING AT THE COUNTER in Bountiful Billiards one Christmas vacation day in 1953, Daniel was explaining to Leo Séguin that the Duplessis era would soon end. Duplessis, he said, had made too many enemies. Still, Daniel was a secret admirer of Duplessis. Duplessis was a demagogue and colourful, living proof that Canadian politics was not boring. So were the anti-Semite Social Crediters in Alberta. Daniel also loved Huey Long and his Ontario imitator, Mitch Hepburn. Daniel loved demagogues and Canada had plenty of them.

Pinchus Weisman interrupted him. "My secret sources," he said, "tell me you are first in the Christmas exams in the university."

From the dummies class in high school to first in the university was impossible. Daniel blew up. "Look," he said, "I'm lucky if I'll pass five out of five."

Pinchus offered to bet. "Why don't you go down to the college and my source will show you the results," said Pinchus, and Daniel agreed.

The source, a file clerk taking a flier on one of Weisman's secret financial ventures, had Daniel's results: a straight A average with a 97 in logic-philosophy. Daniel refused to believe him. He burst into the dean's office and demanded to see his marked exams, and the dean obliged him. The dean returned with five exam papers, marked as the clerk had said.

Perusing them one by one, Daniel realized that his life had altered. Menachem's sword of Damocles had just fallen to the floor, with no harm to Daniel. The scourge of the dummies class was now . . . a scholar? Most important, the fulfiller of Menachem's wildest dreams.

Still, the Christmas results might have been a fluke. Daniel behaved himself at home, until he could see the spring results. Now they were in, and Daniel was still number one. This was no fluke; Daniel was an untouchable.

But negative, even bitter, thoughts began to surface in the heart and mind of Daniel Shtarker. He knew that Menachem would soon be home, perusing the papers and savouring the eighteen scholarship citations. There would then be phone calls to all the important people in the Menachem Shtarker galaxy. Nothing would give Menachem more pleasure than to have Daniel at home to witness Menachem's elaborate network in action, but Daniel was in no mood to provide this pleasure. Daniel the socialist, the believer in the equality of men, thought that the scourge of the dummies class deserved more affection and attention than any goddamn scholar. Menachem's worship of success revolted Daniel; it made him love and respect his father less than he had imagined was possible.

Instead of heading home to give Menachem his *naches*, his joy, Daniel took a streetcar to a bar, where he and two football players he met proceeded to drink Portage Avenue dry. Daniel awoke in the basement of an empty house in the Eastgate section and ransacked the fridge for breakfast. Revived in strength, his anger still burning bright, Daniel waited until the bars opened. Once again, he went drinking. He repeated this pattern for a week, sleeping every night at the empty Eastgate house. On the eighth day, a Sunday, bleary-eyed and unshaven, he appeared at the home of Menachem Shtarker and Zipporah.

Menachem greeted his son as the prodigal returned. Hugging

Daniel as if it were a habit of his, Menachem said, "The phone hasn't stopped ringing! Zipporah can't walk down the street without being beseeched by well-wishers. Eighteen citations, Daniel, it's wonderful!"

"Proud of me now, Pa?" asked Daniel. "Now you really like me? You didn't talk to me for three years but now you like me? Pop, you're a bit of a shmuck and you'll always be one. I'm sick of living my life to prove something to you."

Menachem's response was to run for a congratulatory telegram and hand it to Daniel. Daniel realized his words had meant nothing to Menachem, now a prisoner of *naches*. Daniel went berserk. He leapt on Menachem and grabbed him by the throat. Zipporah put her whole body between them and eventually he let go. But he didn't say he was sorry. Menachem returned to his congratulatory phone calls, Zipporah to the kitchen.

But things had definitely changed. The ever Orthodox Menachem was now confronted by the ferociously secular Daniel. From now on, Daniel came and went as he pleased, and returned home at whatever hour he pleased. If Zipporah's dishes did not please Daniel, he hurled them over his head into the sink. "Geniuses, like rabbis, are so moody and complicated. We have to humour them," said Menachem when Zipporah grew weary of Daniel.

Still, the real winner was Menachem. Used to mad rabbis in the Old Country, he could put up with a crazed secular rabbi at home. He knew there would be more fights ahead, but he was sure he could handle them. Now, when asked about his family, Menacham would say, "I have two married daughters and two sons. One, Saul, is the close financial adviser of the philanthropists the Belzbergs. The other, Daniel, is the top student at the University of Manitoba."

Summer Jobs

*I*n Menachem's view, a summer job might save Daniel, who in his high school days was not only in the dummies class but was also close to being a full-fledged low-life. A summer job could give him the work ethic, instill a sense of ambition, perhaps make a *mensch* out of him. Daniel, of course, had little to say in the matter. Menachem spoke to On the Ball Saul, who had a client called Concord Blouses. Mr. Ehrlich, the proprietor, said he needed a general gofer, and Saul said Daniel would fill the bill.

Fifteen going on sixteen, Daniel reported for duty one day at 8:00 a.m. He had to deliver cartons of Concord Blouses on a bicycle, sweep up, and clean out the factory toilets. He decided to clean the toilets first and get a head start on the week's work. In an hour, he had the men's toilet spic and span. That job done, he headed down the hall for the women's washroom, in the rear of the factory. It was opposite the room where women did piecework at their sewing machines.

"Look, we've got a new kid!" yelled Maria Moldovich. "Like your job so far, kid?" she asked. "I hope you don't run into any surprises." Maria laughed and the other women stopped their sewing to howl in unison. Daniel wasn't sure why the women were laughing, but understood that it wasn't good news.

He was right. In the ladies' toilet, the smell was overpowering. There were at least sixteen turds in the toilet bowl; stuffed down it were sanitary napkins. The toilet now could not be flushed. One by one, the Kotex and Modess pads had to be retrieved.

Daniel recognized class warfare when he saw it. The other two toilets were the same. This was deliberate defiance by the women workers.

Moving quickly, a handkerchief over his mouth, Daniel got the sanitary napkins out of all three toilet bowls and into a garbage bag. He flushed the toilets many, many times.

As he quietly left the sewing area of the factory, Maria Moldovich yelled, "Covered in shit? I hope you enjoyed it, kid." The other women stopped their sewing to laugh with her.

Outside the sewing room, Daniel checked his wallet. He found five dollars, his emergency fund, and went next door to Al's Cafeteria. There were fifty women doing piecework. Daniel ordered fifty cups of coffee and boxes of doughnuts. The bill was five dollars. He marched back into the factory and said to Maria Moldovich, "I've got coffee and doughnuts here and I'd very much like the girls to have them."

Maria called a break. As the workers ate and drank, Daniel said, "I admire your rebellion against the bosses. I'm on your side. I'm only here for the summer because my father insists on it. I'm in the dummies class, the slow learners. I'm maybe the first dumb Jew you've ever met. I respect you all. I hope we can get along. Oh, by the way, in my short life I've been covered in shit many times. I hope it won't happen to me again here."

The following week the women's toilets were clean. Daniel's bargain with the female proletariat had been signed and sealed. Women's liberation, working-class style, had entered Daniel's consciousness.

ONE SUMMER Menachem used his influence to get Daniel a job at the 7 Up bottling plant, an assembly line operation where the workers' jobs varied from one hour to the next.

The first job was to get empty bottles out of the wooden cases they came in and put them on a conveyor belt. That was simple, except that there were many broken bottles. A fellow worker reached into a case too quickly and sliced off his middle finger. Daniel, in response to this episode, removed bottles slowly and very carefully. When the foreman told him to speed up, Daniel did a clever job of faking speed motions but in fact picked up the bottles at a deliberate pace.

In the second phase of the operation, the worker sat on a chair for an hour and watched an electronic device that screened bottles of 7 Up as they passed. The screen would register the presence of old condoms, dead mice, or other detritus that had accidentally or otherwise got into the soft drink mix. It was the worker's job to remove such bad bottles. This was another opportunity for class struggle. All of Daniel's fellow employees let 7 Up bottles pass with condoms, dead mice, and dog shit in them, and Daniel was certainly no exception to this rule.

AT SILVERWOOD'S DAIRY Daniel found himself in a Chaplinesque *Modern Times* operation. Daniel had to be at the job at 6:00 a.m., and until eight, when the ice cream makers arrived, Daniel was alone with the refrigerator pipes, conduits, and levers, charged with cleaning the equipment. Daniel was given highly detailed and complex instructions, which he chose to ignore. He threw into the pipes whatever mix of chemicals and cleansers he thought appropriate. When Daniel heard some employees claiming the Revelos tasted bitter, and the Fudgicles a bit harsh, Daniel smiled wistfully to himself. Daniel liked his ice cream job, but concluded there was no future in the business for him.

IN UNIVERSITY, Daniel held a super summer job, Storekeeper I in the Department of Education. He shipped exams, soccer balls, and information about Newfoundland to all the high schools in Manitoba. His boss, Gus, was not only a veritable saint but also clever. For example, when Daniel was shocked to discover that examination papers were coming back written in Ukrainian, Gus would say, "Son, this is politics. We don't want to upset the Ukrainian vote. Take these exams up to Mr. Wawryko, the assistant deputy minister. He'll mark them." Gus also introduced Daniel to the Press Gallery, but warned him to tell the reporters nothing. "If you're a civil servant, son, never trust the press. They're your mortal enemy. They'll print anything about you, especially your sex life."

That was a sore point. Daniel had little sex life. A preoccupation with the size of his nose didn't help. He did have a Swedish girlfriend, but every time they kissed their teeth bumped and somehow Daniel felt their relationship wouldn't last. But the job at the provincial government had a profound impact on Daniel Shtarker's sex life.

One day he noticed a stunning young creature standing on tiptoe, a nice ripple running through the calves of her legs. She was peering into the film censor room, where the dirty movies were being screened. Daniel joined her, tiptoe to tiptoe. Her name was Dahlia Devon, and they quickly became fast friends. At first there was nothing carnal in their relationship. Daniel assumed Dahlia had a handsome WASP boyfriend and wouldn't be interested in The Nose That Walks Like a Man. Then one day he saw the boyfriend, clearly a wimp. Daniel therefore pursued Dahlia, and one night she gave him his first French kiss. At once Daniel knew he was in love. They began a secret romance. They made love in empty football stadiums, apartment block staircases, empty swimming pools, abandoned coal storage sheds, empty grain elevators, abandoned factories, public parks, and bushes anywhere.

At last Daniel had a real girlfriend. Menachem was right. Summer jobs weren't really all that bad for you.

Three Hairy Black Tomatoes

*I*n the late summer of 1956, Daniel was dreaming a variant of the Canadian dream: the president of Harvard had just given him his Ph.D. in Canadian-American Relations. Sitting in the audience was Daniel's beloved Dahlia, wearing a bikini. Her legs were long and slender, her bosom ample. Since neither Daniel nor Dahlia could swim, the bikini obviously promised amorous pleasures when the ceremony was over. Dr. Daniel Shtarker could hardly wait.

"Wake up, Daniel! Wake up!" Daniel sat bolt upright. It was Menachem in his room, at 4:00 a.m.

The night before, Daniel had told a secret he had kept from Menachem for over two years. Daniel was in love, and his love was not Jewish. There were recriminations. Why had Daniel deceived his parents for two years? He was ready for questions like that. He said he didn't want to hurt his parents; if they knew, there might be sustained quarrels; that could have affected his marks and stopped him from being what Menachem wanted, a success.

The arguments went on for hours. Menachem appealed to Daniel's Jewishness, his fears of anti-Semitism, his Zionism. Nothing worked, so the Shtarkers, exhausted, headed for their beds.

But Menachem didn't sleep. By four o'clock he decided Daniel shouldn't be sleeping either. They would get dressed and go for a walk. They walked in silence, and finally came to rest in St. John's Park.

What approach would Menachem use now? Menachem's worship of success had helped drive him further and further into conservatism. He had become a right winger with a rabid dislike of socialism. The fact that he worked for a socialist newspaper made things worse. He felt like a *marano*, a Spanish secret Jew, hiding his true sentiments. Worse, Daniel's love of socialism was at its peak. Daniel's hero was Professor Harry Raven, a fierce socialist who used to scare his children by telling them Senator McCarthy was coming to get them. Good socialists in Harry Raven's classes got A's. A conservative was lucky to get a C. As Daniel saw it, socialism stood for peace over war, an end to racism, and a concern for the working man. Daniel saw in his love for Dahlia an affirmation of socialism. As the young socialist, Menachem had wooed and won the strong, silent Zipporah; so Daniel, the socialist, had wooed and won the strong, silent Dahlia.

The link between intermarriage and socialism made Menachem all the more bitter. Socialism was not only wrongheaded, it was now actually threatening his family. "Socialism," said Menachem, in the park, "is a great snare and a delusion. Socialism says everybody is the same. Try telling that to the Ku Klux Klan. Blood is thicker than water. The Jewish people must live. They will die if their sons marry Gentiles."

"Moses married a Gentile; so did Boaz," said Daniel.

"The Talmud says neither marriage came to a good end," said Menachem. "Mixed marriages don't work. You'll wake up in the middle of the night craving a salami sandwich; she'll wake up in the middle of the night craving — pork!" Pork, Menachem had often told Daniel, gives the Gentiles constipation, stomach ulcers, glaucoma, heart attacks, and hemorrhoids.

"You'll be walking with Dahlia down Selkirk or Main or Portage and you'll hear the pealing of church bells," said Menachem. "That sound will remind you of the pogroms, the beatings inflicted on the Jewish people by the goyim. Your Dahlia will hear the church bells ring and over her will come the need for communion. Dahlia will leave your side and answer the call of the bells. The bells are ringing for Dahlia and not for you."

"I guess I'll just have to give up salamis and long walks with

Dahlia, Pa," said Daniel, trying to control the sarcasm in his voice.

But Menachem had more tricks up his sleeve. He had contacted On the Ball Saul, and Saul was flying in from Edmonton. He also called Sweaters Shoshannah. She and Phillip were flying in from Wichita. That night all of them would gather at Too Good Teibel's, and family solidarity would win Daniel over. The starting pitcher would be Saul, whose close business contacts with the Belzbergs and the Singers had made the old shiksa-chaser a success. He had given up chasing for a talented and beautiful Jewish girl. Saul would show Daniel the error of his ways.

Menachem told Daniel to bring Dahlia to the family gathering. Only Zipporah would be absent, because of the weakness of her heart.

It was dawn as Daniel and Menachem left the park and silently headed home.

TEIBEL AND HER HUSBAND greeted Daniel and Dahlia at the door. Sitting on the sofa in Teibel's small living room were Shoshannah, Menachem, and Saul Shtarker. It was Dahlia's first encounter with the family.

Saul began. "If you marry Dahlia now, aren't you worried that your children will marry Negroes?" he asked.

Daniel was as ready for that as he had ever been for anything in his life. As a stand-up comedian on the campus, he had a routine about Jewish fear of intermarriage. It went something like this: "It's not the marriage to a shiksa that Jews really worry about, ladies and gentlemen. What Jews are worried about is taking those first steps down the biological ladder. Sure, Jews know that the children of the shiksa will marry blacks, but Jews can live with that. At a party they can introduce their half-WASP kids, and half-Negro grandchildren, who at least all speak English and keep clean. The half-WASP kids can read from Shakespeare aloud, the half-black grandchildren can sing the blues. Now obviously, the half-black grandchildren will take a further step down the biological ladder and they will of course marry apes or monkeys, the next logical step. But that doesn't worry the Jews so much. The

Jewish bubba can still hold a party for her half-WASP grandchildren, her black great-grandchildren and her ape and monkey great-great-grandchildren. The only thing that the bubba has to worry about are the monkey and ape great-great-grandchildren swinging from the chandelier. But at least these Jewish apes and monkeys are lively and fun to be with. What really worries the bubbas is the final step down the biological ladder — the plant kingdom. To introduce her great-great-great-grandchildren, the bubba will have to go to the fridge, open the door, and say, "Here they are." Lying there in the fridge are *three hairy black tomatoes*. It is this fear of the inverted biological ladder and the three hairy black tomatoes that underlies the Jewish fear of intermarriage."

Daniel delivered this stand-up routine to the Shtarkers and added, "Are you not the same On the Ball Saul who chased shiksas by the hundreds?"

"I chased them but I didn't marry them," said Saul.

"No, but you had one kill herself over you," said Daniel. "I think you should butt out of this argument and leave it to Pa and me."

At this point, Shoshannah offered her argument. She shouted hysterically at Dahlia, "If the Nazis came here, whose side would *you* be on!"

Dahlia burst into tears, and Daniel answered. "First of all, Shoshannah, Dahlia would kill Zipporah, then Menachem, then Teibel and her children, and then Saul and his children, and then for the end, the climax so to speak, she would save for you, Shoshannah. Dahlia would kill you, then throw your babies up in the air, and catch them on her bayonet."

This outburst led to a bit of a scuffle between Daniel and Saul, which Menachem broke up. Keeping his temper, Menachem asked Dahlia, "Why do you want Daniel? He's lazy, sleeping all morning whenever he gets a chance. He picks his nose, he's a dreadful dresser, he can't swim or even dance. He doesn't brush his teeth; when he eats, his cheeks are a forest of crumbs. He's sarcastic and has a foul temper. He's fickle and could easily leave you. He talks too much and never listens. His socialism is phony. He wouldn't give a beggar a dime. He talks class solidarity but how many of his friends are from River Heights? Can't you see that a beautiful, clever girl like yourself needs a better person than Daniel?"

Dahlia burst into tears again. Menachem was not used to making beautiful women cry. He could see that things were not going well for his side.

He tried another ploy. Daniel wanted to take law in Toronto at Osgoode Hall. Why not have Daniel go to Toronto while Dahlia stayed behind in Winnipeg and thus could get to know the Shtarker family better? "Oh," said Daniel, jumping in, "now we have the duke and the scullery maid routine. To get the duke off the idea of marrying the scullery maid, you send the duke on the grand tour. Well, I want the grand tour of Europe, all of it, and nothing less, and you're paying for it, Pa. That will take a year. After the grand tour, I'll come and fetch Dahlia."

Menachem could now see that the stubbornness for which he himself was famous was now a streak in Daniel that couldn't be blunted. The confrontation had gone about as far as it could; the curse of intermarriage was staring him in the face — and there was nothing he could do. Reluctantly, he concluded that he could somehow live with the situation. Toward the end of the evening, he announced that intention, and more tears poured from Dahlia. Menachem and Daniel nodded at each other warily.

Daniel started talking to Saul and, grudgingly, to Shoshannah. Tea and cookies were served and politics discussed. Dahlia had dried her tears and was into Zipporah's sponge cake and a glass of hot tea. The Shtarker family was once again a unit — and Dahlia, for better or worse, was now a part of it.

Gone with the Wind

I n the operating room, at the Mayo Clinic in Rochester, Minnesota, Menachem lay unconscious, knocked out by an anaesthetic fed intravenously. He had survived a polyps-in-the-bowel operation five years before, and now had a recurrence that had to be removed. The surgeons were up for this one. They all knew and liked Menachem Shtarker.

He was a bit of a star at the Mayo. He would wander around in his wheelchair, with or without Saul or Shoshannah in tow, talking to patients in his broken English, reassuring them, building up their courage and confidence, as a proper street fighter should do. Once, on a wheelchair tour, sitting awkwardly on the rubber doughnut that kept his rear end comfortable, Menachem escaped from Saul and Shoshannah and greeted what he thought was a long-lost friend. "You look familiar," Menachem said. "Have I seen you before? Maybe Winnipeg? Perhaps Toronto? New York possibly?"

"You could have seen me in a movie. My name is Fred MacMurray. I'm a Hollywood actor." His wife was in the Mayo Clinic with cancer of the liver.

"Fred MacMurray — the name doesn't ring a bell," Menachem said, "but if you're an actor you must have acted with beautiful actresses. Give me their names and I'll see if I can remember."

Fred MacMurray, understandably impatient, nevertheless played along. "Let me see. I acted with Katharine Hepburn in *Alice*

Adams and with Sylvia Sidney in *Trail of the Lonesome Pine*."

"Sylvia Sidney? She's a Jewish girl, isn't she?" asked Menachem. Saul and Shoshannah, who had finally caught up with him, blanched with embarrassment. "You're not married to a Jewish woman, are you?"

"I believe Sylvia Sidney is Jewish," said MacMurray, "and no, I'm not married to a Jewish woman. That of course doesn't mean I wouldn't — under the right circumstances."

Menachem, enemy of mixed marriages, was relieved that he hadn't stumbled on another one. He didn't notice that MacMurray had been placed on the defensive, having to prove he was no anti-Semite by promising to marry a Jewish woman.

"Any other actresses you can tell me about?" Menachem pushed further.

"Well, I did a movie, *Double Indemnity*, with ah, with ah, Barbara Stanwyck."

"Barbara Stanwyck. She's *good*." The implication, somehow, was that MacMurray wasn't. Menachem spun his wheelchair around and headed for the cafeteria. The friendships Menachem made at the clinic were sometimes as bizarre as his encounters in the corridor. Menachem had such a friendship with Dalton McCarthy, a Mayo patient and a Texas oil millionaire. After they met at Mayo they corresponded frequently. Once McCarthy, aware of Menachem Shtarker's battles with his *Street Fighter* bosses, offered to resettle Menachem and his family in Houston. There he would establish a Yiddish-English newspaper for Menachem.

Daniel translated Menachem's letters to McCarthy. "There are no Jews in Texas," Menachem wrote.

I have seen sixty, seventy Western movies and in not one of them is there a rabbi or a garment cutter. How can you expect me to live in a wild Western world without Jews! Come to Winnipeg, Dalton, and start a Jewish paper here.

But when I get well, I'll fly to Houston. Guarantee me there'll be no shootouts at the airport when I land. I love you and I miss you, Dalton.

Your Comrade in Mayo Clinic Arms
Menachem Shtarker
Captain, Kerensky Revolutionary Army
— and still in there fighting.

IN THE MAYO CLINIC, on the operating table, the old fighter was losing. During the operation an infection set in and spread rapidly. The surgeons tried, vainly, to contain the damage. The next day the *Jewish Street Fighter* proclaimed in a front-page obituary:

> Menachem Shtarker, author of *And So Help Me, God* and thousands of features and signed editorials, is dead. All of Canadian Jewry mourns his departure. Reruns of his best work will appear in this newspaper every day for the next two weeks. There will be three services: one at the El Mole Rachmim Synagogue, one at the Butchers' Synagogue and one at the United Left Labour Zionist Freedom Workers Temple.

The service at the El Mole Rachmim was in perfect harmony with the kind of man Menachem was. The Pious Ones danced and whiskey was consumed in copious amounts. Spontaneously in all corners of the synagogue, people stood up to tell Shtarker stories. The Torah was passed around the hall and the kisses on the Torah flowed upward to the angels who were welcoming Menachem back home.

At the Butchers' Synagogue, Rabbi Yakov Weisman paid tribute to the decisive role Menachem had played in the famous Kosher War and laid great stress on Menachem's conversion to orthodoxy in the last years of his life. "This was a victory for God and for the Jewish people. Once Menachem Shtarker had toiled only for the Jewish people. But that is not enough. At the end of his life, Menachem Shtarker toiled for the Jewish people and for God."

The eulogy of teacher Zolf at the Workers Temple was a classic. Teacher Zolf and Menachem Shtarker had become close friends when they realized they were both steering from socialism to orthodoxy. Teacher Zolf's efforts to get bar mitzvah lessons and training instituted at the United Left Labour Zionist Freedom

Workers Temple were heartily endorsed in a signed editorial in the *Street Fighter* by Menachem. Feivel Festung, the realtor-loanshark-socialist chairman of the board, tried to fire teacher Zolf over the bar mitzvah affair, but his attempt at intimidation was exposed in the *Street Fighter* by Menachem. "Menachem Shtarker was not a man," said teacher Zolf, "not an institution, not a god. Menachem Shtarker was Jewish essence itself. Menachem seeped into your pores and poured into your soul. He loved his people, but above all he loved this country, Canada, its British heritage of freedom and fairness. He believed, as did Disraeli, that Britishness without a leavening of Jewish life and laughter was an empty shell. Menachem could make people laugh; he could make them cry; he could make them angry. But always Menachem Shtarker moved people, with an absence of malice truly astonishing.

"We Jews loved Menachem Shtarker back. We'll never forget him. He's in our hearts to stay forever. He will never disappear. Of him, in truth it can be said — 'gone with the wind' will never be his epitaph."

Teacher Zolf had just seen a rerun of the movie epic and knew the title would make a great closer. The weeping and wailing that followed the eulogy was heavy and widespread.

WHEN THE FUNERAL procession left the Chesed Shel Emes near Manitoba and Main and headed for the burial ground, the flood of cars produced one of the North End's largest traffic jams. People lined the streets as the procession made its way slowly to the cemetery. Even Coke Lavish and Boozy Roth and the boys at Bountiful Billiards stopped their pool games and stepped outside to wave.

At the cemetery itself, telegrams were read from the mayor, the premier, and the prime minister. From New York, Buenos Aires, Warsaw, Paris, and Jerusalem, fellow Yiddish writers sent condolences.

Daniel couldn't help noticing that among his fellow pallbearers were the sons of the three men Menachem had most quarrelled with — Feivel Festung, Vladek Cheeribim, and Shmuel Fartick. If Menachem knew that, he'd soon be turning over in his grave. But there was no way to tell him, now, was there? There was so much Daniel wanted to tell Menachem but hadn't. Daniel would have settled for the chance, just once, to tell him how much he loved him. But as the coffin was lowered in the grave, Daniel's mind drifted back to the last time he had seen Menachem, and the amazing consequences thereof.

"I FOUND AN APARTMENT," Dahlia had announced enthusiastically, six weeks after their wedding. Technically, they were living apart in rented rooms on Wells Street in Toronto. Daniel had a single room at 42 Wells. Dahlia had a one-room flat with kitchen across the street at 47 Wells. The arrangement was part of the promise made to Menachem that Daniel would wait a year before marrying Dahlia — just in case he had second thoughts about marrying a Gentile or she woke up one morning and called him a bloody Jew. Now finally they were newlyweds, a year having passed. No one on either side of the family had attended the wedding, to the immense relief of Daniel and Dahlia. Now all they needed was a place to call home.

The home Dahlia had found was not palatial. It was a basement apartment on Wychwood Avenue; it was, as Daniel told his friends, a subbasement in search of the lower depths. The door of the basement apartment opened up on a tiny landing, and then twenty stairs led to the basement floor. Down there were, first, a tiny kitchen with a small stove, a half refrigerator and a small table with room enough for just two chairs, then a small space that served as TV room, bedroom, dining room, and living room. There was one closet. There was one sofa, which folded down into a bed. There were no chairs. The room was so small that when Daniel sat on the sofa the toilet door had to be kept open to accommodate his feet. When two people sat on the sofa, both had to stand up if either wanted to go to the bathroom. Someone sitting on the sofa could reach into the kitchen and fetch a cookie.

The bathroom held one person, barely. When Daniel took a shower, he did so on hands and knees. But Daniel and Dahlia were in love in their first home. They saw only the charms of being alone at last, of setting out on a long life together.

For Dahlia, the apartment provided a chance to demonstrate her cooking skills and fatten up her new husband. Daniel was 130 pounds, much too skinny. Dahlia's pork roast, pork chops, pork spareribs, and pork cottage roll were consumed voraciously by Daniel, now at least a culinary convert to Pauline Christianity.

One day, after four months had passed, Daniel was sitting at the kitchen table alone. He was alone because the kitchen could hold only one person. He was eating pork cottage roll and cold potato salad.

The doorbell rang and Dahlia went to get it. From the landing, she called, "Your father is here." The news so flummoxed Daniel that he gulped quickly and a chunk of cottage roll stuck in his throat. Coughing, gasping for breath, perhaps for life, Daniel went to greet his father. Menachem descended the twenty steps to the basement slowly, majestically, as if attending a public hanging. When he hit the basement, he cast his eye over the apartment, peered into the kitchen and bathroom, and uttered his first word on Daniel's Toronto turf. The word was "Phoohhh!"

Daniel was still coughing, and Dahlia was slapping his back, trying to get the cottage roll to go down. Menachem observed, "You've got some food stuck in your throat. Maybe it was not properly prepared. Is it perhaps unkosher? That can cause problems, you know! Thank God, with Zipporah's cooking, I've never had any trouble!"

Turning to Dahlia, he said, "This place is a pest-hole. It won't do. I'll find you another place. I'll call cousin Rivka. She'll know of places. Is there anywhere to sit?"

The only place to sit was the sofa. Menachem sat down first, Daniel beside him. The act of sitting down, Bless the One Above, dislodged the chunk of pork cottage roll. Dahlia was in the kitchen preparing tea, and Menachem sat silent, waiting for her to reappear. When the tea was served, she joined them on the sofa. Menachem then had to go to the toilet. That meant Daniel and Dahlia both rose so he could get off the sofa.

Eventually, Menachem launched into the setpiece he had mulled over on the flight from Winnipeg. "Daniel, Dahlia, we've had our time of troubles, but that is past. Your mother and Teibel have become good friends, and that is a good thing. What we Shtarkers and Devons need is a giant celebration, a *simchah*, which will symbolize the end of our time of troubles, our sorrows, our despondencies, our depressions. In two years, Joshua, Teibel's son, will turn thirteen, and we'll have a huge big bar mitzvah. In two years, you, Daniel, will have your law degree, will be a lawyer, a servant of the court, of her Britannic Majesty the Queen. We will have a double celebration, a double *simchah*, the likes of which Winnipeg has never seen!"

Menachem's eyes were glistening with joy. But there was a flaw in his scheme.

Daniel had just finished first year in law, but to get his degree he would have to take second year, then article for a year, and then take fourth year. Daniel would have his law degree a year after the bar mitzvah. Gently, he pointed this out to Menachem. Menachem was mad. "What do you take me for, a fool? Of course you're going into second year, then articling, then fourth year. I know that. I am no fool."

Daniel said he was sorry. Menachem then talked about interesting subjects. The increase of intermarriage among Jews in Paraguay. The connection between homosexuality and socialism. The wonders of Zipporah's cooking. Bert Pearl, the Happy Gang, and the Jewish question. (Bert was a Winnipeg Jewish boy — the question was why he had hired only Gentiles for his Happy Gang on the CBC.) And of course the business successes of Saul Shtarker and Pinchus Weisman.

Then Menachem sighed. "Ah, I can hardly wait. Two years from now, Joshua will have his bar mitzvah and Daniel will have his law degree and we'll have a big celebration."

Daniel jumped in. "But, Pa, I told you in two years I'll have finished third year. I won't be a lawyer until a year later."

"What do you take me for, a fool? We'll have two separate celebrations, one for Joshua's bar mitzvah and one, a year later, for your law degree. What's the matter, you don't think I can wait a year? I can wait forever!"

Menachem then talked about Israel. Its air force was the best in the world, its women the most beautiful in the world. Ben-Gurion and Golda Meir were the smartest people in the world. Moshe Dayan the greatest general since Wellington. Then, once again, he lapsed into his two-years-from-now-double-celebration routine.

Infuriated, Daniel stood up from the couch. "Goddamn it, if it kills me, I'll get my law degree in two years and you, Pa, will get your goddamned double celebration!"

Menachem, apparently angered by this outburst, said nothing. Still, he gave Daniel some piercing looks. Soon he had to leave for the airport. Menachem was flying to Montreal and from there back to Winnipeg. Daniel escorted him back to the airport. There was little conversation in the cab. In the lounge, just before Menachem was to depart, he told his son, "I'm worried about you, Daniel. Your temper, your nervousness is not natural. I want you to see a psychiatrist. I have already called one, Dr. Ripstein in Toronto. He will see you tomorrow at three."

In shock, Daniel felt his anger suddenly turn to rage. "Fuck Dr. Ripstein. You go see him. Or better yet, why don't we go together? Somehow I think our stories are entwined." Menachem smiled, shook hands with Daniel, and said goodbye.

Daniel never saw him alive again.

THE OFFICE of Dr. Vladimir Varim in the Metcalfe Institute was a friendly place, tastefully decorated. On the couch, at a right angle to Dr. Vladimir Varim, sat Daniel. Dr. Varim, the celebrated psychiatrist, was a Jewish Hungarian expatriate, famed for his capacity to treat writers, particularly funny ones. Varim's most famous book was *Laugh and God May Laugh with You: A Freudian Probe of Laughter and Lunacy*. It was this work that first attracted Daniel to Dr. Varim. "Did I tell the Menachem story right, Dr. Varim?" Daniel asked the shrink.

"It sounded good to me," said Dr. Varim. "This is the first time you've ever really talked about your father. We're making progress. Your problems are manageable, Mr. Shtarker."

Daniel was relieved, as always, by talking with Dr. Varim. But as he left the Metcalfe Institute and headed for the Bagel and a cold beet borscht, he decided that he'd give a dozen Dr. Varims to be able to tell Menachem how much he really loved him. Just once.

The Last Sir John

O
n his first day on the job as Archivist I for the Province of Ontario, Daniel was invited to a screening of the microfilming of the Orillia *Packet & Times*. That newspaper was special, at least as far as the archives were concerned, not because Orillia was the hometown of Stephen Leacock but because it was the hometown of the premier, Leslie Frost. He had gone to great trouble to obtain copies of the newspaper back to its origins in the early 1820s. Once these were microfilmed, the originals would go back to Orillia where they belonged.

The premier's interest in the project was so keen that he came to the archives to share in the joy of the microfilm launching. Screening the microfilm with him were Dr. Noah Narrow, the Ontario archivist, a patronage appointee from the 1920s; Samuel Simp, a patronage appointee of Dr. Narrow's; and our fledgling archivist, Shtarker, no longer a law student but now a graduate student in history and the University of Toronto history faculty's recommendation for the archives job.

The screening was not a success. The first roll began with page twenty of a 1920 edition, and the next seven pages were from an 1827 edition; pages were upside down, some blurred.

Premier Frost had seen enough. "I do know you're busy, Dr. Narrow," he said, "but *The Packet & Times* is important to me. I think tighter supervision is called for. Do you have anyone in mind?"

"Samuel Simp is our best man, Premier," Dr. Narrow said. Daniel smiled inwardly. If Simp was Dr. Narrow's best man, God help the institution. The premier's pipeline had also told him about Simp.

"Oh, no," he said. "Mr. Simp is too busy on too many valuable projects to worry his head about this. I hear the university has sent you a new man. Why not give Mr. Shtarker the job?" Dr. Narrow nodded reluctantly.

Dr. Narrow had hated Daniel on first sight. After consulting the history department before filling his vacancy, Dr. Narrow had taken the name Shtarker — German for "strong one" — to indicate that his new archivist was of the Teutonic persuasion. The sight of the Semite Daniel had not pleased him, but he had hired him because it would look strange to turn down the leading graduate history student at the university while keeping on staff one of Simp's obvious lightweightedness. He had hoped, however, to make Shtarker's existence as difficult as possible.

"Are you free, Mr. Shtarker, to do this Orillia assignment?" asked Premier Frost.

"Free, able, and willing, Mr. Premier." Daniel, basking in the glory of a premier's imprimatur, could hardly wait to get at the project.

THAT AFTERNOON, he went to the microfilm room in the basement of the Sigmund Samuel building on Queen's Park. Daniel cast his eye from one end of the room to the other. The far left-hand corner was the most interesting part. There stood a six-foot framing stand, the kind from which to hang huge geological or topographical maps. This framing stand was different. Hanging from the top of it, in a kind of fetal position, was a drunk, sleeping off his intoxication. This was the official microfilmer. His distinguishing mark was a Terry-Thomas handlebar mustache. He was wearing the jodhpurs Daniel had seen at so many British India movies at the Odeon.

Daniel pulled up a chair and waited for the microfilmer to awaken. An hour later, the man stirred, lifted himself off the framing stand, and landed on his feet. He said, "I'm Pembroke

Potts, Indian Army Fifth Division — and you're a Jew!"

"Right on, Potts. My name is Daniel Shtarker, Counsellor, Habonim Camp, Winnipeg. And you're a drunk. I don't give a sweet fuck what you think of the Jews, Potts, and I suppose you don't care what I think about drunks or the Indian Army. But there are now, Potzie, new rules to be enforced and obeyed. You fucked up Premier Frost's Orillia stuff, Potzie. Now I've got the job and I'm not going to let you do it again. You come in at eight in the morning, sharp — and sober. We work from eight to one. The afternoons are yours, Potzie, to piss away as you see fit." Pembroke agreed.

Daniel rode herd over Potts like some mad Nazi *Gauleiter*. Soon all the pages of *The Packet & Times* were in order, and right side up, on the microfilm. The premier thanked Daniel personally and told Dr. Narrow that he would be calling on Shtarker for further services in the future. Dr. Narrow tried to smile.

DANIEL ENJOYED solving the premier's historical problems. Once he asked what was the difference between the Lubavitcher Chassidim and the Setmar Chassidim. Daniel found out, and told the premier, but added, "I don't think these Chassidim vote, Premier. They see democracy as a threat that could assimilate them."

"Well," said the premier, "maybe they'll change their minds when my canvassers get at them. These Chassidim sound a lot like Quebeckers."

On another occasion the premier wanted to refer to being a Mason at a Jewish Conservative party gathering. He wondered if the Masons had Jewish members. Yes, said Daniel; his uncle was the head of the Masonic Lodge in Miami Beach. "Jews and Masons have to stick together should be your theme, Premier. Hitler hated both."

One day the premier called Daniel in with an odd request. He escorted Daniel into a huge vault beside his office. Standing there were ten statues of Sir John A. Macdonald, ranging in size from three feet six inches to about six feet. These were models the sculptor worked on before he finally came up with the statue that stands outside the legislature.

The premier said, "My problem is this, Daniel. I have to have the vault for office space and these statues must go. Any idea of how much they're worth, Daniel?"

"About five hundred to seven hundred dollars each, Mr. Premier, I'd say."

"Well, then, its all the more important we find homes for all these Sir Johns — there are ten of them. I know you can find sanctuary for them, if anyone can." The words *home* and *sanctuary* were perfect examples of the Frost elegance.

Daniel wondered if there was an element of danger for the premier in this. "Mr. Premier," he said. "I'll try my best to find them homes. But should I fail to do so in one or two cases, then there could be a political problem involved. I'd hate to see that Tory rag, *The Toronto Telegram*, with a headline reading 'Tory Premier Takes Axe to Sir John' or 'Tory Premier Demolishes Tory Father of Our Country.'"

The premier laughed and said, "Oh, there will be none of that." Daniel went off, determined to find loving homes for all ten Sir Johns.

In the first week he did well. He got rid of two Sir Johns at the University of Toronto right away — one to the chairman of the history department, and another to Hart House. One Sir John went to the Albany Club and another to No. 10 Toronto Street, home of the Argus Corporation. Queen's University took two; the Oddfellows in Napanee graciously accepted one. At last, nine were gone.

But finding a home for the tenth Sir John, six feet tall, was a problem. The University of Western Ontario declined it, and so did the historical societies Daniel contacted. It was too big, too clumsy, to be an object of affection and love in a permanent home. Desperately, Daniel kept at the job, and hoped there'd be no calls from the premier's office. Perhaps the premier would forget and let the last Sir John call the vault his home. But a phone call came from the premier. "You are an utter marvel, Mr. Shtarker. Nine homes for nine Sir Johns. What a salesman! Still, Mr. Shtarker, there *is* the last Sir John. He must leave the vault."

"I know, Mr. Premier," said Daniel. "But no one wants him. I'm afraid, despite my previous advice, that we will have to . . . dispose of him. The deed must be done quickly. I suggest tonight, under cover of dark. If you'll leave the main office key under the mat for me, Mr. Premier, I'll come and fetch the last Sir John at nine sharp. If we're careful, no one will catch us in this act of — dare I say it — Tory deicide."

"Sir John will forgive us I'm sure, Daniel," said Premier Frost. "But don't forget the *Telegram*. Be careful and good luck!"

At nine sharp, Daniel and three helpers entered an absolutely empty premier's office. The last Sir John was carried out, the door locked, and the key put back under the mat. Sir John was put into a panel truck. "Head for High Park!" said Daniel, and they were off. The largest park in Toronto would be the perfect place for the deed.

In High Park they drove around until Daniel was sure they weren't being followed. Finally he called a halt. The helpers went to work with sledgehammers — the head fell first, then the arms. Finally, body and legs collapsed in a heap. As the truck drove around High Park, they scattered the remains. What was still left, and possibly recognizable, was dumped into the harbour. The disappearance of the last Sir John remained a mystery. Neither the premier's role nor Daniel's role ever saw the light of day.

Here Come the Sixties

O ne day in 1956 Daniel Shtarker found the TV page in the *Winnipeg Tribune* mysteriously missing. Not that such a page was really indispensable — the CBC was all you could get in Winnipeg, and the absence of choice produced fighting words among Manitoba's hardy breed of sod busters. One story in the *Trib* had been headed, "Winnipeg Man Builds World's Largest Antenna on His Roof." Abner Snively had explained, "I'm sick of all the faggots and commies on the CBC. With this antenna, I can pick up Fargo, North Dakota. At last, I'm a free man!" Two weeks later, the *Trib* reported, "World's Tallest Antenna Collapses into Living room." Abner, watching Fargo at the time, suffered a broken leg and three broken ribs. "It's those fags and commies at the CBC that did this to me," he was quoted as saying. "I was in the middle of watching 'The Jack Benny Show' from Fargo. They did it deliberately, the CBC bastards."

Daniel sympathized with Abner. Daniel was a CBC-phobe too. But, while perhaps the place was riddled with faggots, there were certainly no communists at the CBC. Communism reeked of Jewishness and the CBC was as free of Jews as Vienna or Warsaw in 1956. The CBC brass in Winnipeg were notorious anti-Semites — or so North Winnipeg felt.

Even so, like most Winnipegers Daniel watched the CBC every night, always looking at the TV listings page, as if he had a choice of programs. Daniel hated surprises, especially on the tube.

That night Daniel looked everywhere for the listings. He asked Zipporah about it, and he peered into every corner. Searching Menachem's study, he shoved aside the large blotter pad on his desk. And there was a single sheet of that day's *Trib*, page 22 and 23. On page 22 was the TV listing. On page 23 was a more interesting story, from New York: "Senator Joseph McCarthy Says Communists Run the New York Times." Daniel hated McCarthy with a passion and was familiar with his crazy accusations, but the bottom paragraph of the story contained a surprise. "Named by Senator McCarthy as a communist was the *New York Times* chief proofreader, Isaac Shtarker. Mr. Shtarker, on advice of his counsel, Leonard Boudine, refused any comment to the press. Mr. Boudine said Isaac Shtarker would plead the Fifth Amendment . . . "

Finding the torn-out sheet of newspaper saddened Daniel. It was clear that Menachem Shtarker, fearless Kerensky soldier, Nazi-baiter deluxe, was so ashamed of his communist nephew that he had hidden the newspaper story under his blotter. In a small way even Menachem Shtarker was a victim of McCarthyism.

"WILL YOU, DAHLIA DEVON, take this man, Daniel Shtarker, to be your beloved husband, to love, cherish, honour, and obey, until death do you part?" asked Toronto's Red Rabbi, Ezekiel Eneg, of the Shrine of the Mystic Petal. It was the spring of 1960.

Six months before, Rabbi Eneg had asked Daniel Shtarker whether he and Dahlia would have a civil wedding ceremony if he declined to marry them. "We will," said Daniel.

"In that case," said Rabbi Eneg, "it is better that I perform the wedding and do so in a House of God."

The rabbi even agreed to give Dahlia a kind of quick immersion in Judaism, an almost-conversion. "Dahlia is a quick learner, Rabbi," said Daniel. "You'll love her. She's crazy about Jews and Israel. What's even better, she's for nuclear disarmament, racial integration, and unions. She's also against pollution and capital punishment. Your kind of woman, Rabbi."

The Red Rabbi, who was forever picketing the American consulate on one or all of these issues, nodded. He then cast a quick look at Dahlia's magnificent face and figure and readily agreed that she was his kind of woman. The author of two classics, *Petting in the Pulpit* and *Torah between the Sheets*, knew a good prospect for Judaism when he saw one. He gave Dahlia a reading list and told her to come back and see him when she had finished. A quick reader, Dahlia was back in a week. An hour later, she told Daniel the news. "I'm a Jew! God, it's hard to believe! Once Rabbi Eneg said I would be an asset to the Jewish community. Twice he said I was a worthy successor to Ruth in the Bible. And three times he said I was really cute!"

The wedding was performed in the cavernous and empty Shrine of the Mystic Petal. Rabbi Eneg's secretary, Mindel Mishne, and Agatha Waishunt, secretary to the synagogue's rabbi emeritus, Gideon Platitude, acted as witnesses. Rabbi Eneg, by now almost half blind, used a magnifying glass to read the service. "And do you, Daniel Shtarker, take this woman, Dahlia Devon, to love, honour and cherish — sorry I missed a line — to be your lawful wedded wife, to love, honour, and cherish all your living life till death do you part?"

"I do," said Daniel. As he placed Rabbi Eneg's magnifying glass back on the podium, he let his mind race to the joys of his New York City honeymoon, just hours away.

Totally bereft of funds, a penniless thesis writer by profession, he had a great plan for a cheap honeymoon. Daniel had phoned his communist cousin, a man he had never spoken to before. Isaac was niceness itself. Isaac and his wife, Mindel, welcomed Daniel and his new wife, Dahlia. There was a spare room they could use. Daniel thanked Isaac profusely. Daniel and Dahlia would spend a week in New York and then go to Washington for a day. They had never been to either place before. Their bus tickets were marked Toronto – New York – Washington.

Cousin Isaac was fun. Like Daniel, he enjoyed arguing and meant nothing personal by it. One day Isaac and Daniel argued about what is a Jew. "A Jew is a religion," said Isaac. "I'm not religious. I'm not Jewish, I'm a communist."

"Tell that to Stalin," said Daniel. "He's been murdering Jewish poets and writers for years."

"Zionist propaganda," said Isaac.

"If being Jewish is a religion," said Daniel, "so how come nobody looks Protestant or Catholic. Given my schnoz, I look Jewish and every anti-Semite knows I am. Jews don't define who's Jewish. Anti-Semites and Nazis do."

Isaac had a treat in mind for Daniel and Dahlia. That night the Communist Party was having an affair for all the leaders who were going to jail. Hyman Lermer, the party's organizing genius, and Herbert Aptheker, the leading intellectual, would be making speeches. Both were going to jail.

As Isaac, Mindel, Daniel, and Dahlia approached the St. Nicholas Arena, the scene of many prize fights Daniel had listened to on radio, they were greeted by a raucous crowd of American Nazis, with swastika insignias. They were chanting:

> *Ikey kikey, go to bed*
> *Ikey kikey*
> *Wake up Red!!*

Inside the arena there was a huge vat about four feet deep and full of — chopped liver. A Ritz biscuit dispenser was beside it. There were about three hundred at the rally, most of them Jewish, most in their sixties and seventies. For them, the Soviet dream had not yet turned nightmare. They applauded lustily the speeches of the martyrs on their way to prison.

Corned beef sandwiches and coleslaw and a fruit cup were served to one and all. Daniel and Dahlia, exhausted by all the communist rhetoric and emotion, ate lustily.

DANIEL LOVED Isaac's handling of his status as Red Menace. Knowing his phone was tapped, he would lift the receiver and say, "Hello, Freddy, are you there? Good. Look, we have some relatives, Daniel and Dahlia from Toronto, and me and Mindel are taking them to see the Bronx Zoo. We'll be back by 7:00 p.m. sharp. You can take the afternoon off, Freddy. No sense you sitting there for hours, tapping for nothing." Isaac had a civil relationship with his FBI men. As he told Daniel, "Freddy's okay, he's just doing his job!"

One afternoon, cousin Isaac's son Vincent paid a visit to the apartment and brought his best friend, Paul Robeson, Jr. Vincent was in an American army uniform, and Isaac was proud of Vincent. Communists were good American citizens and patriots, Isaac argued. While American Jewish liberals were dodging the draft, Vincent was proving Reds were no cowards. It was hard to argue with Isaac's sense of pride. Vincent was harassed because of his father's appearances in the papers, but he fought back and broke some noses.

The day the visit ended Daniel and Dahlia deposited their luggage in a locker at the bus depot and killed the two hours before departure time. Dahlia decided to shop at Klein's and Daniel decided to browse at the second-hand bookstores nearby. In one store he reached onto a dirty shelf and pulled out a two-volume first editon of *Living My Life* by Emma Goldman, one of his heroines, priced at five dollars. Daniel bought it. He waited for Dahlia to return so he could show off his purchase. When they met again Dahlia reported that she had bought nothing at Klein's because she had discovered she had no money.

Did Daniel have any? He checked his pockets, and found them empty. Dahlia was furious about the fate of his last five dollars. "Who the fuck is Emma Goldman? Another of your Jewish nuts? Damn it, we need that money." They quarrelled so bitterly that a passing Jewish policeman had to break it up.

Finally, Daniel said, "We'll be okay. We'll skip Washington. We'll cash in the difference on the tickets and have enough money for a good ride home."

But at the bus depot the news was bad and final. The only place the bus tickets could be cashed in was back in Toronto. On the tickets they had, you went to Washington first, if you wanted ever to get back to Toronto.

Worn out, discouraged, and frightened, Daniel and Dahlia boarded the 10:00 p.m. bus to Washington. All the seats were taken, and they hung from straps for six hours. Dahlia, in the process, developed a severe cramp in her leg.

Sleepless, they arrived on a Monday morning in Washington.

Dahlia wanted to just lie down and await the return bus at 11:00 p.m. But when Daniel arrived in America's Rome his fatigue and anxiety disappeared and his curiosity took over. Suddenly, he was brimming with life. Better than that, he had a plan for survival.

Senator John F. Kennedy had addressed the students of the University of Toronto earlier in the spring. Senator Kennedy was terrific and Daniel almost forgave him for his father's notorious anti-Semitism. Kennedy was running for the Democratic presidential nomination and though Daniel favoured Adlai Stevenson, Kennedy was a great second choice.

Daniel's problem was money, and Senator Kennedy had plenty. Surely the senator would give some to a starving pair of Torontonians. The Shtarkers simply had to get to Kennedy and all would be well. Bizarrely, Dahlia agreed. Dragging her cramped leg, she followed Daniel to the public gallery of the Senate. It was almost empty, and Daniel and Dahlia sat in blessed relief. At two sharp, the bells rang; Vice President Richard Nixon, the shoo-in for the Republican nomination that year, was presiding officer.

Nixon called the roll, and Kennedy was the first speaker. His aides were on the Senate floor beside him, handing him notes for his speech. A Senate cop had already told Daniel that Senator Kennedy would be leaving the Senate in about an hour. The senator would then head to his office, a block away.

The speech over, Daniel went to the Senate washroom while Dahlia rested her sore leg on the grass outside the Capitol building. As Daniel was relieving himself at the urinal, the door suddenly opened wide and Secret Servicemen scoured the place, obviously in search of drug pushers, army deserters, and subversives. By the skin of his teeth, Daniel was none of these.

The agents having finished their inspection, Nixon entered. In Daniel's demonology in those days, Nixon was holding hands with the likes of Stalin and Hitler. Now he was sharing a washroom with the devil himself. Since Nixon was only two urinals away Daniel couldn't help noticing that Nixon was circumsized and was just short of six inches in length (like Daniel). But he made up for it in width. The similarity in their penis size made Daniel feel a bit warmer about Nixon than he had ever felt before.

Nixon went to the sink, washed his hands and dried them. Daniel did the same. Nixon stuck out his hand and said, "I'm Richard Nixon and I'm running for President. I'd very much like your vote."

Daniel shook Nixon's hand. "Gee, sir," he said, "I'd really like to vote for you but I'm a Canadian and I can't vote here."

"That's all right, son, but you must have relatives in the United States? Why don't you get them to vote for me?"

"I'll try that, sir," said Daniel, thinking of Isaac, Mindel, and Vincent voting for America's leading Red-baiter. But Daniel was too flustered to remember to ask Nixon for money so he and Dahlia could eat breakfast.

Dahlia hobbled with Daniel to the Senate office building to trap Kennedy. Soon Kennedy and his friend, Senator Mike Mansfield of Montana, were on the sidewalk just ahead of them. Daniel poured out his tale of woe.

"Senator Kennedy," he said, "we're starving students from the University of Toronto and we haven't eaten in a day. We're big fans of yours, Senator, and we have lots of relatives in the United States and we'll make them vote for you. Some people I know, Senator, would never forgive your father's anti-Semitism. But I know you're one of Israel's best friends. You're so right for the presidency. We only need a little money, Senator, so we can have breakfast. We're really hungry!"

Senator Kennedy turned to Daniel. "Never before has a senator been so eloquently panhandled." He then pulled out his pants pockets and found them empty. He searched the rest of his seersucker suit and came up with nothing. But Senator Mansfield produced $1.75. Daniel and Dahlia grabbed it. The closest food was a machine selling chocolate bars in the Senate office building. They bought $1.75 worth and swallowed them all.

In the evening, as they sat on the knoll across from the Senate building, killing time till their bus left, Daniel asked Dahlia a big favour. "I've never seen the Lincoln Memorial. To me, Lincoln is the greatest man who's ever lived. I want to see Lincoln before we leave. We can just make it." It was 9:00 p.m. Daniel dragged the crippled Dahlia down the knoll, down fifteen city blocks, through several rose gardens and one illuminated pool. At last they were at the steps leading to the statue — a hundred steps, which they mounted painfully, one by one.

At last they reached the top. Daniel took what was perhaps a two-second look. Then the lights on the Lincoln Memorial went out. It was ten o'clock, and closing time.

At 11:00 p.m. they boarded the bus for Buffalo and found it empty. They stretched out and slept like babies. Daniel had mooched half a dollar from a friendly Marine whose views, for the occasion, he completely agreed with. The fifty cents bought coffee and doughnuts in the Pittsburgh bus terminal the next morning. Finally the bus hit Buffalo. Daniel and Dahlia were exhausted and starved, but as they crossed the Peace Bridge into Canada they knew they would live and endure. "Dahlia," said Daniel, "here come the sixties. Damn it, we'll be ready." They had survived America — indeed, America at its McCarthyist worst. Then and there Daniel decided he would never live in America because pokey old Canada, though WASP to the core, was a fairer and a nicer place to be.

THAT NIGHT, in their apartment in Toronto, Daniel dreamt that he was before the McCarthy committee. Roy Cohn asked him, "Are you now or have you ever been a communist?"

"No, sir."

"Do you have the names of communists that you would be prepared to give this committee?"

"Sure, I've got tons of them. There's all the boys at the Ukrainian Labour Farmer Temple and the Freiheit Temple in Winnipeg. They're communists. Just go ask them. They'll tell you. Then there's Skip Tregebov — he's a proud communist and the most successful tinman canvasser ever in Canada. The suckers are lining up to deal with Skip and he's rolling in dough. He's a free enterprise communist. Then there's my communist second cousin Vincent. He's in the U.S. Army to fight for democracy — so you guys can be the pigs you are. Then there's his dad, Isaac, and his mother, Mindel. Anyway, they're all proud communists."

He woke up in a cold sweat, and after Dahlia calmed him he

went to sleep and dreamt an older dream, from his boyhood. He was with the Partisans, fighting the Nazis. In that bloody battle, nobody asked for names, nobody gave them. At last Daniel found himself in a quiet and peaceful sleep.

Citizen Cane

A t noon on a Friday in March 1966, Don Dash, the executive producer of "All in an Hour," called Daniel into his office.

Daniel did not realize that the conversation would change his place in history. Indeed, that morning Daniel — now transformed into a producer and interviewer for the CBC — was busy lining up midgets for an item he called "The Little People." Daniel proposed to interview the midgets on all subjects of the day; democracy would be fulfilled in that at last the little people, beset by bureaucracy, politicians, and the press, would get their chance to air their views on bilingualism, the birth control pill, and Vietnam. Daniel was sure the item would work. He thought this was what Don Dash wanted to talk about.

Don Dash's grandfather had been a rabbi's son, inducted into the czarist army. He had deserted, made it to Canada, and married a Jehovah's Witness. Their children married Witnesses, and Dash was a Witness. Once Daniel told Don, "You're one-quarter Jewish and you work it to death." Don laughed. Don was crafty, cunning, single-minded and lovable. He had hired Daniel on the suggestion of Heather Zieskeit, Daniel's old camp counsellor and now Dash's right-hand woman. "All in an Hour" was Daniel's first job in six years. He saw himself as a loyal soldier in the service of "All in an Hour" and its executive producer.

Now Don spoke quietly but quickly. "In the House this morning, in some sort of heated argument, the justice minister, Napoleon Nordique, said a magic word, 'Ventruh.' Nordique had it a bit wrong. He meant Von Tren, Veronika Von Tren, the biggest untold story in the recent history of Ottawa. Veronika Von Tren is a whore. She may also be a Soviet spy. Some say she slept with half the Diefenbaker cabinet. Possibly she slept with the Hon. Tim Tidbit, but for sure she put out for the Hon. Sylvestre Scaramouche, Dief's patronage boss in Quebec. Now that Von Tren's name is on the public record, we can go after the story.

"What I want you to do, Daniel, is get a crew, go to Montreal, knock on Scaramouche's door with the camera rolling, and ask him, 'Do you know Veronika Von Tren?' If Scaramouche says yes, keep probing. Mention the spy stuff. If he says no, thank him and leave.

"Scaramouche is a hard drinker and a war hero. Be careful."

Daniel regarded Dash's request as legitimate but the "be careful" made him do a little research. From friends in Montreal he learned that Scaramouche had already turned away from his door reporters from *The Gazette*, *La Presse*, *Time*, and *Maclean's*.

He wondered about his legal position, and called Osgoode Withers, one of his closest friends. Osgoode warned Daniel to remember his first-year law about trespassers. "Knock on Scaramouche's door once and you're like any other vendor. Knock on his door twice or more and you can be a trespasser." Having a camera rolling, Osgoode said, was legitimate. The camera was a part of the TV trade, like a pencil and a notebook for a print journalist.

Daniel phoned Montreal and booked Grattan Garvey, the dean of Montreal's TV paparazzi. Grattan had covered mob funerals and nationalist demonstrations by the hundreds. He was perfect for this job. "We'll have no problems," said Grattan. "We'll use mag stripe reversal. That way you're always in sync. Just lift the soundtrack and match it up with the picture. It's perfect."

Daniel liked hearing that. A technical screw-up on this assignment would not be welcome. This exercise would have to be fast: quickly in, quickly out. Daniel was getting into just the right mood for this derring-do raid on the beachhead of Westmount.

While he sat in the Toronto airport, waiting for his flight to Montreal, he reflected on the Hon. Sylvestre Scaramouche. Daniel admired Scaramouche's wartime courage but had not forgiven him for betraying Diefenbaker by resigning in 1963. He also found Scaramouche's constant defence of his family's honour a bore.

"Do you know who my father was?" Scaramouche shouted in a TV interview.

The interviewer didn't pursue the question, but Daniel, yelling at his TV set, did: "Yeah, I know Armand Scaramouche, your father. He was the only French-Canadian politician to support conscription in 1917. He was the most hated man in Quebec. Soldiers had to guard his house." Daniel's sources indicated that Sylvestre Scaramouche had a dangerous temper. Well, Daniel had faced hot-tempered, hard drinkers before.

Daniel met Grattan and the sound man, Alphonse Letellier, a block from the Scaramouche house. Grattan then parked his station wagon in front of Scaramouche's home and they got ready for action. Daniel, of course, had the microphone, but over his shoulder he also carried a frezzolini, a sixty-pound device that instantly sheds a cold, harsh light on its subjects, making them all look like hardened criminals.

It looked like snow, and Daniel was wearing a Burberry wool sport jacket and wool Burberry overcoat he had bought in England. He and the crew stepped forward and Daniel rang the bell. The camera and sound were rolling, and the frezzolini was on. Looking through the leaded glass in the door, Daniel could see Scaramouche sitting in his study, a large glass in his hand.

Mrs. Scaramouche opened the door and peered into the glare of the frezzolini. "Excuse me, Mrs. Scaramouche, we're from CBC's 'All in an Hour,'" said Daniel. "Could we please speak to your husband?"

"He's not here," said Mrs. Scaramouche. It was as brazen an on-camera lie as Daniel had run across in his short journalistic career. But it seemed to indicate that Daniel should stop asking questions and retreat.

"Thank you for your trouble," he said. The crew and Daniel switched off the equipment and left.

Daniel was relieved. The problem was now over and Daniel could head home. But inside the station wagon, Grattan said, "Shit, we don't have an establishing shot." In television, every item needs a shot telling the viewer where the action is taking place. Since Don Dash might want to run Mrs. Scaramouche's words, an establishing shot was needed. The three of them got out of the station wagon once more. By now it was snowing heavily. Grattan proceeded to take a beautiful establishing shot, while Daniel held the mike and the frezzolini. Grattan panned the cherubim statues on the front lawn, the bay windows, and the imposing walls. The shot came to rest on the front door.

A man stood in the doorway, his hand on a cane and his finger beckoning. Because of the snow, Daniel couldn't see the finger beckoning or the cane. But when he heard Grattan say, "Hey, he's at the front door. I think he wants to talk to you!" Daniel rushed forward, in search of a scoop.

As he reached the door, still blinded by the snow, Daniel could barely make out what was happening. Only instinct made him see the up-from-the-floor swing of the cane at Daniel's head. Only instinct made him duck. The blow landed on his heavily padded shoulders and did no damage.

Grattan and Alphonse started to head for the station wagon, but the duel in Westmount wasn't over. Scaramouche took another swing, this time missing completely. Daniel then launched a vigorous kick at Scaramouche, the force dislodging Scaramouche's wooden leg. Hopping on one leg, he was still swinging his cane and Daniel was now yelling angry insults. "Listen, you can fuck Veronika Von Tren but you can't fuck me, you drunken old fart."

Scaramouche swore back in a French that Daniel could not comprehend; Daniel thought he heard *"Maudit juif"* but he wasn't sure. Scaramouche was obsessed with swinging his cane. Daniel was obsessed with getting great footage for Don Dash.

Finally Daniel retreated to the station wagon. Scaramouche followed and was now on the road, hobbling on one leg and smashing his cane on the station wagon hood. Daniel told Grattan, "Roll up the window and tell the old fucker if he doesn't get out of the way, our car will run him over. Give him a count of five."

Grattan did just that, but Scaramouche kept swinging. The car nearly knocked him over as it took off for the airport. The ten-minute roll that recorded the duel was put in a package for Daniel, who shoved it in his overcoat. "I'm sure Scaramouche is calling the Westmount Police," said Daniel. "They'll probably try to grab the footage. I'll take the first flight out at Dorval, no matter where it's going." At the airport he stepped on a plane to Ottawa. From there he phoned ahead to the film processing lab to tell the owner to be ready for him. "Look, I've got a real hot potato here. I'll be in Toronto soon and I'll drop it off. This is all hush-hush!"

"What do you want to call the item?"

"Call it 'Potato Famine,'" said Daniel, thinking the luck of the Irish was with him. Daniel had a scoop, a real scoop. No one was going to stop him from letting the world know about it.

AT THE EDITING house, Clive Clever — the senior editor and a BBC veteran — picked up the can labelled "Potato Famine: Daniel Shtarker" and screened it. It was Friday at midnight on the day of the Scaramouche caper.

Clive was subject to an asthmatic condition that made him almost choke if he laughed really hard. Daniel, of course, had often tried his best jokes on Clive just to watch the phenomenon of ecstatic choking. Now Clive began laughing dangerously hard. He could not believe what he was seeing — and hearing. Although Daniel hadn't known it at the time, the sound equipment had run through his entire meeting with Scaramouche and the tape had picked up all of Daniel's insults to a Privy Councillor.

As Clive howled with laughter, Freddy Fife and other men working at the editing house gathered around. They howled too. Fife, the boss of the place and an old Winnipeg friend of Daniel's, decided the "fucks" and other insults would hurt Daniel at the CBC. Fife sat down and cut them out, replacing them with sound effects; flamingos cooing, monkeys chattering, cows mooing. What flamingos, monkeys, and cows were doing in Westmount on a winter night was somebody else's problem, not Fife's. Fife did something else. He edited the picture to show first a pan over the verandah, then a cut to the door and the Mrs. Scaramouche interview, then back to the house, then the caning. It now looked as if Daniel had approached the Scaramouche house only once, not twice.

This became an issue three days later when Daniel was visiting Emile Chartrand, chief legal counsel of the CBC, at his luxurious office in Ottawa. "How many visits did you make to the Scaramouche house?" Chartrand asked. Paintings by Paul-Emile Borduas and Jean-Paul Riopelle stared down at Daniel.

It was a friendly inquisition, preceded by lunch at an elegant restaurant. Emile had told Daniel how much he admired his work, and how much the president of the CBC also admired Daniel's work. Daniel was beside himself with happiness at these observations.

Now Daniel's answer to Emile in the office was vague. "I'm not sure," he said. "It could have been one or two, but no more than two."

"The film shows only one visit, Monsieur Shtarker. Film does not lie. Why don't we stick with the one visit."

The logic seemed fine to Daniel. "And you never spoke to Monsieur Scaramouche while you were there?" asked Emile.

"If you mean spoke to as in an interview or conversation sense, no," said Daniel.

"You don't have any personal bias or malice toward Monsieur Scaramouche, do you?"

"Considering Mr. Scaramouche tried to kill me, no, sir, no malice at all."

Emile was satisfied with Daniel's answers, and he expressed no interest in the noises of flamingos, monkeys, and cows, all of them still on the soundtrack he had listened to. Daniel, for his part, did not raise that matter. As they left the office, Daniel was greeted by a man named Pierre Fournier.

Fournier said, "You're Daniel Shtarker of 'All in an Hour.' I'm the president's projectionist. I screen all your stuff for him. It's all so controversial and funny. If it wasn't for you, Monsieur Shtarker, my job would be a complete bore."

Daniel thanked the projectionist. Still, it was startling to know that the president was screening all his items. Was the president really such a fan?

THE SCARAMOUCHE footage did not appear on the air the Sunday following the famous Friday. For four or five days there was a ferocious battle over it between Don Dash and the CBC president, Fernand Dubois. The order from on high was clear: no airing of Scaramouche-versus-Shtarker, and no reference to Von Tren. By now the affair had been filling the pages of the newspapers for days. Even the Scaramouche-Shtarker story was out and on the loose. Prompted by the Batman cult, *The Vancouver Sun* ran a headline: "Zam, Zowie, Zap, Zshtartker, Zcaramouche." Below it were the pictures of Dubois, Scaramouche, and Daniel, and a story with all the details.

At the Four Seasons Hotel, the CBC's favourite watering hole, one of the reporters asked Daniel if he had been hit on the head by Scaramouche's cane. Daniel said he had been hit only on the shoulder. The newshounds at the Four Seasons refused to believe him, and Daniel suggested they examine his head for bruises. They did; there were none. Daniel suggested that when they made the movie about all this it would be called *Citizen Cane*. Everybody laughed and then the newshounds and Daniel returned to the business of drinking.

With all the publicity about the Von Tren affair and the Scaramouche incident mounting, and "All in an Hour" kept out of action by CBC fiat, Don Dash was getting frantic. He decided on defiance.

"Do you have any ideas," he asked, "about an item on Von Tren? We can't get your stuff on the air. But I want something on the air, something funny. That will piss them off, those humourless bastards in the president's office."

"Actually, Don, I do," said Daniel. "I'll have it for you to screen tomorrow afternoon."

Daniel called a friend, the principal at Upper Canada College. Daniel had interviewed the UCC boys many times. He loved their erudition and their ability to disgorge on air the sentiments of their famous fathers or grandfathers. The school, in turn, loved the publicity Daniel provided. "I wonder if you can help me," Shtarker said to the principal. "I want six boys, from twelve to fourteen. I want each of the boys to have famous fathers or grandfathers, preferably in politics."

"No sooner asked than done," said the principal.

Later that afternoon, on the playing fields of Upper Canada College, six stalwart lads looked into a TV camera. A remote videotape machine and truck were there ready to record.

After Daniel gave them a long briefing, they began. "My grandfather was the first Jewish member of the Quebec National Assembly and one of this country's most distinguished advocates. He had an OBE and a DSO and degrees from Oxford, Harvard, and McGill. Under no circumstances would my grandfather ever date a woman like Veronika Von Tren!"

The second boy said his grandfather was a cabinet minister in the Diefenbaker government. "My grandfather wouldn't touch a woman like Fräulein Von Tren even with surgical gloves," he announced.

The other four all rattled off their pedigrees and ended with a similar tag line: "Grandpop wouldn't touch Veronika with a barge pole."

When the item ran on the air, the studio audience was delighted — and so, apparently, was the TV audience. Daniel received a producer's credit and was pleased. The program's staff, and Don Dash himself, voted it the best item of the show.

But one Canadian was not laughing: the CBC president, Fernand Dubois. Dubois refused to watch "All in an Hour" on the Sunday nights when it was aired because it ruined the weekend at his Gatineau Hills retreat. Instead, he had a special screening every Monday at 11:00 a.m. in his office. He was outraged. Reaching for his phone, President Dubois dialled Emile Chartrand. "Emile," he said. "These people at 'All in an Hour' do not understand a presidential order. This Shtarker is a loose cannon — put him on the list of those who have to go. The war is beginning — let's be ready for it, Emile!"

Back in Toronto, Daniel Shtarker now had a son, Nathan; the three Shtarkers were now living in a nice rented house; Zipporah, his mother, could see him on TV in Winnipeg. His name was almost daily in the papers. Could anything really happen to such a lucky man? Of course not, thought Daniel.

Miss True North
Strong and Free

D aniel," said Don Dash, one day in 1965, "we've simply got to do something about the Miss True North pageant. The Dominion Broadcasting Network runs that god-damn contest against us. They make a major dent in our ratings — all those pretty girls competing with a big-nosed Jew like you, Daniel, how can we possibly win?" That was one of Don Dash's rare jokes — so rare that Daniel laughed uproariously on the simple grounds that his boss was always entitled to a laugh. "What we have to do is send up the Miss True North contest on our show the same Sunday DBN airs the Miss True North contest. Casey McGee has been working on the story but he has to be in Prince Albert covering Diefenbaker for election night. Casey is hard to reach now. You're on your own Daniel — the sky's the limit. I want this story badly."

"*Jawohl, mein Fuehrer,*" said Daniel, clicking his heels and extending the Nazi salute. Dash saluted and sent Daniel off to his new and intriguing assignment.

Daniel went to a rehearsal at Union Station in Toronto and came face-to-face with the eleven lovelies vying for the title of Miss True North. There were eleven because DBN split Saskatchewan in two, having two affiliates in the province, one in Regina and one in Saskatoon. DBN, Daniel found out, had a considerable stake in Miss True North, but the biggest player was Courtney Cox, a promoter who owned the pageant and with whom Daniel had

135

pissed away many an evening in the basement of the Celebrity Club.

Courtney did not warmly welcome Daniel to the rehearsal hall, even though the event was open to the press and there were press kits giving details of the contestants' movements for the next few days.

"You're trying to send us up," said Courtney. "I can feel it in my bones. I like you, Daniel, but for a buck you'd slit anyone's throat. You're to shoot film only when I tell you and you're to stop shooting when I tell you, understand?"

"I understand," said Daniel. "Relax, I'd only slit your throat for a minimum of, say, ten bucks." Courtney did not laugh.

Daniel waited for about a half-hour and then began peppering Cox with requests. Can I shoot this? How about that? Hey, that's grabby — can I shoot that? The idea was that Cox would soon tire of saying no and would say yes. Once he did, the crew would shoot like crazy until told to stop. Cox at last relented and allowed Daniel to shoot the dispersal of gifts by the Miss True North management to the contestants. Daniel whispered into the ear of his cameraman, "Shoot Miss Quebec, quick!"

Miss Quebec was indeed providing cinematic opportunities. Seemingly unaware of the camera, she reached into her bag of gifts. The first was a bouquet of wax flowers. *"Merde,"* she said, and threw it across the room. She reached into the bag again and this time she came up with perfume. She sniffed it and said, *"Malodorant."* She threw it away. On her third foray into the gift bag she came up with a record album, *The Collected Songs of Doug Crossley*. "Doug Crossley?" said Miss Quebec. "Who de hell is dat?" She threw the record across the room. Daniel thought that was an intelligent question, though he knew Crossley was another client of Courtney Cox's. At this point, Cox ordered Daniel to stop shooting.

When it came time to rehearse the contest's official anthem, "The Miss True North Strong And Free Song," Cox wouldn't allow Daniel to shoot. Daniel pleaded and cajoled and argued that it was the only thing the contestants were doing as an ensemble, so to speak, and thus was indispensable to the item. Cox finally relented, and the camera rolled as eleven voices sang out, in relative harmony,

> *We are strong and free,*
> *We are clever and very beautiful,*
> *As you can readily see!*
> *We believe in Canada,*
> *True north strong and. . .*

The rehearsal was over, and Daniel was overjoyed by what he had on film.

Later he and his crew arrived at DBXY, the flagship station of DBN, located on a moose pasture thirty-seven miles from Toronto. In one of its rehearsal halls they found the eleven Canadian beauties of the Miss True North contest plus a twelfth beauty, the master of ceremonies that year, Peter Jennings. Ah, thought Daniel, if I could only change places with Peter Jennings, the world would be my oyster. But then, I'd have Jennings's brains and he'd have mine.

Courtney Cox wasn't there and Daniel was free to shoot at will. The camera concentrated on Peter Jennings doing his spiel as the contestants displayed their talents, from juggling to tap dancing. As the camera rolled, Jennings announced, "And now from Rathole, Saskatchewan, population 241, the beauteous and brainy graduate of Rathole Composite High School, Angela Antwerp, Miss North Saskatchewan!" She began a soft-shoe routine. Remonstrance Jones, Daniel's cameraman, was virtually on his knees, shooting a low angle shot, when Miss North Saskatchewan crossed her legs badly and tumbled from the stage on top of Jones and his camera. That, Daniel thought, would be a classic shot, but DBN didn't see it that way.

Suddenly, DBN's president, Waldo Wasserstein, was in the rehearsal hall, confronting Daniel Shtarker: "Get out of here," he said. "You're barred from covering this contest. Get out now."

"What did I do?" Daniel pleaded. Behind him Remonstrance Jones was recording all this, following Don Dash's instructions that all such confrontations must be filmed.

Waldo Wasserstein saw what was happening. Looking right into the camera, he yelled, "If you use one word of this, I'll sue!" He then escorted Daniel and the crew out to the parking lot, not knowing that Jones had *still* not shut off his camera.

The next day the staff at "All in an Hour" was delighted by a *Toronto Telegram* story headed, "CBC Crew Bursts into DBXY." God, thought Daniel, the *Telegram* is even sleazier than we are. He remembered that any publicity was better than no publicity.

When Don Dash arrived at the staff meeting that day, he announced, "We've certainly got our teaser now. We'll open the whole show with Waldo Wasserstein pointing his finger at our camera and saying, 'If you use one word of this, I'll sue!'" There was a knock on the door and a man entered with a legal paper for Don Dash. It was an injunction, signed by a judge, prohibiting the airing of any material shot at the Union Station rehearsal hall and DBXY.

Dash immediately suspended the meeting and called Daniel into his office. "You're our legal expert. What can we do?"

"Well, I've got the Miss True North agenda, so we can keep stalking them. If we avoid more injunctions, maybe we can salvage an item."

"That's what I like to hear! No defeatist talk."

The first available opportunity to strike was at supper the following day. The press kit said all the True North princesses would be eating in the Royal York Hotel cafeteria at six o'clock. In the meantime, Daniel came up with some interesting facts. He found out that the beauties had not been chosen in competition in their regions. All of them were secretaries or receptionists in the TV stations across the country affilated with DBN. Daniel also found out that Cox had sold his rights to the contest to a company called Apex Waste Management of Clairmore, New Jersey. That company sounded suspicious.

At five-thirty Shtarker arrived at the cafeteria with his crew. The beauties and their chaperones, ignorant of any trouble and assuming Shtarker was going to make them famous on television, were affability itself. He approached one young lady who turned out to be Miss Manitoba. Daniel started to ask careful, general questions, trying to give no cause for complaint. "Do you think the birth control pill can cause moral problems in the future?" asked Daniel.

"Yes, I do," said Miss Manitoba. "It could lead to promiscuity and ruin family life."

"What do you think of the war in Vietnam?"

"It's a mess and America should pull out as fast as it can."

Daniel was feeling a surge of pride over this display of brains by a fellow Manitoban, but his brief reverie suddenly ended. A huge, fat arm was around his throat, pulling hard; someone punched him in his private parts. Nausea spread over Daniel, but the will to resist took over. The lighting man wrestled Daniel free. "So the boys from Apex Waste are here, are they?" yelled Daniel. "Well, you guys have seen too many Mafia movies or are you the *real thing*? What do you want to do — put us all in waste containers?" The bruisers demanded the film and tape. "Fuck you, Mafia gorillas, the tapes and film belong to the CBC. Let us go or I'll lay charges." Daniel's crew, film intact, exited carefully from the cafeteria and quickly from the hotel. As usual, Remonstrance Jones had filmed the entire sequence.

Naturally, Dan Dash was overjoyed. Now, again, he had an item. But soon a second injunction arrived, this one forbidding the use of the Royal York cafeteria caper. Well, the next hit was obvious. The press kit said, "10:00 p.m. — the princesses prepare for bed." The princesses were sleeping on the eleventh floor of the Royal York.

Daniel arrived there with camera rolling. The girls, all clad in kimonos, once again greeted him pleasantly. The security guard, a fan of "All in an Hour," was equally welcoming. But from the corner of his eye Daniel noticed Cynthia Sweet, the famous CBC broadcaster of shows for women, now chief publicist for the Miss True North contest. Sweet was hiding behind a wall and signalling "Pssst! Pssst!" to the guard. The guard was too busy talking to Daniel to notice. So Cynthia Sweet darted forward, saw the camera, screamed, "Oh, my God!" and reached for the phone to call her old friend, Arthur Zeboulian Longhorn, vice president and general manager of English Language Services at the CBC. "'All in an Hour' is here with that crazy man Shtarker!" she screeched. "He's trying to film the girls half-dressed. He's nothing but a peeping Tom! You're right, Zeboulian, I'll call the police!"

That advice of Zeboulian's wasn't necessary. Daniel retired rapidly, if not gracefully — and of course a third injunction the next day prohibited the use of Daniel's film and barred Don Dash and his employees from the entire Royal York Hotel.

Daniel had a fresh plan. Part of the sidewalk in front of the hotel was public property. With the help of the hotel management Daniel marked off in chalk a safety zone where he could operate. The press kit said that at ten-thirty the princesses would return to the hotel, and Daniel was waiting with his crew. A beaming couple in their fifties came out of one car, parents of a contestant. Daniel rushed forward, his tiny wireless microphone in hand. "Which one of these Canadian beauties are you the proud parents of?" he asked.

"Miss Manitoba."

"Hey, that's great," said Daniel. "I'm from Manitoba too!"

"Yes, we know, we see you on TV. You're great!"

"Not as great as your daughter." Daniel was well on his way to being the most charming interviewer on television, when suddenly the conversation ended. A female flunky of the contest suddenly grabbed the microphone out of his hands and put it down her blouse. The crowd broke into laughter, but the camera could record only silent laughing faces; the tape was picking up nothing but the thumping heartbeat of the flunky.

Daniel told Remonstrance to focus on him as he tried to retrieve his mike.

The Nose That Walked Like a Man, Daniel Shtarker, stuck his nose into the midriff of the female flunky — he had no choice if he wanted his voice to get onto the tape. "Could I please have my microphone back?" he asked, bent over nearly double. "You have no right to it. It's CBC property. I don't want to have to call the police."

The flunky hesitated, and then slowly and carefully withdrew it from her bosom. Daniel pried it from her hands.

IN OTTAWA, the CBC president Fernand Dubois, and his chief counsel, Emile Chartrand, finished screening the Miss True North footage. "Do you think that Shtarker fellow tripped that poor woman when she fell off the stage?" asked Dubois.

"With that character, all things are possible," said Chartrand.

"Is that Shtarker a peeping Tom like Cynthia Sweet and Zeboulian say he is?" asked Dubois.

"I don't think so, Fernand, but the height of discretion Shtarker is not."

"Well, Shtarker didn't sexually attack that woman in Toronto, thank God! What do we do with him?"

"Nothing now. Time is on our side. Don Dash has acted foolishly. Soon the public will see how irresponsible the Dash people are. They'll see the program as sleaze, as shameful. Our polls tell us there is a growing disenchantment with 'All in an Hour.' Our time will soon approach."

That Winter in Paris

D ANIEL SHTARKER had absolutely nothing against the French as a people. His father, Menachem, had often pointed out that Napoleon gave the Jews citizenship. Corinne Calvet, the sultry, steamy, sexy movie star was French *and Jewish*, said Menachem. Finally, Menachem noted, in *The Life of Emile Zola*, a Jew, Paul Muni, played Zola, and another Jew, Morris Carnovsky, played Anatole France. Daniel remembered that movie well. The abuse taken by Captain Dreyfus had frightened him. The French mobs in the movie seemed as nasty and as deadly as the Nazis, and later he heard that in wartime, Vichy France was at best fascist and at worst Nazi.

These thoughts returned to Daniel's mind when Thor Teifelblut, his boss, called him in one day in 1967. "Your old rabbi, Eneg, and three other holy men have been invited to Hanoi," said Teifelblut. "Buddy up to Eneg and get the North Vietnamese to let you and the crew go along with the rabbi. The four holy men are in Paris. You leave tonight. The crew will follow, once you get the North Vietnamese permission. This will be a 'Target Up' spectacular, a world first. You'll be famous."

Famous maybe, Daniel thought to himself, but also probably dead from an American bomb on Hanoi. Still, there was the chance to see Paris, and Daniel expected no real problems there. Sure enough, the meeting with his old rabbi was pleasant. Though the rabbi's crusades for nuclear disarmament, feminism, and public broadcasting might at times be a bit tedious, Daniel had to admit he agreed with him on most things.

But in Paris, the rabbi could not help Daniel. He told the North Vietnamese embassy that they should let Daniel and his crew come on the trip to Hanoi, but his influence seemed minimal. The influence of the French Communist Party was of a higher order, and Daniel was sent to see Armand and Ariane Bourget. Armand was managing editor at *L'Humanité*, the French communist newspaper; Ariane was a TV playwright. The Bourgets lived in a four-storey mansion on the rue Foch, with three maids and a manservant. They certainly didn't resemble the poor communists Daniel had grown up with.

In his political discussions with the Bourgets, Daniel was careful never to steer beyond the left-liberal clichés he had comfortably digested in his years at the CBC, and Ariane agreed to act as his interpreter and supporter at the North Vietnamese embassy. Things started off well. The diplomat agreed at once that Daniel could accompany the holy men to Hanoi. But when asked whether Daniel could take along a film crew, he grew vaguer. Ariane translated his reply as "The wind blows, the tree bends, the leaves fall." When Shtarker asked Ariane to put the crew question again, the reply came back: "The sea is vast, the fish are plenty, but one must first catch them."

Daniel found this frustrating. Worse, to get close to the North Vietnamese he had to attend their cultural events. Ariane took him to a North Vietnamese feature film festival, where he found a theatre full of exquisitely gowned, coiffed, and jewelled members of the upper bourgeoisie, all members in good standing of the Communist Party. Daniel had rarely seen such opulence.

Ariane translated a few words of the film, but she didn't really have to. Anyone could follow it — the Americans were all evil and were all played by Russians. They spent their time bombing, looting, gambling, and raping. The brave North Vietnamese jumped out of the bush and successfully attacked one American jungle base after another.

Everybody but Daniel loved the film.

Soon Daniel was sick of French communists, of diplomats, of

North Vietnamese, perhaps even of Paris. One night on the Champs Elysées he noticed a sign advertising *Triple Cross*, with Chistopher Plummer. By this time, Daniel was starved for an unaccented English word. The idea of *Triple Cross* — a film about Nazis, a favorite subject, starring a Canadian, Christopher Plummer — was attractive. Daniel had to see it. He joined a long line-up, wondering whether the film had French subtitles. If it were dubbed into French, Daniel would be lost and humiliated. When he approached the ticket window, his heart fell. The ticket taker was an old harridan, a perfect Madame Defarge.

To Madame Defarge he said, *"Excusez moi, je ne parle pas français, seulement anglais."* Then, putting his finger to his mouth, he asked, *"Les mots dans la bouche de Christopher Plummer sont anglais ou français?"* Naturally the ticket taker understood nothing of what he said. She shouted at him to get out of the queue. He refused to move and began shouting back. As she was phoning the police, a young American girl miraculously appeared.

"Are you having some problems?" she asked.

"The Frogs won't tell me if the goddamn movie is dubbed in French or not!" Daniel shouted. The American spoke briefly in French to Madame Defarge and reported that the movie had French subtitles. She also bought his ticket for him. Daniel sat through *Triple Cross* twice, savouring every nuance of English.

Afterward, strolling down the Champs Elysées, Daniel saw what he at first thought was a mirage — a neon sign proclaiming The Sir Winston Churchill Pub. Could it be? It could and it was: an authentic London pub, full of Londoners, all talking English. Daniel could not believe it. Soon, with a table of fifteen Brits, he was busy singing "Rule Britannia, Britannia rules the waves . . ." At last, in Paris, he had found a home.

Two days later, the holy men left for Hanoi. Daniel spent three more excruciating days listening to aphorisms from the North Vietnamese, without getting permission for his crew. But the boys at the Sir Winston Pub, God bless them, made the time pass. Finally Daniel Shtarker flew home, and that winter in Paris was over.

No Sense of Timing

*I*n the fall of 1972, when Pierre Trudeau called for his second
majority government, Daniel Shtarker, Ottawa correspondent for the CBC's flagship current affairs program, "Target
Up" — one of the series of programs that replaced the long-since-
banished "All in an Hour" — was not one of those cheering him
on. He had nothing against Trudeau — he agreed with him on
most things, even the War Measures Act. But somehow Trudeau
wasn't political enough. Shtarker hated his critical path flows,
participatory democracy, and functional bilingualism. These
things all seemed Brave New Worldish, McLuhanish, tech-
nocratic, and dull.

Of course, there was nothing to be done about it — until, in a
telephone conversation with Dalton Camp, a ray of hope appeared. Said Dalton: "We'll carry the Maritimes, hold the Liberals
to a draw in Toronto, and carry the rest of Ontario and the West.
Half of Trudeau's seats will come from Quebec. Trudeaumania is
dead — and really dead in English Canada. This will be the closest
election in history." Camp and his secret polls were never wrong,
and Daniel waited for the chance to use his information. CBC
News gave him that chance by assigning him to cover Trudeau on
election night 1972.

Certain that Camp was right, Daniel predicted at 8:05 p.m. "the
closest race in Canadian history," a difference between the Tories
and Liberals of only two seats, with the NDP holding the balance

of power." The pundits in their booth pooh-poohed this prediction, but the anchorman, Floyd Donaldson, kept reminding the audience of Shtarker's prediction as the race got tighter and tighter and Shtarker grew more joyous and irreverent as the evening unfolded. In one of his appearances, Shtarker told the audience, "The average Trudeaucrat working in the East Block on Parliament Hill weighs a hundred and seventy-five pounds, man or woman. Tomorrow, do not wander anywhere near the East Block. A suicidal Trudeaucrat landing on you will do you severe harm." When sent by CBC News to the sixteenth-floor Trudeau headquarters at the Skyline Hotel, Daniel reported: "I was greeted by two Mounties who, after talking into their shirtsleeves, would not let me into the Trudeau room. Still, I noticed Marc Lalonde sitting in a fetal position in the middle of the floor. The Hon. Allan J. McEachen was up against a wall reciting either a Thomistic chant or a mantra. Trudeau was going around the room shrugging everybody. Margaret was sitting on a sofa sucking a cigarette of an unfamiliar brand."

Floyd laughed heartily at this report. Floyd laughed even more when Daniel Shtarker announced on air that Trudeau, who had just stepped into an elevator in front of the TV cameras, had done so in the company of six Mounties, four communists, two Trotskyists, and a Maoist. Floyd again reminded one and all that Shtarker had predicted the result.

As usual there were mixed reactions to Shtarker's performance. Hundreds of viewers wrote to the CBC demanding his dismissal. "Boor!" "Not fit to be in our homes!" "Rude, crude, obnoxious!" "Clever — almost too clever!" "What ugliness!" "Is that Shtarker's face, or did his pants fall down?" These were some of the more forceful expressions of dissent. Others lavished praise on him. "Wonderful!" "What a tonic Shtarker is to WASP wailing and woe!" "That Shtarker is a visible minority if ever I saw one! Let his nose flick like a thousand whips!" Shtarker's supporters warned of incendiary activities if any harm befell him. In a typical CBC compromise, he was allowed to keep his job, but denied a merit pay increase that year.

He was happy. Trudeau had been humbled, there was a minority government, and his colleagues in the Parliamentary Press Gallery held the real balance of power. Still, somehow, Shtarker sensed that he had engaged in overkill — and that he had wished for Trudeau's blood simply because he was a North Winnipeg underdog and Trudeau an Outremont millionaire. A touch of guilt set in, and refused to go away.

A CHANCE TO ASSUAGE it came sooner than he had expected. Shtarker was called to the office of Trudeau's press secretary, Gaston Gavroche. An old friend, Gavroche wanted Shtarker to write the comedy speech the prime minister would deliver at the Parliamentary Press Gallery dinner. Daniel leapt at the opportunity, and for three weeks was obsessed by the project. In no time, he had what he felt was a brilliant opening. When Trudeau made his deal with David Lewis and the NDP and formed his minority government, the Tory leader, Bob Stanfield, had attacked both Trudeau and Lewis and asked, "Who is the organ grinder, who is the monkey?"

Shtarker seized on that line. Trudeau's speech began: "Ladies and gentlemen, half my week is now spent taking organ grinder lessons. Do you think that's easy? Have you ever tried feeding a banana to David Lewis, especially with a hungry Stanfield waiting in the wings!" Daniel, like all his contemporaries, remembered the pictures of Stanfield publicly eating a banana at the convention that made him leader. The image of Lewis and Stanfield wrestling for Stanfield's beloved banana would lift the gallery dinner audience to its feet.

And, in fact, Trudeau delivered the opening gambit very well, to a good laugh. But then, for some reason, he lost interest and proceeded to read Shtarker's speech like a grocery list. He never paused to wait for a laugh, thereby letting a second or third joke die under the laughs from the first one. It was still Trudeau's funniest performance at the gallery dinner, but to Shtarker it was a travesty, a pogrom on the high art of comedy. He drank himself silly that night, and made a pest of himself by showing copies of his speech to members of the gallery so they could see how really funny it was.

Weeks passed. One day, as Daniel waited for Question Period in a corridor of the Centre Block, Trudeau walked by. Noticing Shtarker, he said, "I gather you wrote my Gallery speech. I'd like to thank you."

"That's okay," said Shtarker.

Then demurely, almost shyly, Trudeau asked, "How did I do?"

"How did you do?" shouted Shtarker. "You couldn't deliver a joke if it was in a Brink's truck. You, sir, have no sense of timing." He spun around and left. Confused, Trudeau was not at his best in Question Period that day.

Months passed. At a Western barbecue party in the nifty Rockcliffe home of a cabinet minister, Shtarker saw Trudeau in a corner surrounded by a bevy of beauties and guarded from intruders by the legendary Two Tits Malone — the wife of one of Trudeau's aides, a formidable woman who had reportedly bedded half the male Liberals in Eastern Ontario, Quebec, Saskatchewan, and B.C. When Trudeau noticed Shtarker, he beckoned him over, waving aside the attempts of Two Tits to keep a mere reporter from the great man. Trudeau obviously had something on his mind. "The last time we spoke," Trudeau recalled, "you said I had no sense of timing. What did you mean by that?" Shtarker explained that when you deliver a joke you must wait for the laugh. "How long?" Trudeau asked in some puzzlement.

"Ten minutes," said Shtarker.

"Ten minutes! That's a long time," said Trudeau.

"Well, Prime Minister, by the eighth minute the tension in the room will be so high the place will be about to burst. In the meantime your aides will be going from table to table explaining the joke. By the tenth minute, massive fear of you will drive the audience to hysterical laughter."

"What do I do then?" asked Trudeau.

"That's easy. Wait for the laughter to die down and then say 'And now for my next joke.' That line will bring the house down. Remember this, you are the prime minister and as the prime minister you're entitled to a goddamn laugh!" A beaming Trudeau laughed at that line.

DANIEL WAS PLEASED with his pupil's performance in the 1974 campaign. Daniel delivered more comedic material for the exclusive use of Trudeau, and Trudeau delivered the jokes, waited for the laughter, and was grateful when he got it. He got a majority government victory too.

One day Trudeau emerged from the House of Commons and stepped into the government lobby. Shtarker and the press corps were waiting for him. Trudeau's mood was the most ferocious anybody had ever seen him in. His eyes were a squint, his face screwed up tight. No one dared to say a word to him — except Daniel. "Excuse me, Prime Minister," Shtarker said.

Trudeau screamed, *"And What Do You Want?"*

Though this was not exactly the proper way for the prince to treat his jester, Shtarker, a true Westerner, said, "I want nothing. I just wish to compliment you on that great cowboy suit you're wearing."

"Do you like it?" said Trudeau, appreciating a Western compliment on his Western attire. Trudeau pirouetted around and showed off the cowboy suit.

"Oh, by the way, Prime Minister," said Daniel, "I've watched you lately and your sense of timing is very much improved. That bad temper act you've got is also really terrific." Trudeau laughed and headed off for another day of saving the nation, in the best of moods.

M.

D aniel Shtarker hated typing. In Lord Mount Stephen High School, he had tried to learn. He had enrolled in the typing class in grade 10, the only boy in a room with thirty-four girls. Bunny Senesh and April Stryk were in the class, and Daniel was in love with both of them.

The first day was a nightmare. Miss Wilson, the typing teacher, entered the room, faced the class and said, "Today we'll do a basic speed test. Ladies and gentleman, put your fingers on the keyboard and we'll begin in five seconds. One, two, three, four, five." At five, Miss Wilson blew a whistle and 340 nimble female fingers hit their keyboards simultaneously. Soon Bunny and April had finished three pages of accurate typing; at the rate they were going they could have typed *War and Peace* that morning. The other thirty-two girls were also moving along at a merry rate.

But Daniel could not finish even one sentence. He felt impotent and useless. He waited for the class to end and told Miss Wilson he'd like to drop out of the class. "Why?" said Miss Wilson, an early feminist. "Do you find typing, like cooking and cleaning, to be women's work? Typing is the wave of the future. Mastery of the keyboard will affect worldwide communications. The world will be divided into those who can master the keyboard and those, the helpless and weak, who can't." Daniel eyed the alternatives and chose the helpless and weak. There were more of those than the strong, he thought. United, the helpless and weak would someday rule the world — or so Menachem Shtarker had always said.

And the inability to type did not really hamper Daniel Shtarker in his journalistic career. In the early 1970s, while stationed in Ottawa and working for the CBC news department, Daniel was expected to type on the teletype machine. Instead, he made alliances. Sarah Sims, a beauteous radio reporter, once told him she was interested in marriage. In a matter of days, Daniel introduced her to a prominent Ottawa Conservative. They fell in love and got married. Sarah, knowing Daniel's problems, would type up his stories and sign them S.S. for D.S. As a back-up measure, Daniel enlisted the aid of another reporter, Robert Right, a gallant fellow who had the most interesting sex life in Ottawa. To that sex life Robert devoted an enormous amount of his time, particularly in the afternoons, in the Château Laurier. The deal Daniel made was that he would do Robert Right's stories as well as his own. In return, when Daniel called, Robert would cease his amorous activities, come back to the Hill, and type up Daniel's stories as well as those Daniel covered for Robert Right. Right agreed at once. Promptly at four, Right would show up and hit the teletype keyboard with a flurry of stories. The ones he should have prepared were simply signed R.R. Daniel's were signed R.R. for D.S. This arrangement worked perfectly. Robert Right was a great guy, a wonderful womanizer, and a terrific typist. Sad to say, Daniel was none of these.

ONE DAY Daniel was sitting in the Press Gallery, directly above the Speaker's Chair, listening to the end of Question Period, the time when all the questions on timber, fish, fur, and wheat are asked. Daniel had to stay on top of what was happening, because this part of Question Period produced the regional stories Robert Right was supposed to cover. His concentration on Question Period was interrupted by Napoleon Savoie, the Press Gallery messenger, who had a note for him. Daniel opened the note. It read: "I am here. I await you. M."

Daniel, in his career, had received many strange messages and a great deal of hate mail, not all of it pleasing to him. In fact, Daniel hated his critics with a passion; he could be teased, but his thin skin often made him vulnerable. The M. message simply seemed outlandish, and therefore hostile. Daniel put it in his pocket and continued to listen to Question Period. Soon Napoleon Savoie delivered another. It read, "You don't know what you're missing! M." M.'s persistent, Daniel thought, as he stuck the second note in his back pocket. A half-hour later, Naopoleon Savoie delivered a third message: "Why are you forsaking me? M."

Daniel began trying to figure out who the mysterious M. was. M. could be a last name. M. could be a first name. Daniel tried first names first: Max, Murray, Manny, Mervyn, Melvin, Morris, Marvin, Morley, Mordecai.

Mordecai Richler, that's it. Daniel knew that Richler, famous for his savaging of creative writing courses, was now teaching creative writing in Ottawa. That ambivalence alone would drive Mordecai to drink, but of course virtually anything drove Mordecai to drink. Mordecai Richler, the smiter of all things provincial in Canada was in Ottawa, the most provincial Canadian city in the country. Mordecai would hate that, Daniel knew. Daniel equally deduced that Richler was in the National Press Club where not a single person knew or recognized him. That, too, would hurt.

Daniel guessed that Richler would need rescuing fast. He phoned Robert Right and told him to come to the Hill right away; it was an emergency. Robert Right came at once. The teletyping done, Daniel rushed to the Press Club.

His detective work was perfect. M. was indeed Richler and M. was indeed being ignored, lonely, and grumpy. As usual, Daniel wasn't sure exactly how to handle Richler. Richler hated Western Canada and Winnipeg; Daniel was a Winnipeger and a Western Canadian. Richler found Canada parochial and boring; Daniel loved Canada and had taken his M.A. in Canadian history. The one thing Shtarker and Richler had in common was a love for Richler's talent. On that basis, they got along. The favourable reviews and defences of Richler's work written by Daniel in newspapers and magazines didn't hurt the relationship.

Daniel greeted Richler with the irony Richler deserved. "Well,

M., nobody knew who M. was up on the Hill. I gather these louts, these vermin, these paparazzi assembled here at the Press Club have been ignoring you. Forget them. They can't even spell Proust, much less read him. But I know who you are, M. Let me buy you a drink."

Seven cognacs later, M. was becoming steadily more uncommunicative. Daniel took him home, and the presence of Dahlia and the children cheered him a bit. M. relaxed and became almost human.

He of course hated his Ottawa creative writing course. On the dining room table he dumped various copies of writing assignments he had to mark. Daniel read only one — it was awful — and felt at least a bit sorry for M. He was reminded of Menachem Shtarker, having to sell or do things he hated to make a buck.

But another one of Richler's students' submissions caught Daniel's eye. Its title was "Safe in the Arms of Harry." "What a title for a movie!" said Daniel. Why don't you offer the kid fifty bucks for the movie rights to the title?" M. smiled his dour smile and said nothing.

Eventually, well fed, Richler was ready to go. A taxi was called. Shtarker said goodbye to the man called M.; he had done his duty to Richler — and, more important, had once again survived.

MANY YEARS LATER, in the spring of 1989, when Daniel came to write the story of M., he found it hard to come up with an appropriate ending. Like typing, the ending to the story was something that Daniel could not manage. He found it hard to sort out his emotions. Dealing with M., he knew, was always dangerous. Perhaps a *deus ex machina* ending would do it? Let's see: Richler leaves the Shtarker house and gets into a taxi. The driver is Margaret Atwood. Without uttering a word, Peg, while still driving, takes off all her clothes. Unperturbed, Richler says, "To the airport, Ms. Atwood. You better put your clothes on. You'll catch your death. I don't want to be held responsible for the sudden demise of the priestess of Canadian culture!" Fade in music and the flashing of images of Mordecai in his Westmount home, playing with his children, as his wonderful Gentile wife brings him a hot, steaming bowl of chicken soup.

Not bad, thought Daniel, not bad. But maybe it could be Christmas. Instead of a cab driver at the door of Daniel's house, there could be, standing at the door in a red Santa Claus suit, white beard and all, Robertson Davies.

"Come with me, my son," says Santa Robertson to Richler, "and I will take you to see Canadian Christmas. Look down there, Mordecai — all the factories are shut, the rivers polluted, the streets teeming with skinheads. No one reads, everybody watches television. This is what Brian Mulroney and Free Trade have wrought, Mordy. You should not have supported Free Trade, Mordy! It was a naughty, naughty thing to do!" They look in at the CBC, now strictly a warehousing and merchandising operation. Daniel Shtarker is standing outside the building in dishevelled clothes, a begging bowl in his right hand. Neither Santa Robertson nor Richler puts a coin in Daniel's begging bowl.

"Tightwads! Yankee lovers!" shouts Shtarker, but no one listens. Santa Robertson takes Mordecai to Washington, where Conrad Black is being sworn in as president of the United States of America and Canada. *Saturday Night* now has a circulation of 200,000,000. Ontario is the fifty-first state. Quebec has the status of Puerto Rico.

That ending Daniel liked better. But somehow Daniel felt it wasn't good enough. Then the answer came quickly. Daniel sent a note to Richler: "Dear M., you who have finished a thousand tales — please finish this one! Do not forsake me! D."

The Vengeance of
Daniel Shtarker

Y ou've heard of the Oglethorpe family — Orson Oglethorpe and Sons? The people who own half of Western
Canada? Dahlia Shtarker's family, the Devons, were nuts
about the Oglethorpes. Dahlia's father, Sidney, gave his life for
them — a teletype operator, he pounded a keyboard for the Oglethorpes for thirty years, till finally he died of angina on a St.
Boniface Hospital bed.

Like many good Anglo-Saxon tycoons, the Oglethorpes were
as tight-fisted as two clam shells riveted together, so Sidney's
loyalty was rewarded by a firm handshake provided by the chief
Oglethorpe, Oscar, for the widow Margaret. There was no pension
for Sidney, had he lived, and no widow's allowance for Margaret.
In the Oglethorpe world, the bottom line ruled, with a little help
from the law of the jungle.

At fifty-four, after thirty years as a housewife, Margaret Devon
took her first timorous steps into the Winnipeg marketplace. No
one at Eaton's, the Bay, Birks, or the Royal Bank could manage to
fit her in, but a tough Jewish garment manufacturer, Itzik Flink,
took her on. "Okay, I'll hire you. I'll pay you by the day, and only
if you show up. If you don't show up, even if you're sick, you don't
get paid. Understand?"

Margaret was good at her new secretarial job. She ignored
Flink's bad manners, piled into his correspondence, straightened
out the bills and files, and made herself thoroughly useful. But she

dreamt of a WASP working environment, and several times she sent out feelers to Orson Oglethorpe and Sons. She wasn't exactly rebuffed, but she wasn't given a job either.

All this bothered Margaret. Vaguely, she desired not only an Oglethorpe job but an Oglethorpe in her family, wed to her beautiful and brainy daughter, Dahlia. Alas, no Oglethorpe sought out the charms of Dahlia.

Needless to say, Margaret was not overjoyed when confronted at her door by The Nose That Walked Like a Man. Never, not even with Itzik Flink, or in a museum under glass, had Margaret seen such a Jewish person.

"Hi, Mrs. Devon, I'm Daniel Shtarker. Is Dahlia here?"

"Yes, of course. Come in. Have a cup of tea. I just made it."

Daniel entered the den of lions, hoping the tea was free of dangerous potions.

"How are you?" Mrs. Devon asked. "How's the university?"

"I'm fine and so is the university."

"Have you known Dahlia very long, Mr. Shtarker?"

"Three weeks, four days, eighteen hours, and twenty minutes," said Daniel, checking his watch, "and I've never had so much fun in my life before."

Images of Daniel's fun popped into Margaret's mind, looking precisely like stills from a porn movie.

"Isn't today Yom Kippur?" she asked. "My boss, Mr. Flink, took the day off. Can you have tea and cookies?"

"I'm a socialist and to be a socialist you have to eat every day, even Yom Kippur, so you can be strong and fight the capitalist enemy — people like the Oglethorpes. Dahlia tells me your husband slaved for them for thirty years but there's no pension — no help provided to you by this wealthy cartel that every day holds Winnipeg to ransom by the throat."

Margaret grew queasy. Daniel's odd looks and his communist views were equally repellent. What could Dahlia see in him? Perhaps he was casting some secret Jewish spell over her.

"Where are you and Dahlia going tonight?"

"To a movie, *The Golem*."

"Golem, what's that?"

"Well, it's about a rabbi who casts a spell on a mound of clay in the Jewish cemetery in Prague in the Middle Ages. The clay turns into a giant Golem — a monster who then goes out and slays all the Gentiles who've been picking on the Jews. It sounds like fun. It's my kind of movie!"

Margaret felt faint, but by the time Dahlia came home she was ready for a bitter argument over Daniel. Hair was pulled, blouses ripped, ankles kicked. Still, Margaret, a perfect Anglo-Saxon, was always pleasant when Daniel called. Tea was always served, and the conversation was always polite.

Eventually, Margaret made room for a Jew in her Scots-Irish family, and when Daniel became something of a TV star, she was impressed. On his visits to Winnipeg, Daniel would visit Margaret. In 1972, when Daniel visited her in the hospital during her last illness, he was pleasantly surprised to find that Mr. Flink was continuing Margaret's salary even though she was sick.

BUT HE NEVER SHARED his mother-in-law's regard for the Oglethorpes. Not only had they treated the Devons wretchedly, they had led the Winnipeg business community into Red-baiting and fascist behaviour in the Winnipeg General Strike of 1919. Finally, they had the Hon. Ovid Oglethorpe, the federal minister of personnel and procurement. In 1972 *Maclean's* had caught Oglethorpe saying that Eskimos were stupid and dragged everything behind them on a snowshoe. "Snowshoe" became Oglethorpe's nickname in Ottawa. *Maclean's* also pointed out that while aboard a government helicopter, Oglethorpe failed to properly strap himself into his seat. As a result, Snowshoe fell out of his seat three times, banging his head on the dashboard on each occasion.

Daniel loved the *Maclean's* exposé. As a member of the Press Gallery, he hoped that he, too, could come up with a good Oglethorpe story. One afternoon in 1972, his chance came. The former prime minister, John Diefenbaker, stood up in the House and asked the minister of personnel and procurement a question. "Why has the government dared to remove the royal coat of arms from all government cheques?"

Flustered, Oglethorpe rose and said, "Mr. Speaker, after checking with the RCMP—" Oglethorpe got no further. The MPs roared with laughter. They were laughing because Dief's beloved Mounties had approved — or recommended? — the removal of the royal coat of arms from government cheques. They were amused because, for once, Diefenbaker had been bested.

The Press Gallery laughed too, but not Daniel. Shtarker knew that turkeys do not become swans overnight; certainly Oglethorpe was no swan. Grabbing his tape recorder, he cornered Oglethorpe in the lobby. "Excuse me, sir, did you say the Mounties approved the removal of the royal coat of arms from the government pay cheques?"

"No! No! The coat of arms removal was a cabinet decision."

"Trudeau's?" Daniel Shtarker asked. "Yours? Not the RCMP's?"

"Yes," said Oglethorpe. "Trudeau's, mine, not the RCMP's." Daniel then asked what the RCMP contribution to all this was. The Mounties, said Oglethorpe, asked that the colour of the cheques be changed from blue to green because green cheques are harder to forge.

For dramatic effect, Shtarker repeated his question. The answer was the same — the Mounties had not recommended removal of the royal coat of arms from government cheques.

Running to Diefenbaker's office, his tape recorder in hand, Daniel thought fondly of Margaret Devon.

IN DIEFENBAKER'S office, Daniel faced the Chief's legendary secretary, Miss Ely. A prim, tough spinster, she was awesomely loyal to Dief, did not suffer fools gladly, and sometimes saw fools where there were none.

Shtarker, she thought, might just be a fool. "Mr. Diefenbaker is flying to Winnipeg on the four-thirty flight," said Miss Ely. "He is ready to go now and will see no one."

"He'll see me, Miss Ely, and he'll listen to my tape. When he hears my tape, he'll order two stenographers to type a transcript of it. Mr. Diefenbaker will then cancel his reservation and tell you he can go on the six o'clock flight and still be in time for the Winnipeg rally. Let me in now!"

Reluctantly, Miss Ely ushered Daniel into the great man's office. Diefenbaker was putting on his overcoat.

"Mr. Diefenbaker," said Daniel, "I realize you're busy. I simply want to play you a short tape."

When he heard it, Diefenbaker grasped its significance quickly. "They laughed at me," he said. "Those Grits *laughed* at me. Well, I was right about the coat of arms — and they were wrong! Miss Ely, change my flight to six o'clock and get me two secretaries to transcribe this tape. That ninny, Oglethorpe, is on the chopping block tonight. I'll be dining off this story for years."

He turned gratefully to Daniel. "Tonight," he said, "we're going to make mischief together. You'll be there in spirit, Mr. Shtarker. I'm sure of that." That night Dief read copiously from the Shtarker transcript and his audience howled at Oglethorpe's evasiveness. The *Winnipeg Free Press* headline the next day said, "Diefenbaker obliterates Oglethorpe."

The Chit-chat Seat

D aniel first met Peter Reilly, the legendary journalist, in the offices of the Toronto Labour Council in the early 1960s. Reilly was then a tough feature writer for the local newspaper that was owned by Col. Burton Barrelblast, royalist, militarist, and Conservative extraordinaire. This employment caused some inner turmoil for Peter Reilly, who was in complete rebellion against royalism, militarism, and conservatism, as well as his own Irish Catholic heritage. For fun and relaxation, Reilly naturally gravitated toward the labour movement and a tenuous relationship with labour's illicit stepson, the New Democratic Party.

Reilly's appearance and behaviour matched the vigour and flamboyance of his prose. He had a perpetual scowl, and fierceness was his normal demeanour. But these superficial characteristics were more than cancelled out by a heart of pure gold and a fondness for conviviality, wit, and good company — accompanied, alas, by a drink too many.

Heavy drinking in the labour movement — Reilly was the representative of the Newspaper Guild — was endemic. Every Thursday afternoon a liquor salesman came to the Toronto Labour Council office from Adams Distillers to replenish the liquor bottles that Jock Brannigan, One Eye Wally, Two Fingers Muldoon and the others emptied in the week past. In this drying of the well, Reilly had done his fair share — and so had Daniel, at that time the Toronto Labour Council's public relations adviser. Daniel had never believed in the ancient anti-Semitic canard that Jews don't drink. In Winnipeg, he had grown up with Boozy Roth and Speedy Feirfly, both two-bottle-a-day men, and both as Jewish as Barbra Streisand. Daniel also remembered the lectures on booze he had received from his father, Menachem.

"Booze is a bad business," said Menachem. "Take an average Polack. Sober, the Polack is clean and sensible — and just an average anti-Semite. Feed the Polack some of Bronfman's medications and that same Polack turns into a murderous pogromchik. Give an Irishman too much whiskey and he begins to weep and say nasty things about Oliver Cromwell, who let the Jews back into England. Give a German some schnapps and he votes Nazi. Jewish strength lies in moderation, my son, if not in abstinence. In our new state of Palestine the milkshake will be the strongest potion you can get!"

Despite this lecture, Daniel adopted the drinking habits of the leaders of Toronto's proletariat. Drinking rye with Jock Brannigan, the nicest ex-member of the Ku Klux Klan Daniel had ever met, in the mornings, vodka tonics with One Eye Wally for lunch, and double Scotches with Reilly in the evening meant that Daniel sometimes slept in his office in the afternoons and rarely at home at night. Falling face forward into empty soup bowls and getting abusive with 250-pound football players in strange bars were equally unfortunate side effects.

Still, the camaraderie of the labour movement was vital to Daniel. He admired Reilly not only for his colourful prose and flamboyant strike tactics but for his obvious manliness. Reilly was a man's man. The women he squired around were beautiful, delightful, and interesting; his speech was always pungent. "Diefenbaker," Reilly would say, "is the lyingest, thievingest purveyor of falsehoods this fair Dominion has seen since the McGreevy scandal." "Pearson," Reilly would say, "is a mouse, so timorous that he needs an executive assistant like that midget Jim Coutts, just to cast a shadow for him."

In the late 1960s Shtarker and Reilly became not only drinking buddies but also colleagues on various CBC programs, the first of these being something called "Circle Square." Its executive producer was Reggie Regent, who liked doing television items on hermaphrodites, neo-Nazis, Otis Redding, the Staple Singers, and silicone breasts. This was a far cry from the Alabama integration crisis and the Vietnam war stories that Reilly had covered for CBC News. But Reilly lived as best he could with the new pop journalism. Then there appeared a new executive producer, Thor Teufelblut, an Icelander from Varnish Red, Prince Edward Island. Thor and his family were the only Icelanders on PEI and this uniqueness had traumatized young Thor and made him crafty, willful, and stubborn. These qualities of course served him well at the CBC and enabled him to outlast Reggie Regent and Rodney McTavish, two executives producers who had preceded him in the ten-to-eleven hour slot on Sunday nights. Thor's Sunday hour, "Target Up," featured items with titles like "Homosexuality: Dilemma or Destiny" and "The Womb: Trap or Triumph?"

Thor hired Reilly and Shtarker as co-hosts, and they prospered in their new roles as prophets of gloom and doom. But Daniel tended to be sharper than Reilly in spotting trouble ahead. For example, it was Shtarker who first heard the rumour that Thor Teufelblut was cooking up an independently produced series of his own. The series was to feature the great British iconoclast, wit, journalist, and gadfly, Malcolm Muggeridge. In particular it was to feature Muggeridge's reconversion to Christianity, an event central to the very core of the universe, an event that deserved thirteen hours of television — or so Muggeridge and Teufelblut felt. The first hour was to be a demolition of Marxism from the point of view of St. Francis of Assisi.

Muggeridge kept popping up in person at CBC parties in Toronto; more important, he kept appearing on "Target Up." Frequently, Daniel found himself telling his audience things like, "Tonight on 'Target Up,' a look at Judaism and capitalism, 'Wailing Wall and Wall Street: Judaism and the Rise of Capitalism,' with Peter Reilly and Malcolm Muggeridge." Daniel was joined by Muggeridge in "Organized Labour and Christianity — the Parting of the Waves," and "Child Abuse: Is Christianity the Cure?" Reilly was not happy about sharing TV time with Muggeridge, but knew nothing about the Muggeridge-Teufelblut series. As for Shtarker, while conceding Muggeridge's brilliance and erudition, he still found him a boring old fart, smitten with self-love. Still, Shtarker said nothing.

In those days, programs like "Target Up" went on the air twice, once to the Maritimes, Sunday from nine to ten Toronto time, and again from ten to eleven for the rest of the country. "Target Up" varied in length considerably, and at the end the time would be filled by chit-chat between the announcer, Floyd Donaldson, and either Reilly or Shtarker. One night, when "Target Up" featured Muggeridge in conversation with three Chassidim in a Brooklyn condo, Reilly was in the chit-chat seat. As the Maritime feed drew to a close, Floyd Donaldson asked Reilly, "You've just seen Malcolm Muggeridge. What do you think of him?"

Reilly replied, "Malcolm Muggeridge is a horse's foot, a snake oil salesman, a prevaricating fabricator of the snide and snively, a prince of darkness who cannot light a room, a man who can bore you to death by saying hello." All of this, live to the Maritimes.

In the control room Thor was beside himself with anger. He and his coterie rushed down to the studio floor as Shtarker followed them, knowing history in the making when he saw it. "You drunken son of a bitch," Teufelblut said to Reilly. "How dare you talk that way about Malcolm Muggeridge, one of the great men of the century? I'll tell you what I'm going to do. You stay in the chit-chat seat for the next fifty-four minutes. You'll be asked the same question about Muggeridge for the rest of Canada, but your answer better be different or you're fired! You've got fifty-four minutes to think."

Reilly seemed to take this outburst calmly, although his scowl was now even more pronounced. The tension back in the control room was palpable for the next fifty-four minutes. Then, for the viewers from Quebec to B.C., Floyd Donaldson asked Reilly, "You've just seen Malcolm Muggeridge. What do you think of him?"

Reilly sucked in his tummy, took a deep breath and said, "Well, Floyd, lately I've become quite a fan of Muggeridge's." He then went on to praise Muggeridge for the allotted time. The control room by this time was in fits of laughter. Thor broke out into a raucous, triumphant laugh.

As for Reilly, he fled to his favourite bar across Jarvis Street. There Daniel was waiting to greet him. "Now everybody in the Maritimes thinks Muggeridge is an asshole," said Shtarker, "and everybody from Quebec to Vancouver thinks he's a saint — and it's all because of you, Reilly. I've never been more proud of you!"

Reilly agreed it was a great day. "That Muggeridge crap will be the greatest CBC story ever told," he said.

"And I'll do the telling," added Shtarker. They laughed, and ordered another round of doubles.

The Dinner Party

I n Toronto, in the late 1970s, Daniel and Dahlia Shtarker were busy preparing for one of their rare dinner parties. Dahlia worked carefully on the guest list. She invited, for instance, Northrup (Thrup! Thrup!) Archibald and his wife, Agatha. Northrup got his nickname from the *thrup! thrup!* noises he made with his size-sixteen shoes when he walked across a crowded room. He was finance minister and the obvious heir to Trudeau, but somehow he and everyone else knew he would never make it — even though his wife, Agatha, was the toughest Liberal woman in the land. Daniel loved the Archibalds for themselves, and not only for the aura of power they so convincingly exuded.

Also on the guest list was Flemingdon Will, maker and breaker of Tory leaders for twenty years. Bald as a billiard ball, Flemingdon could send signals back and forth to his henchmen during Tory conventions by having flashlights beam Morse messages off the top of his dome. Flemingdon and his new wife, Ivanka, said they would come in for the party from their retreat in Wilno, Ontario. The third man invited was Dulmadge Ditto, critic, sportsman, memoirist, translator, bibliophile, and publisher of the Canadian literary and political magazine, *Phoenix Ablaze*. Dulmadge and his wife, Sarah, producer of the CBC radio program, "Lethargy," promised to come. Dulmadge, too, was as bald as an eagle and a hulk of a man whose suits were ill-fitting and whose shoes squeaked. Sarah was pretty, though her false teeth protruded on occasion and often made clicking noises. Although few read *Phoenix Ablaze* and fewer still listened to Dulmadge Ditto's radio programs, and none at all watched Ditto's CBC-TV show, Daniel knew nevertheless that Ditto was the most influential intellectual in Canada, a man under whose umbrella Daniel could safely spread his wings. Daniel had submitted to *Phoenix Ablaze* an article titled "Pockets of Plenty — the Pool Hall and Canadian Nationalism." Ditto had held the article for weeks and had not yet responded. Daniel hoped the dinner party invitation would turn hesitancy into resolve.

Rounding out the guest list were the Gotliebs, Allan and Sondra, for it was in their honour that the dinner party was being held. And there was one more guest, added to the list by Daniel over Dahlia's objections: a veteran CBC cinematographer and landed immigrant from India, Gandhi Nepal. "Why Gandhi Nepal?" Dahlia had asked irritably. "Why does he have to be at my dinner party?"

"Our dinner party," said Daniel emphatically. "Let me see, did you see 'Sword of Sorrow' on CBC's 'Nature of Things'? It was a one-hour study of circumcision and other rites of passage all over the world — in Canada, Turkey, and New Zealand."

"No, I didn't," said Dahlia.

"How about 'Harvest of Repentance,' a 'Man Alive' special on hunger among fundamentalist Christians in Armenia and Shiites in Iran. Did you catch that? Or maybe you saw 'How Dark Is My Mountain,' a docudrama about sexual repression in Kamloops?"

"No, I didn't catch any of those turkeys," said Dahlia. "They sound awful."

"Well, they won the Samuel Bronfman Award for cultural integrity, the Conrad Black Award for responsible iconoclasm, and the Anne of Green Gables Award for the best feminist picture of the year.

"And" — Daniel added the clincher — "Gandhi Nepal shot or directed or produced all three of those films."

"I don't care if he directed *Gone with the Wind*," said Dahlia, "I don't want him here."

"I do," said Daniel. "Please, I owe Nepal this invitation. It's important to me." Dahlia reluctantly agreed.

WHY DID HE want Nepal on the guest list? Daniel had just done a documentary on immigration, breaking the story of Vincent Massey's anti-Semitism. It also told, for the first time, of Mackenzie King's cowardice on the Jewish refugee question and pinpointed King's refusal to allow the S.S. *St. Louis*, full of Jewish refugees from Europe, to end its voyage in Canada. Daniel's documentary, *Storm Before Tomorrow,* brought tears to the eyes of Canadians from coast to coast. The ratings and reviews were great.

Nepal was quiet, terribly polite, anxious to stay out of the limelight. But he was determined and stubborn, a man with set ideas about what he wanted and set ideas about how to get it. He had volunteered to help on the immigration project, and Daniel was grateful. After it was aired, Daniel invited Nepal to his office and told him, "You made my film live and sparkle. I owe you one. If there's something you want me to do for you, ask." Nepal smiled enigmatically and said, "Daniel, you must know a lot of powerful people in Ottawa."

"That's true, I do," Daniel acknowledged.

"I want to speak," said Nepal, "face-to-face with the deputy minister of immigration."

Daniel paused as he absorbed this request. Nepal, no doubt, had relatives back in India and wanted to get them into Canada. The immigration bureaucrats were probably holding things up. Well, thought Daniel, I can clear that up. Face-to-face with the deputy minister of immigration is what Nepal wants, that's what Nepal will get, he said to himself. The deputy minister of immigration was Allan Gotlieb, Daniel's lifelong friend and his godfather in Ottawa. "Consider it done," said Daniel.

His connections to the deputy minister of immigration were manifold. Gotlieb had been Daniel's counsellor at summer camp, and when Daniel was posted to Ottawa in 1970 Daniel and Gotlieb renewed their relationship and became great friends. Dahlia and Sondra Gotlieb got along like sisters. At legendary Gotlieb parties in their Rockcliffe mansion, the Shtarkers tripped over the powerful and famous.

NEPAL ARRIVED last at the party, wearing a Nehru jacket, baggy Indian pants bound tightly to the ankles, and a Nehru cap. For the dinner table he brought a small bouquet of wax flowers.

Dahlia greeted him with less than her usual warmth, because she wondered what he and Daniel were up to. "Good evening, may God be with you," said Nepal. "Thank you for inviting me." He bowed gracefully to each of the guests in turn, his hands folded.

At the table, the conversation was sparkling. "I've always believed that tax policies should be neutral, but I never thought you had to neuter the finance minister to do it," said Thrup! Thrup! to Sarah, Ditto's wife.

To Agatha, Archibald's wife, Flemingdon Will said, "Charisma is a two-edged sword. You can fall on it twice."

The wine flowed, the conversation flowed, and the *bon mots* went rat-tat-tat. On federal-provincial relations, Allan Gotlieb said, "Sharing power is like wife-swapping in daylight. You wind up with your own wife."

Dahlia's sweet-and-sour spareribs were the smash of the evening. Daniel, busy being the amiable host, poured wine, cracked the odd joke, laughed at everybody else's, and behaved himself. Nepal sat quietly smiling and nodding. Around midnight he told Daniel he'd like to talk to Gotlieb soon. Daniel had of course told Gotlieb that Nepal probably had relatives he wanted to bring over, and that Gotlieb could simply pass this problem to his officials. Daniel added that Nepal had made *Storm Before Tomorrow* the great film Gotlieb had said it was.

When Daniel whispered in his ear, Gotlieb got up from the table and escorted Nepal to the living room for a private chat. He lit a cigar and offered Nepal one. He declined. "A good Hindu does not smoke or chew tobacco; the only smoke the Hindu approves of is that of the funeral pyre, which reminds the Hindu of the mortality and fallibility of man. That smoke sends a message to the Engineer of the Universe that man is a mere smoked replica of the All-Seeing One."

Gotlieb patiently stored that information in the part of his memory bank marked, "Hindus and Other Third World Citizens."

He smiled at Nepal expectantly. The quicker the request was made, the quicker the resolution thereof. He was eager, as always, to pull Daniel's chestnuts from the fire.

From the dining room table, Daniel could see, but not hear, the conversation. When Gotlieb smiled Daniel thought things were going well. But as Nepal made his pitch, punctuating it with Indian gestures of supplication, Daniel could see that Gotlieb was getting more and more flushed. He seemed to be on the edge of his chair, like a coiled spring. Fortunately, Nepal's argument was short. When he finished, he rose from his chair, put his hands together, pointed them politely at Gotlieb, bowed, and prepared to leave.

At the door, Nepal turned to Dahlia and Daniel and said, "You know, as a Hindu, I, like the Jews, do not eat pork, in particular pork spareribs. But I could tell from the expression on the faces of those around me that everyone loved your spareribs. The tuna you gave me was also very delicious. I thank you. May this feast tonight be the first of many." He left.

In the living room, Gotlieb asked plaintively, "Is he gone? Please say he is!" When assured of Nepal's departure, Gotlieb returned to the dinner party, visibly shaken by his experience. "In my twenty-five years in the government business," said Gotlieb, "I've never had a more bizarre request!

"Nepal does *not* want to bring his relatives from India. In fact, he doesn't want any Indians to bring their relatives into Canada, ever. What he wants me to do is *stop* letting Hindus into this country. He says there are way too many already. Some, he says, should be deported. He says the Hindus in Canada are loud and vulgar and stick together."

Gotlieb gulped down a cognac. "For a while I thought Nepal was putting me on — all that bowing and hand clasping! But he's for real!" Gotlieb relit his cigar and puffed two circles into the sky. "Anyway, Daniel, you no longer owe Nepal anything. I told him I'd consider his suggestion to bar all Hindus, Sikhs, and Moslems from Canada, if he would put his request in writing. He'll get my standard form letter in reply."

Everyone toasted Daniel's new-found freedom from the demands of Nepal. Ditto then told Daniel he'd read his article, and liked it. "It will be published in the Christmas issue." The Archibalds told Daniel that the prime minister loved Daniel's line, "Wage and price controls if necessary but not necessarily wage and price controls," and planned to use it in a speech soon. Flemingdon Will told Daniel to watch out for young Brian Mulroney. Mulroney, said Will, was building a coalition that could win the Tory leadership someday. Daniel could use that tidbit of information on his radio and TV shows. There was no getting around it, thought Daniel, this was probably one of the best dinner parties ever held.

How Odd of God

O ne morning in the early 1940s, Daniel answered the doorbell at the old dump in Winnipeg. "Can I speak to your father, please?" said a stranger. Daniel fetched Menachem. "My name is Bob James," the stranger said, "and I'm an Albertan. I bear witness to Christ Almighty."

"How can I help you?" Menachem asked.

"Sir," said Mr. James, "have you ever heard the couplet, 'How odd of God, to choose the Jews'?"

"No, I haven't," said Menachem.

"God chose the Jews," said Mr. James, "to lead the way to Christ. They sort of blew their first chance, sir. But if the Jews choose Christ now, then there will be no more obstacles to the Second Coming of Jesus and the reign of the saints on Earth can begin!"

"Well," said Menachem, "I hate to be a stick in the mud, but I don't intend to declare for Christ. But should I ever become a Christian, I'd be a Roman Catholic, never a Jehovah's Witness." Mr. James blanched; the great Satan beast, Rome, was next to the Jews in the demonology of the Jehovah's Witnesses. Mr. James accepted this double whammy from Menachem, excused himself, and left.

Young Daniel, who found the conversation interesting, asked why it was odd of God to choose the Jews. "Well," said Menachem, "I'm not sure He chose us. We certainly chose Him. But the people who say it's odd of God to choose the Jews mean it's ludicrous to believe that Jewish people who gave the world the sins of capitalism, the sins of communism, and the pornography of Hollywood could ever be chosen as His People by God. People who say this are anti-Semites, Daniel. They're not our friends. Anti-Semites never are." Daniel had received his introduction to the mysteries of Chosenness.

DANIEL WENT OFF to play stick ball, alleys, and "Red Rover, Red Rover, I Call You Over" with his best friend, Teddy Wyrko. When the games were over, it was time for lunch. Mrs. Wyrko prepared a beet borscht, Polish sausage, lard-fried potatoes, and *kapusta* Polish-style sauerkraut pickled in brine for weeks. When Daniel came home, Zipporah casually asked where he'd been. "At the Wyrkos, Ma," Daniel replied.

"Did you eat lunch there?"

"Yes, Ma."

"What did you have?" When Zipporah heard the reply, she was so alarmed that she whipped Daniel off to see Dr. Redbelly at once.

Dr. Redbelly, amused at Zipporah's fears, examined Daniel and concluded he was just fine. "Pork sausage and *kapusta* are quite healthy and nourishing," he said. "They can hardly harm Daniel. If we don't trust other people's foods and delicacies, they won't trust us and that breeds anti-Semitism, Mrs. Shtarker."

On the way home Daniel wondered what *kapusta* had to do with anti-Semitism. Zipporah said she wouldn't touch Polish *kapusta* and Polish sausage ever, and expressed the hope that Daniel wouldn't either, ever. "If that spreads anti-Semitism, so be it," said Zipporah.

Anti-Semitism — the same word twice that day. There must be something to all this, Daniel thought. One Sunday morning, the Wyrkos took him to Sunday Mass at St. Stanislaus the Avenger's Polish Roman Catholic Church, across the street from where the Wyrkos lived. It was a huge church, with many altars. There were Christ statues everywhere. Father Lazlo was in charge. Daniel watched as Mr. Wyrko, Mrs. Wyrko, and Teddy approached Father Lazlo at the central altar. Having taken a sip of wine, Father

Lazlo slipped a wafer down each Wyrko throat. Then Father Lazlo gave a sermon in Polish, which Mr. Wyrko translated for Daniel. "He says Poland will one day be free. The communists must also be watched. Communism is a Jewish idea and no true Pole would embrace it!"

After the service, Daniel asked about the wine and wafers and was told they were the body and blood of Christ. The Wyrkos, by taking communion, were at one with Christ, said Mr Wyrko.

"What happens to those who don't take communion?" asked Daniel.

"They're damned and go to hell," said Mr. Wyrko. "But don't worry, we'll take you with us when we go to heaven."

What about Menachem and Zipporah, Daniel asked. "Oh, they'll be taken care of by the International Jewish Fund in Zurich," said Mr. Wyrko. "Every Jew in the world gets a payment every third week in April. The amount depends on how well the Jews have been doing in loan-sharking, stock swindles, and peddling real estate. The rich Jews kick in their share. The poor ones get their share."

Then Daniel asked, "Why did the priest say communism is Jewish?"

Mr. Wyrko replied, "Dr. Redbelly is a communist, isn't he, and he's Jewish."

"But Dr. Redbelly is your doctor and treats you for nothing."

"That's just a Jewish trick," said Mr. Wyrko. "Dr. Redbelly will be charging us soon enough — triple, probably triple to everybody else."

Wasyl Wyrko was the janitor at the United Left Labour Zionist Freedom Workers Temple, and he spoke perfect Yiddish. Often he cursed the Jews in Yiddish to their faces. "Maybe Hitler isn't wrong after all," he would say. "Jews are okay individually, but as a group they run everything."

When Daniel, in real excitement, told his father that the Shtarkers would soon be receiving a large sum of money from the International Jewish Fund in Zurich, Menachem just laughed. "The day I see rich Jews giving their money to poor Jews is the day I know the revolution has come," Menachem said. "There is no fund in Zurich, and no money coming. What you heard is Polish nuttiness about Jews — like everything Polish, not terribly deep or original. Still, Teddy is a nice boy, the Wyrkos like you, so keep on playing there. But watch out for Father Lazlo, he's a tiger."

THERE WAS a new addition to the neighbourhood in 1943. The Lamp unto the Jews and Other Lost Tribes, under the guidance of Rev. Salter Salmon, opened up right across the street from St. Stanislaus the Avenger's. Every Sunday afternoon, the Lamp had a Jewish kiddies' day. Jewish parents, anxious to get rid of their kids for a while, dumped them with the Rev. Salmon. Soft drinks, chocolate milk, and cookies were served to a dozen or so Jewish children. A movie about the passion of Christ, like *King of Kings*, was shown, followed by an animated cartoon in which Jesus was shown as a boy, playing in the fields and preaching to the animals. Afterward, there was a brief sermon by Rev. Salter Salmon and then a question period. Daniel once asked: If Christ were Jewish, as Rev. Salmon said, why did all the Christs Daniel had seen look like Gentiles? "All the Christs in this place look British," said Daniel.

"If the Christs looked Jewish," said Rev. Salmon, "then they'd all have large fat noses and thick heavy lips. They wouldn't look attractive and the Christian faithful might be less inclined to worship."

When Daniel told this to Menachem, there was a roar of laughter. Pointing to his own enormous, protruding nose, Menachem said, "I can never be Christ, thank God! Who needs to be nailed to a cross every Easter? You tell the good Rev. Salmon I don't mind you going to the mission. You're learning something new and that's good! But you tell him his nose joke is anti-Jewish and Menachem Shtarker has duly noted it."

In truth, Menachem didn't mind Daniel being exposed to other faiths. He would need that exposure if he were to grow up and be a street fighter like Menachem. And if Daniel got fed by the Wyrkos and the Lamp unto the Jews, it made balancing the budget that much easier.

Daniel was slowly absorbing these lessons about what was or

was not anti-Jewish. Someday, he thought, he might even find out why it was odd of God to choose the Jews.

IT WAS MANY YEARS later, in Toronto, that the full significance of Oddness and Chosenness came home to Daniel. Strangely, it was at one of the highest windows of Canadian culture that the lessons came fast and furious.

Daniel first met Royce Roarshack at the University of Toronto in the late 1950s. Royce was the son of Rupert Roarshack of Roarshack, Dimwitty, Uptight, and Flake, stockbrokers. Rupert Roarshack was also the author of *Not This Cow*, a novel dealing with the sex life of Laura Secord, which Daniel had read for a research paper on the War of 1812. The sexual material — the dirty parts, that is — was terrific, but Daniel wasn't sure whether Rupert was kidding.

Perhaps Royce was also kidding Daniel. Who knows? They met at the university film society screening of *Potemkin*. Royce and Daniel were the only two people in the room who applauded heartily when the baby carriage, plus baby, tumbled down the Odessa steps. They alone understood the historical implications of that montage. Daniel was a leading socialist, Royce a flaming liberal — a potential socialist, really. And that's not all they had in common. Both loved literature and Royce was a well-known campus poet. Above all, Roarshack and Shtarker prided themselves on their sense of humour.

Royce asked Daniel to join him after *Potemkin* for a drink at the Park Plaza Hotel. Testing Daniel's sense of humour, he asked, "Why do all you Jewish kids sit together in the front three rows of the lecture halls?"

Daniel asked in reply, "Why do all you WASPs sit together in the other twenty-seven rows?"

Royce enjoyed this sally. Later he had a new twist on an old theme. "I was listening to a Jewish writer on CBC radio last night, Mordo Reichler. He was telling a funny story about a Jewish ball player called Zalman Zehrow. Zehrow, says Mordo, played ten games for the Cleveland Indians, and got zero hits, a zero zero zero batting average, and no catches, no fields, no throws. Zero for Zehrow. I just love Reichler. He's a Jew who's not afraid to laugh at his own people."

Daniel always found the idea that Jews were bad at sports hard to handle. Shtarker the wit was also sensitive, often to the point of humourlessness, and he carried a list of famous Jewish athletes with him: "Max Baer, world heavyweight boxing champion; Hank Greenberg, 58 home runs; Marshall Goldberg, fullback, Chicago Cardinals; Sid Luckman, quarterback, Chicago Bears; One Eye Louie, Canadian lacrosse champion." In 1972, when Mark Spitz, an American Jew, won more gold medals at the Olympics than the entire British and Canadian teams put together, Shtarker added Spitz to his list. But Shtarker did not want to show his list to Roarshack — perhaps because he was sure Mordecai Richler did not carry around such a list.

Instead, Shtarker turned the conversation to Alex Levinsky, the Toronto Maple Leafs' Jewish hockey legend. Unfortunately, Royce had to ask who Levinsky was. Frustrated, Shtarker said, "Aw, fuck it." He switched the subject to John Milton's love of the Jews. Roarshack had never heard of that either, but it was the kind of stuff he was willing to listen to.

Roarshack was doing poorly at university because he spent all his time working on the *Thinker*, the student cultural newspaper. Shtarker helped Roarshack with his courses and in return Roarshack published in the *Thinker* virtually everything Shtarker wrote: letters to the editor, book reviews, essays, diatribes, and sermons. But the Roarshack-Shtarker relationship was prickly, and as the years passed became pricklier. Roarshack believed the Jewish people were special, and this meant that no Jew could be a liar, a thief, a rapist, or a terrorist. If one Jew were any of these things, somehow all Jews were all these things, in the Roarshack calculus.

Obsessiveness was the key to the Roarshack-Shtarker relationship. Roarshack was obsessed with the Jews, and Shtarker was obsessed with Roarshack's ability to blend savage criticism of the Jews with extensive use of Shtarker's talents as writer and broadcaster. When Roarshack went to work for the CBC he often got

Shtarker guest shots on CBC culture programs like "Totality: The Arts in Conflict."

DANIEL IMAGINED that Royce would be a fount of financial information, and he did as he was told when Royce suggested that Daniel invest his money in XYZ Properties run by the Roarshack family's Jewish financial adviser, Moishe Shlacter. When Shlacter went bankrupt and Daniel lost the $5,000 he had invested, he was annoyed to discover that Royce had pulled his own money out just in time.

"Why didn't you warn me Shlacter was in trouble and tell *me* to get out?" Daniel asked.

Royce replied, "You're Jewish. Your people have a smell for money. I assumed you'd know in your marrow, so to speak, when to get out."

This, of course, was no doubt unconsciously uttered. Still, it was the old canard about Jews as financial wizards. The gathering at which Daniel's question was asked was attended by the illuminati always invited to Royce's lavish downtown pad. The guests all howled at Royce's *bon mot*. Daniel, looking at Royce, said, "Well, when it comes to Jewing someone, I'll have to take lessons from you." That Jewish anti-Semitic remark also drew big laughs; besides, it reinforced the fact that in business matters Daniel, the Jew, was a klutz, and the Gentile Royce was a financial maven.

The Roarshack-Shtarker relationship exploded in the late 1960s when Royce interviewed Arieh Deharget, the Holocaust novelist and poet, on "Totality." In preparation, Roarshack whipped himself into a frenzy. Deharget was his usual calm, hypnotically serene self.

Roarshack: Would it not be fair to say, Arieh, that in your poems and novels you portray the Holocaust victims and survivors as a kind of collective Christ figure?

Deharget: I make no such claims.

Roarshack: Are you not really saying, Arieh, that the Holocaust is the ultimate crucifixion and its victims and survivors are the ultimate Christs?

Deharget: You are arguing, Mr. Roarshack, from an experience with which I am completely unfamiliar. Sorry.

Roarshack: I'm asking these questions, Arieh, because if what I'm saying is true, then it follows that you're saying all Holocaust survivors are Christ figures, and that's rubbish. I know a Holocaust survivor who won't pay his employees the legal minimum wage. I also know a Holocaust survivor who's a notorious wife-beater — his own and everybody else's!

Deharget: Your views, if you do not mind my saying so, Mr. Roarshack, are a bit astonishing.

Roarshack: The Holocaust survivors came to Palestine as victims of Nazi persecution. Now they persecute the Palestinians. Aren't the Israelis, at least in a metaphoric sense, really today's Nazis?

Deharget: Jews are not in any sense, now or ever, Nazis. No Palestinians have been put in crematoria; no Palestinian faces Israeli gas chambers.

Two days after the interview was aired, an item on the front page of a Toronto newspaper said Arieh Deharget had just won the Nobel Prize for literature. Much of the rest of the page dealt with a rally in Maple Leaf Gardens, held by the Jewish community to demand the dismissal from the CBC of Royce Roarshack. The CBC soon threw him to the wolves, and his career in broadcasting was over. Royce took his crucifixion by the Jews badly. This strained his friendship with Daniel for quite a while, but it wasn't over yet.

Some months later Royce and Daniel were invited to read from their works-in-progress to the culture-vulture set at the Sandshore Reading Club, a government-subsidized cultural spa on Lake Ontario. Daniel read "Clarissa's Caliban," a love story about a five-foot Canadian senator and the gorgeous, statuesque and *zaftik* six-foot Clarissa, an assistant director on Canadian films and documentaries. She worked, for instance, on *Navel Gazed*, a romance about the amorous adventures of a Canadian plastic surgeon in war-torn China. Clarissa's Caliban, the diminutive Senator Strom Stirrup, was a legend. He had deliberately lost a safe downtown Toronto riding, knowing that this would enable the prime minister to put him in the Senate.

Daniel's tale described Stirrup's campaign and his slogan, More Power to the Little People. He also described in detail how Stirrup overcame his physical handicap to make love with the statuesque Clarissa. He tantalized her with flowers and expensive cocktail dresses. When Strom and Clarissa felt the need to neck, Stirrup would stand on a chair. In bed they were perfect. Clarissa could get all of Stirrup to rest comfortably between her breasts and lower extremities. "It's like making love to a koala bear," she often said. "Clarissa's Caliban" was a nice story with a happy ending. The Sandshore Reading Club seemed to get Daniel's message — never sell short the short.

Royce, by now famous for his obscurantism, read one of his new poems, "Enema of the People." His deep voice, rich and mellifluous, played with the words like a cat with a ball of wool. The phrasing, the emphasis were exquisite. The imagery didn't flow, it bounced and exploded.

Shove /push /pause /re-enter /squish /
roar / release /
enema of the people /
deny / lie /
cry / spy /
war measures / arrest / prison / two weeks / release /
fury / vote PQ /
the enema of the people is me / you /
Catholic / Protestant / Jew /
him / her / it / them / they / everyone /
the enema is within us /
all enemas have hidden agendas /
getting the shit out is only part of the problem /
just getting the shit out is no solution /
you are the enema of the people /
I hate you.

Daniel just loved it. When Romo Sapyenz, the roly-poly master of ceremonies, called for a standing ovation for Royce, Daniel leapt to his feet, applauding wildly. As he was the only one doing so, he was certain that Royce had noticed his enthusiasm.

Royce had noticed. Later, over coffee, he rewarded Daniel with a detailed analysis of "Clarissa's Caliban." Royce concluded, "It's a good folkloric story, the kind that can get *you* a multiculturalism grant — you know, the grants I can't get because I'm only a Scot. But I won't go into that!" Daniel was grateful that Royce didn't. He was even more grateful when, a month later, Royce called to invite him for dinner at his father's mansion.

This was a signal honour. Rupert Roarshack, the Bay Street stockbroker, knew all the major Toronto tycoons — Bud McDougald, E. P. Taylor, Hal Jackman — and, being a historical novelist, knew the Canadian literary establishment as well. Morley Callaghan, E. J. Pratt, and F. R. Scott had all dined at the Roarshack table. For Daniel, this was one great leap forward.

Royce would pick Daniel up at seven on Friday night. Dinner would be at eight, drinks between seven and eight. As Royce's car passed over the Glen Road Bridge, across the Rosedale Valley ravine, Daniel noticed that the weather had changed for the better. A cold wind had permeated the city that afternoon, but now it had disappeared. The trees fronting the stately Rosedale mansions were tall and proud. The pines and poplars saluted Royce's car and whispered, "Welcome to Rosedale, where bad becomes good, dishonest becomes honest, and richness and chosenness are definitely not odd."

Rupert Roarshack's home was a stately mansion deep in Rosedale, and his greeting to Daniel was elegant too. The conversation ranged over the universe and Canada's connection thereto. Royce began to talk about the Canadian treatment of Indians. "What we did to our Indians was genocide, pure genocide — as bad as the Holocaust and no one talks about it," said Royce, and Rupert agreed.

Money, literature, now even the fate of the Indians: with Royce, everything somehow came back to the Jews. Flattering, in a way. Also, not flattering. Daniel, coming from Winnipeg, Canada's largest Indian reserve, said nothing. Maybe that was because he believed the Holocaust was unique and Indian suffering not quite the same. In any event, Daniel was always more Jewish than he was liberal.

After dinner, after the brandies were poured, Rupert Roarshack turned the conversation to publishing. "Thank God for Macmillan," he said. "A good Scottish firm. They know good Canadian stuff when they see it. They published *Not This Cow*. They publish Canadians — Morley Callaghan, for instance — all the time. I tried to publish my book in New York, but the Jewish publishers there don't publish Canadians. They don't publish Callaghan either. Those New York Jewish publishers just hate all things Canadian."

Daniel was stunned — particularly because, to his knowledge, no one loved all things Canadian as much as he did. Now the Jews were doing in his beloved Cancult. Was there no end to Daniel's suffering — as a good Canadian, and as a Jew? He surveyed the room. Rupert Roarshack was a remarkable fellow, Daniel thought. So was Royce. The Roarshacks had taught Daniel a lot, especially about Jews and Gentiles. Daniel had learned that WASP liberals ask the impossible from the Jews, and frequently that makes the WASPs insensitive. Jewish liberals, for their part, expect too much of the WASPs and often wind up too sensitive. And perhaps there was something deeper. The Canadian WASP had a garrison mentality, his identity pure un-Americanism. The Jew was North American assimilationism incarnate, therefore a threat. Still, Daniel wasn't sure of the value of these lessons. A gnawing fear told him that the Roarshacks might teach him more things he didn't really want to know.

And at that moment Daniel realized why it was *not* odd of God to choose the Jews. The answer was simple. Nobody else wanted the job.

Smoked Salman Rushdie

T he phone rang in Daniel Shtarker's cluttered, messy, and revolting CBC office in Toronto in the late winter of 1989. "Felicia Farthing calling," said the pert little voice. Daniel was immediately on his guard. Though he liked Felicia, she was the executive secretary of Phalanx Canada, the official lobby for Canadian writers.

Everything about Phalanx Canada had made Daniel nervous, ever since its founding by Canada's most famous literary couple, Waldo Wafer and Bonnie Bratwood, co-authors of *The Petulant Pendulum: Canadian Patriotism 1880-1980*, a classic in nationalist literary criticism. *Orville's Fire*, their jointly written novel, was a delightfully saucy story that proved that the House of Commons fire of 1916 was deliberately set by an American annexationist, Orville Orbit, a third cousin of Teddy Roosevelt. Years ago, at a chi-chi party in Rosedale, Daniel Shtarker — the author of only one book, *No Sissies They — An Unauthorized Sexual Biography of J. S. Woodsworth and Stanley Knowles* — had approached Waldo Wafer. "I've written a book," said Daniel. "I wonder if I'd be eligible to join Phalanx Canada."

"How old is your book?" Waldo inquired. "Has it been out in paperback yet?"

"My book is *only* a paperback," Daniel replied, cringing with shame. "But it was condemned by the New Democratic Party convention and the executive council of the Canadian Labour

Congress. Also a woman writer in *Feminist Forum* said I was a fascist."

"Is your book still in print?" asked Waldo, pursuing the scent that the increasingly uncomfortable Shtarker was giving off. Daniel said it was. "That's good," said Waldo. "We don't want any more Unicorn Ginsbergs in Phalanx Canada." Unicorn Ginsberg had written one travel book twenty-two years before. She refused to leave Phalanx Canada, even though the rule was crystal clear: one book every ten years or membership suspended.

Indeed, it was this Phalanx Canada deadline that in 1989 was spurring Daniel on to finish his second book: *Hail And Farewell: A History of Canadian Crop Failures*, and thus secure his membership in Phalanx Canada. Daniel loved Phalanx Canada; he loved its secret newsletters, for the eyes of members only, which he often used in making CBC programs. He liked his fellow members, such as Fels Naptha, author of *The Swede Smell of Success: A Multicultural Look at Swedish Canadians*.

Felicia Farthing's call was worrisome. "Daniel, we'd like to add your name to a list of writers to a petition in support of Salman Rushdie. Can we go ahead?"

The request unnerved Daniel. Haltingly, he asked, "How many other writers are on the list?" With Daniel's luck there would be five and all five would be visited by the sword and flame of Allah.

"Oh, there are several hundred," said Felicia, ruining that excuse. But there was always the old CBC employee ploy. The CBC had a guide book telling employees to refrain from public comment on issues. Daniel had said the guide book prevented CBC employees from being "ists" — communists, Zionists, capitalists, optometrists, florists, or journalists. Still, he knew no one at the CBC would object to supporting Salman Rushdie.

But he hated signing petitions and had never done it. Daniel preferred to express his own views his own way. This time, though, he put his name down. At least it didn't start with a Z like that of his old schoolteacher, Falek Zolf. Kooks and cranks always started with the last name on petititions when they wanted to get their man. With a name like Shtarker, Daniel would be buried somewhere in the middle and thus be fairly safe.

Maybe, just maybe, Daniel said yes to Felicia Farthing because he felt he had a bond with Salman Rushdie. Rushdie was a lapsed Moslem married to a WASP and branded a Moslem self-hater. Daniel Shtarker, lapsed Jew, married to a WASP had on all too many occasions been branded a Jewish self-hater. Rushdie had a price on his head; Daniel had once had a price tag on his too.

IT WAS A SATURDAY afternoon in the late 1960s when the phone in the Shtarker house interrupted Daniel's nap. "Hello? Is this Daniel Shtarker, CBC?"

"Yes, it is."

"You are a Jew, are you not?"

"Yes, I am."

"You're not a Jew, you're a Nazi lover! You vant to put Volfgang Von Volfpack, the new Hitler, on Canadian TV. My family went to the gaz ovens. This time you'll go. I tell you, Mr. Shtarker, that you and your kind are worse than the Nazis. For two cents I blow you and your house up!"

For two cents? thought Daniel. My God, I have a price on my head — and a pretty low one at that. But Daniel did not call the police. The call couldn't be be traced anyway. Besides, the caller was a Holocaust survivor and had been hunted enough. Daniel would just have to ride this one through by himself.

Just before Daniel's flight to Frankfurt, 14,000 Toronto Jews assembled in Maple Leaf Gardens to protest the Von Wolfpack interview. They all shouted, "Yes! Yes!" when David Lewis, NDP MP, branded Shtarker "a man ashamed of his race and heritage" and demanded his dismissal from the CBC. But Daniel and the CBC went ahead anyway. At the Frankfurt airport, Wolfgang Von Wolfpack, the former Wehrmacht tank commander, met Daniel.

"Welcome to the new Germany," he said in flawless English. A Mercedes limousine waited to drive them to the Hanover estate of the Prussian. Along the way, Wolfgang was effusive. He loved the controversy generated by his upcoming interview on the CBC.

Wolfgang was proud of the turnpike the Mercedes was driving over. "This autobahn," he said, "was built by *der Fuehrer* — I mean Hitler. It's an excellent design, very durable. It could easily last a thousand years. The infrastructure left behind by Hitler is a precious legacy. In the new Germany, we must build on that infrastructure.

As the Mercedes sped on, Wolfgang babbled, "The Jews are not a factor in the new Germany. There are no Jews in Germany now. Hitler solved that problem. People say I hate the Jews. How can I hate what isn't there?" Wolfgang went on to tell his own horror stories about a sister and brother-in-law executed for trying to kill Hitler. Wolfgang insisted he himself had never been SS. Hitler's orders toward the end of the war made no sense, Wolfgang said.

"The real enemies of the new Germany," he said, "are the Beatles, the Rolling Stones, and the German youth who wear long hair, play guitars, and won't listen to their parents. Germany was built on discipline. We must return to discipline."

God, Lord and Master of the Universe, thought Daniel, please rescue me from this all-consuming bore!

THE INTERVIEW, done in the spacious living room of Wolfgang's ultramodern space-age home, went well. Daniel, after all, was an experienced Nazi interviewer. Anytime the CBC wished to interview a Nazi they called on Daniel. His huge Jewish nose and kinky hair provided all the balance and objectivity these interviews required. And weeks later at a debate at the Shrine of the Mystic Petal Synagogue ("The Wolfgang Von Wolfpack CBC Interview: Jewish Self-Hatred or Jewish Spite?") Daniel Shtarker was doing not too badly. He had packed much of the hall with friends. He also had a transcript of the interview, and when asked why he did not put a certain question to the Nazi, he would read from the transcript and prove he had indeed asked it. Then he would say, "I work for goyim. The goyim took out that question. I don't know why. I don't run the CBC. Why don't you ask the goyim who do run the CBC your questions, rather than going after me — the token Jew in the CBC woodpile!"

This didn't soothe the crowd, but it got some laughs for Daniel. Then a short stocky woman stood up. Showing her tattoo numbers to the crowd, and speaking in a calm and deliberate way, the woman quickly let all the hot air out of Daniel's balloon. "Mr.

Shtarker, on air I heard you say that Wolfgang the Nazi likes kids. Is that right?" Daniel, seeing the trap, lamely agreed. He had filmed Wolfgang with some kids and pets and remarked (he thought it funny at the time) that someone who liked cats, dogs, and kids couldn't be, tee hee, all bad. "You also said Wolfgang the Nazi likes cats!"

"Right," said Daniel.

"You also said he likes dogs. And then you said he can't be all bad. Well you're wrong, Mr. Shtarker. All Nazis are bad. Ask the right people in this room and they'll tell you. You and the CBC stink to high heaven — *you*, sir, are all bad."

WAS HE ALL BAD, Daniel Shtarker wondered, in the winter of 1989. Was he really a Jewish self-hater, perhaps an unconscious Nazi lover? Or did his stupid remark to Wolfgang Von Wolfpack simply prove the ultimate horror — that Daniel Shtarker, celebrated wit, was in fact an insensitive fellow who stepped on other people's toes just for the hell of it? Was it possible? Perhaps the answer lay somewhere in the past. Daniel let his mind drift back to the early 1960s when he was a penniless standup comic in Toronto's bohemian cafés.

"LADIES AND GENTLEMEN, tonight the Sack and Ashes, the café that brought you poet Al Purdy, is proud to present one of Canada's brightest young comics, fresh from gigs in the Braless Cloister in London, Ontario, and the Ruthless Rivet in Hamilton, I give you Daniel Shtarker, the Lenny Bruce of the North!"

Daniel quickly went into his anti-Nazi repertoire. He would open with a one-liner like "Individually, ladies and gentlemen, Nazis can be nice people, but as a group they can be sudden death." That usually emptied the hall of at least a dozen people, mostly Jewish. A second line had similar effects. "Ve Nazis are a hated, scorned, and persecuted group. You Jews are a hated, scorned, and persecuted group. The solution? Ve Nazis and Jews gotta stick together!" Daniel often wove some of his poems into his routines. One that aroused a certain hostility was:

Roses are reddish
Violets are bluish
If it wasn't for Eichmann,
There'd be six million more Jewish.

This not only upset all Jews, but all members of the Northrop Frye archetypal criticism crowd as well.

Daniel found hostility from the Jews hard to deal with. No one hated anti-Semites more than he did, but he saw himself as a hipster, a gunslinger of wit. Daniel firmly believed that only caustic wit and scabrous humour could keep the fascists at bay. So he soldiered on. After the one-liners and the poems, he usually decided that the audience, or what was left of it, was sufficiently warmed up. He would move into his routines, sometimes surrealist spoofs on documentaries. One began:

"*Achtung, achtung, achtung,* this is the Deutsche Rundfunk Gesellschaft, German National Socialist Broadcasting Corporation. We take you now to our noble warrior soldiers, on duty, keeping the peace in our European possessions. Meet Helmut Kartofel. Helmut is a member of the Wehrmacht, the Katzteufel Division. Helmut is on guard duty in the warehouse district of Amsterdam. Helmut is now walking by a three-storey warehouse. But wait! An object has been thrown out of the third-floor window of the warehouse. The object has landed at Helmut's feet. Helmut is now opening the package. On the front cover of the package it says 'Diary — 1942-1944.' Inside, on the first page, it says: 'Help! I'm surrounded by Jews in an attic. Signed, Anne Frank.'"

That routine would empty the hall of his Jewish audience, leaving behind the hipsters, the junkies, the petty criminals, the bikers, the psychopaths, Zal Yanovsky, Pat the Pimp, and Henry the Gigolo. They cheered it to the rafters.

THE LENNY BRUCE of the North routines were not quite as comforting in the late 1980s as they had been in the 1960s. Somehow it was hard to tell from Daniel's 1960s jokes whether he hated the Nazis, the Jews — or just himself. Thinking about Rushdie after his phone conversation with Felicia Farthing, Daniel had to admit that despite all the years that had passed, he had no final answers to the Jewish questions that had bugged him all his life.

Indeed, Daniel wasn't even sure about good old Rushdie. (If caught and thrown on a funeral pyre, Rushdie would soon be Smoked Salman Rushdie — will you please check that dumb Lenny-Bruce-of-the-North impulse?) Still, even though his own price was two cents, Daniel could understand the price on the head of Rushdie.

The Reunion

One evening in the 1970s Daniel was sitting comfortably on a stool in the Longchamps Bar of the Hyatt Regency Hotel in Toronto. Freddy, like bartenders all over the city, knew Shtarker well. The CBC, after all, was then, by common myth, populated by faggots, communists, creatives, and drunks. Daniel was somewhere between the creatives and the drunks. "How's your double?" Freddie asked.

"Smooth as silk, Freddie. At the rate you mix 'em and the rate I drink 'em, you'll be master of ceremonies at my funeral, Freddie. It's already in the will."

The will had just been drawn up by Skip Tregebov, who had been in the dummies class with Daniel. Skip, too, had been designated for a life in the factories but had escaped through good university marks. The will he drew for Daniel was simple in principle: Daniel left everything to Dahlia, just as Menachem had done for Zipporah. But the details of the funeral were far more complex, at least in Daniel's mind.

Often Daniel had fantasized about his last day above ground; now, at the Longchamps Bar, the fantasy was upon him again. His body was to be flown to Winnipeg, where the funeral would take place in front of the Cenotaph on Memorial Boulevard. Daniel had been too young for the Second World War and Korea, too old for Vietnam. But he had seen every war movie ever made and had listened patiently to dozens of war veterans telling their stories in hundreds of bars across Canada, the U.S., and Britain. He felt he deserved a military funeral simply for listening to hundreds of Norman DePoe's war stories without nodding off. So a Cenotaph funeral it was to be. The burial would take place at the Chesed Shel Emes Cemetery, where the pallbearers would be all the beautiful and stunning women Daniel knew, desired, or worked with: Bunny Senesh, June Kozak, Barbara Amiel, Helga Stephenson, Barbara Frum, Anna Porter, Diane Francis, F. M. Morrison, Susan Teskey, and Azza el-Sissi. They were all to weep and wail and throw themselves at the coffin just as it was lowered into the ground. Azza, a beautiful Egyptian colleague of Daniel's, would show the others how to do it. Those who declined to throw themselves on the coffin would not be invited to the wake, which would be handled by Skip Tregebov and Pinchus Weisman and paid for by a contingency fund in the will.

But why dwell on death, thought Daniel. He was at the Longchamps to meet Skip Tregebov, and they were to go on to the sixth floor, which had been entirely reserved for Pinchus Weisman. Pinchus, the former tinman tycoon, was now a business legend in Vancouver. Daniel had not seen him for eighteen years. This was to be a reunion of North Winnipeg's three ratketeers — Tregebov, son of a communist; Weisman, son of the chief rabbi of Winnipeg; and Shtarker, son of the lapsed socialist, Menachem Shtarker.

Daniel's misgivings had begun the moment Skip first told him about it. Reunions spoil the sense of stories past, of old scenes set, of the right laughter for the right reasons. People always look dumber and more humdrum. Reunions reek of death, or decay.

"WANNA SEE ME sell some tin?" Pinchus asked Daniel one night in 1954.

"Actually I would," said Daniel.

"I'll pick you up on Saturday afternoon," said Pinchus.

Daniel had heard a great deal about the tinmen exploits of Pinchus and Skip. Skip was the canvasser, the man who got his foot in the sucker's door and kept it there. The canvasser went there first to sell the sucker on the value of aluminum windows and doors — "tin," in trade jargon. The canvasser would then set an absurdly high price the sucker couldn't afford, the sucker would balk, and the canvasser would throw up his hands and say it was up to the branch manager to decide on a price. The branch manager, better known as "the closer," would be waiting in a car nearby. Pinchus was always the closer. The canvasser would pretend to make a phone call and would then report back that the branch manager was making calls in the neighbourhood and, with a little luck, could probably be found. He would leave the house and come back ten minutes later with the closer. The closer would listen to the sucker's arguments and let himself be bargained down by ten or fifteen per cent; company rules, he would note, prevented him from going any lower. The sucker was satisfied he had obtained a bargain and would sign. Having made a two hundred per cent profit, canvasser and closer would go in search of other suckers.

That Saturday afternoon, Skip, Pinchus, and Daniel drove to the bungalow of Oleg Grobnik and his wife, Olga, in the Ukrainian section of North Winnipeg. Skip worked his charm on the Grobniks, and he and Daniel were soon in the living room, Daniel being introduced as Skip's apprentice. "The windows will keep you warm in the winter and cool in the summer," said Skip. "They'll raise the value of your house, Mr. Grobnik, by at least thirty per cent. They're not just windows and doors. They're an investment in the future." Grobnik's response was silence, but that wasn't unusual. Stoic bargaining was a traditional Ukrainian ploy. Skip concluded it was time to bring in the closer. Soon Pinchus was there.

"Mr. Grobnik," he said, "for you, the ten aluminum windows and the two aluminum doors with the cocker spaniel doggie engraving in the middle of the doors is $600. How does that grab you, Mr. Grobnik?"

"Feiv nindy-nine," said Mr. Grobnik.

"Done and settled at $599, Mr. Grobnik."

"Feiv nindy-ate," said Mr. Grobnik.

"Five ninety-eight? Well, that's an even round number. Five ninety-eight it is, Mr. Grobnik," said Pinchus.

"Feiv nindy-seven," said Mr. Grobnik. Pinchus stared at him a moment. Then, in a playful mood, showing off a bit for Daniel, he did a crash-and-swerve ploy. "Two hundred for the windows and the doors with the doggies in them," he said.

"Von nindy-nein," said Mr. Grobnik.

This was war, and Pinchus was prepared to fight. "Mr. Grobnik, a special just for you and just for today. The windows, the two doors, and the two doggies — for ten dollars!"

"Nein dollars," said Grobnik. "Two dollars," said Pinchus.

"Von dollar," said the Ukrainian.

"Hell," said Pinchus, "you can have the windows and the doors and the doggies engraved in them for nothing! Just sign here, Mr. Grobnik. Use the windows and doors well. Come, Daniel, Skip. Send our boys out to this house to install the stuff at once, Skip."

Back in the car, Daniel asked, "Why did you give him the windows and doors free, Pinchus?"

"Well, I'm making so much money, I don't give a shit. And this Grobnik may appear to be a silent one, but my research says he's a blabber. He'll tell everyone he knows how easy it was to out-jew the Jew. The Honkies will be falling all over themselves to deal with me now. I'll be up to my ass in Honkies. I've just found myself a thousand new suckers. Understand?" Daniel, the young social-ist, watching for the first time the darker side of capitalism oper-ated by his own generation, said he understood.

ONE DAY Pinchus Weisman introduced Daniel to his good friends the Stoodleigh brothers — Jack the Stick Stoodleigh was the older, Two Dip Stoodleigh the younger. Jack the Stick and Daniel hit it off at once.

"Say, kid," Jack said one day, "Your sweater looks a little ragged. You'd really look good in cashmere." Jack the Stick, easily one of the best-dressed men in Winnipeg, was clad in cashmere cap, Harris tweed jacket, grey flannel trousers, and black Dacks shoes. "Stay here, kid, I'll be right back."

The Salisbury House, where they were talking, had behind it a lane that led directly to the Hudson's Bay department store. Jack the Stick was gone for about half an hour. On his return, he had eight different cashmere sweaters in various sizes. "Try 'em on, kid," he said. Daniel tried them on; none fitted. Jack wasn't upset. "Okay," Jack said, "I've got your size down now." He went off and was back in half an hour. "Try these on," he said, thrusting four sweaters at Daniel. All four of them fitted Daniel. "They're yours, Daniel, wear them in good health," said Jack.

"But you stole them, Jack. I could get in trouble with the law." Jack the Stick laughed and said, "Look, Joe Kennedy is a thief, J. P. Morgan was one, and Sir Herbert Holt was a real crook. The Hudson's Bay Company stole this country from the Indians. Proudhon says property is theft. A little shoplifting only redresses the balance. I'd be upset, Daniel, if you turned down my gift." Daniel left the Salisbury House wearing a Burberry cashmere cardigan, with three other Burberry cashmeres in his briefcase. He felt uneasy but he was persuaded to accept the sweaters by Jack the Stick's obvious erudition.

Once, Daniel even took Jack the Stick to college and palmed him off as a visiting professor of English Lang. and Lit. from the University of Minnesota. Daniel's friend, Bunny Senesh, the Ukrainian beauty, took a shine to Jack the Stick. It was the poetry readings Jack did so well that touched Bunny's heart.

Daniel asked Pinchus how Jack the Stick was making a living. "Jack's a hit-and-run man," said Pinchus. "He gets involved with women, then he and his brother move into their apartments. These are career-type professional women with good incomes. One day the woman goes off to work. When she comes back home the Stoodleighs are gone and so is every piece of furniture in the apartment. The women are too embarrassed to call the police. The Stoodleighs sell the furniture to a fence and keep the dough. It's the oldest scam in town."

Jack the Stick moved into the apartment of Bunny Senesh. One day she went to college as usual. When she returned, her apartment was empty and her furniture was gone. But Bunny wasn't too proud to call the police. The police then paid the Stoodleighs a visit and gave them what was known as a floater — they were told to stay out of Winnipeg for two years.

"Love is blind," said Pinchus. "Bunny should have known

better." Daniel wasn't sure of the ethical base underlying Pinchus's judgement, but said nothing. Love may be blind, Daniel thought, but as clichés went, maybe those who lived by the sword, like Jack the Stick, die by the sword.

Two years later, Pinchus himself was given a floater by the police. By that time, he was the richest tinman in Canada, and his methods were unusual. As early as high school, Pinchus begun managing the considerable fortune his father, Rabbi Yakov, had accumulated. By the time he was in college, he had built a small but efficient mortgage company, which dovetailed neatly with Pinchus's tinman activities. Often he sold tin to the less fortunate — welfare cases, the unemployed — and frequently the less fortunate could afford aluminum windows and doors only if they took out a mortgage — from Pinchus's family company, of course. When the less fortunate failed to keep up their mortgage payments, Pinchus foreclosed. By 1957, he was a major property owner.

The *Winnipeg Tribune* then did a sustained exposé of Pinchus's operation and he became a household word in Winnipeg. Anti-Semitism inevitably followed. The windows in the Butchers' Synagogue and the El Mole Rachmim Synagogue were smashed. A swastika was drawn on the front door of Rabbi Yakov's stately mansion. Soon the provincial government intervened, and the dean of the law school was appointed a one-man commission to look into Pinchus's activities. He found no illegalities, but on ethical grounds he completely condemned Pinchus.

Two days later, a squad car pulled up at Rabbi Yakov's house, where Pinchus was still living. "Is your son Pinchus here, Rabbi Weisman?" Sergeant McDermott of the fraud squad asked.

"Yes, he is," said Rabbi Yakov. "I'll go get him."

Sergeant McDermott and a constable got right down to business. "Mr. Pinchus Weisman, the city of Winnipeg no longer finds you welcome," said Sergeant McDermott. "We're giving you a floater. You are to stay out of Winnipeg for two years. Please pack a bag and get your car ready. Should we find you back here within two years, we will have to act in an unpleasant manner. I hope you understand."

Pinchus did. He packed his bag and, escorted by the police, drove his car to the outskirts of the city. Then, waving jocularly at the police, Pinchus stepped hard on the gas pedal and departed for Vancouver. There he got out of tin and into deal making. In no time at all, he was as rich as Midas and twice as smart.

DANIEL WAS TRYING to remember the rest of Pinchus's story when his reverie was interrupted by a vigorous slap on the back. "How ya doin', kiddo?" Skip Tregebov asked. Skip was doing very well, thought Daniel. The wiliest divorce lawyer in Toronto, now himself divorced, was with a stunning Italian woman, beautifully attired in the best from Creeds. She and Daniel got along at once.

"What's happening, Skip?" Daniel asked. "How's Pinchus going to handle the reunion?"

"I don't know, he won't tell me," said Skip, "but he's got the whole sixth floor reserved and some surprises for us, he says. He'll call down when he wants us." Two doubles later the phone on the bar rang, and the three of them were on their way.

The sixth floor was chaos. Cakes, desserts, and canapé trays were being wheeled around. There were twelve girls dressed in Minnesota Viking football uniforms, there was a plates juggler and a balls juggler, there were six or seven Pious Ones, obviously disciples of the late Rabbi Yakov. There were four reporters and a TV crew interviewing Pinchus. Four enforcers were present to ensure that no harm came to Pinchus or his kind.

As soon as he spotted Skip and Daniel, Pinchus interrupted the media and rushed forward to kiss and hug his two old friends, the ex-socialist son of the ex-socialist father and the ex-communist son of the ex-communist father. "This is for you guys. Watch and enjoy!" said Pinchus. He blew a whistle. The twelve girls in football uniforms lined up; a ball was snapped and they all rushed off. When he blew his whistle again, a horse emerged from a back room. On the horse, sidesaddle, was a beautiful woman with a sash running from the nape of her neck to the end of her mini-skirt — Miss Minnesota Viking 1975 said the sash in gold-and-green lettering. "Yeah," said Pinchus, "it's the real Miss Minnesota Viking 1975. She's my broad. I love her. Ingrid Floist is her name.

Come and meet her." They met Ingrid, a lovable airhead.

Already Daniel was feeling he had been wrong about reunions. This one was spectacular. It was nice to see Pinchus still wheeling and dealing. Pinchus, thought Daniel, may be an exploiter of the masses but he was no exploiter of Shtarker. Daniel still truly loved Pinchus Weisman, the rabbi's son and capitalist.

As Daniel headed home, he wondered how all his bright and beautiful pallbearers, all staunch feminists, would have felt about this reunion. The girls in the football uniforms were certainly proof of male chauvinism. Miss Minnesota Viking 1975, riding in on a horse, was an insult to Lady Godiva and was definitely evidence of male piggery. True, all true, thought Daniel. But if his feminist friends knew the true story of Pinchus Weisman, would they forgive him?

On Avenue Road, Daniel hailed a cab. As always, he asked the driver what he thought of Trudeau. This cabbie was violently Trudeauphobic, and the predictable eruption of his phobia put Daniel gently to sleep. In his dream, they were all there: his feminist beauties, his beautiful pallbearers, all in tears and wailing, and all about to throw themselves on his coffin as it was being lowered into the grave. Barbara Amiel was the first to jump on the coffin, Barbara Frum the second. Diane Francis was third. Azza el-Sissi was as usual last, having done her job of training the others to perfection.

Let My People Go

D aniel didn't really mind the hospital. Given that he had just undergone major rectal surgery and that further problems awaited him down the road, he found convalescence almost pleasant. Maybe it was because the hospital was Jewish, the B'nai Emes in downtown Toronto, and the doctors were Jewish too. Weren't Jewish doctors the best? So his father, Menachem, had always told him. Besides, Daniel got along well with the nurses, though his relationship with Brunhilde Gassenfleisch, the Teutonic enema dispenser, was not ideal. She gave seven enemas the night before surgery, and Daniel had reserved for Brunhilde the first three chapters of a novel on hospital life he intended to write, *Satanic Nurses*. Still, she was under the power, so to speak, of Jewish doctors; Teutonic subservience to the Jews was a comforting thought to Daniel.

Daniel's favourite nurse was the blonde and pert Felicity Stone. During a long talk she disclosed that she had dated three men Daniel knew well — a film reviewer for *Toronto Life*, a man who sold mutual funds only to blind women and deaf men, and a lecherous, bum-patting skirt-ruffling alderman who eloquently represented the poor and downtrodden. In that same conversation, about an hour in length, Daniel and Felicity found they had one hundred acquaintances in common. That didn't surprise Daniel. He was a journalist, and had once been a fanatic socialist, and then a beatnik. In these three categories one meets the best and brightest in our society, as well as some other people.

Daniel's feelings toward Felicity were not carnal. In the shape he was in, he could not have been aroused by Marilyn Monroe and Jane Russell. Felicity was simply Daniel's friend, and a great help in passing time — which, next to passing urine and stool, is the most vital activity in a hospital. But she had to do her rounds, and that often left Daniel to fend for himself.

Getting out of one's room, he knew, was important to recovery. Too much time in the room and on the bed could lead to brooding, self-doubt, and fear. Moving around was the key to success. Right across from Daniel's room was a lounge, and it was there that he thought he heard the sound of Yiddish. Though it was Daniel's paternal language, the only one spoken at home, he had not heard it in years. The sound evoked memories of childhood.

The Yiddish was coming from a couple in their early seventies. The man was a short, wizened visitor; his wife, frumpy and dishevelled, was the patient. The husband, Daniel learned, arrived promptly at seven every morning and stayed with his wife until visitor curfew at 8:30 p.m.

Daniel knew that in Toronto even old Jews usually would speak accented English, not Yiddish. He decided these must be Soviet Jews, refuseniks, secret soldiers against communist totalitarianism. Images of the Gulag danced through Daniel's head. Without meeting the two people, Daniel felt a kinship with them, and felt pride in their struggle for a free Jewry, a fight he had never had to fight.

One day in the lounge, as Daniel was immersed in a *New Yorker* short story, the man sidled up to him and said, in Yiddish, "I'm Shmulik Weinweiss. Are you a Jew?"

Given Daniel's pronounced Semitic features, he wondered why anyone would ask him if he were a Jew. Besides, if he weren't a Jew how could he understand a question in Yiddish? Still, Daniel replied in his imperfect Yiddish that he was a Jew. Then, just to see if his theory was accurate, Daniel asked, "You must be Soviet Jews? Did you come here after the war?"

"In 1967."

"You've lived under Stalin and Khrushchev. You must have many stories to tell."

"Ah, feh, they're all anti-Semites, the whole awful place."

Sympathy swept through Daniel, but when he tried to talk about Soviet atrocities, Shmulik Weinweiss shook him off. It seemed there were more pressing matters on his mind. "I've just sold a condominium at Bathurst Heights and Wilson," he said. "I made a hundred and thirty thousand dollars on the deal. Could you give me some advice about investing my money?"

The question jolted Daniel. All his life, he had been plagued with an inability to handle money. Possibly this was caused by the anticapitalist bias instilled at home. Deep in his heart Daniel believed that stockbrokers were crooks and big businessmen pirates. These biases made him shun financial and business matters. Daniel prided himself on ignoring the *Globe*'s Report on Business and crossing the road whenever he saw Conrad Black emerging from his limousine. Now he tried desperately to explain to the Soviet freedom fighter why he was incapable of offering financial advice. He mentioned that he failed math in high school, had been too scared to take economics in university, and couldn't tell a debenture from a preferred share.

The refusenik soon grew bored and returned to his wife, sitting stoically in her wheelchair. As for Daniel, running down his own financial acumen had also run down his spirits. He felt lethargic and headed back to his bed.

A moment later Felicity Stone appeared at his side. "I see you've been talking to the wife beater."

"Wife beater?" Daniel Shtarker asked.

"Yeah, he beats her every day. We caught him punching her in her stomach while she was still sitting in her wheelchair in her own room. The public relations man in the hospital is really worried about all this. What if it gets in the paper? Can you see the headline: 'B'nai Emes Patient Beaten in Wheelchair.' You wouldn't tell the CBC, would you?" Daniel swore complete silence.

After Felicity left, Daniel was upset. The noble refusenik was now the antithesis of whatever Daniel, a male feminist, believed in. The beating of women by Jews was unthinkable, unless the woman was Ilse Koch — and then only maybe! Daniel began thinking about the Soviet Jews. Maybe there were thousands of Shmulik Weinweisses, taking the cudgel to their womenfolk. Maybe such no-goodniks deserve Russia!

Daniel's thoughts were interrupted by the arrival of lunch and Shmulik Weinweiss, who poked his head into his room and asked to use the phone. "Ours is out of commission in the next room." Daniel gritted his teeth, gave his permission, and listened to Weinweiss's side of the conversation, this time in English:

"The wife? She's a cripple. She'll always be a cripple. I'm stuck with a cripple! Do you want to take my cripple off my hands? Maybe I can stick her in a home somewhere. Cripples are a pain in the ass."

Weinweiss's insensitivity infuriated Daniel. When the conversation ended and Weinweiss started to speak Yiddish, Daniel turned on him, in English. "Look, this is my room and this is my lunch. I want to eat it alone. If you don't get out of here right now, I'll bust your beak!"

Weinweiss left and Shtarker, exhausted, ate his lunch. He crept back into bed. Peace at last. But not for long. Felicity dropped in. "I see you had the wife beater in your room. Why?"

"He said his phone was out of order."

"You bet it was. He picked that poor woman out of her wheelchair and threw her against the phone. Knocked the phone off the wall. She's got a broken rib!"

Daniel was thinking. If the hospital wouldn't have this assaulter of female flesh arrested, maybe he could do something. Maybe an anonymous phone call to the immigration department would send Weinweiss back to Russia. Maybe he could get George Geltfresser, the TV financial maven who had cost Daniel thousands in a real estate deal years ago, to advise Weinweiss on the use of his $180,000. Maybe Daniel could provide Mace to Weinweiss's poor wife.

These pleasant thoughts lulled Daniel to sleep. In his dream Gorbachev was seated on an Egyptian throne. Daniel was yelling,

"Let my people go!"

Gorbachev replied, "Certainly! Why not? We have thousands of Shmulik Weinweisses here in the Soviet Union we'd be only too glad to let go. But let me ask you one question, Comrade Shtarker: How many Shmulik Weinweisses can Western democracy stand?" Good question, thought Daniel. The next moment he was awake, anything but refreshed.

Scorpions for Sale

O n a September afternoon in 1988, Daniel returned from a public reading, his first ever. He had read his short story, "Media Good Samaritan," to gales of laughter from the twelve people assembled at the Belfast Loyalist Ratepayers Association Annual Fun Fair.

The reading was given beneath a piece of canvas rigged up to protect the writers from the sun. Four times during Daniel's reading, the canvas collapsed and landed on him. Four times he recovered quickly and plunged onward. Shtarker loved reading his stories: to CBC producers too drunk to spell CBC, to CBC typists busy at work, to drunks in the washroom at the Hop and Grape. Once, for laughs, Shtarker read a story aloud at the corner of Yonge and Bloor. A man listened, gave him a quarter, and promised to consider conversion to Jehovah's Witnesses. He said that until hearing Daniel's reading he hadn't considered the Witnesses very funny.

So far the reviews of Daniel's new book of short stories were good. "The Canadian Jew Truly Exposed at Last," said *Maclean's*. "A Pilgrim's Progress Through the Pool Halls, Back Alleys and Political Backrooms of Canada," said *The Toronto Star*. "Taking the lint out of the Jewish navel and the mickey out of everybody else, Daniel Shtarker's first effort is a multicultural milestone," said *The Globe and Mail*. "Recommended reading even for WASPs." But Daniel had this nagging feeling he had left something out of his book — a story perhaps about some great event he had lived through. It was too late to change the book, of course, but Daniel still had another story to write. What was it? He was confident it would come back to him.

THOR TEUFELBLUT'S 4:00 a.m. phone call awakened Daniel that day in October 1970. "Daniel, I want you in Ottawa by 8:00 a.m. This is going to be the biggest story in Canada ever."

On the plane the passengers were quiet, seemingly unafraid — no doubt, as good Canadians, seething inside and nervously awaiting the drama closing in on Ottawa. The stewardess, who had seen Daniel on a hundred flights, said, "Hi, Daniel, is Trudeau declaring war?"

"Not on his own people — not yet anyway," said Daniel.

The Ottawa airport looked like Saigon: tanks, armoured cars, and soldiers with machine guns over their shoulders. Wandering through this scene, Daniel raised his arms high and yelled, "On behalf of the CBC, I surrender! What's more, I surrender the CBC as well. You can have them. They're all a bunch of commie faggots anyway."

An officer laughed. "We're just doing our job, Mr. Shtarker," he said. "I promise you we won't occupy the CBC."

Daniel wasn't particularly reassured by this message. A military occupation might do the CBC some good, he thought. A little law and order around there wouldn't hurt.

A few hours later Daniel was looking down from the Press Gallery at Mr. Law and Order himself. As usual, the Right Honourable Pierre Elliott Trudeau wore a red flower, a Saville Row suit, and an expression that was half-Socrates, half-Machiavelli. The phrases "Peace, Order and Good Government" and "Apprehended Insurrection" dropped like pearls from his lips. Good, thought Daniel; never a bleeding heart, Daniel concluded that Trudeau's decision was the right one. The situation was deteriorating fast. Willingness to condone violence had become almost a credo of the Quebec left.

BUT, WAR MEASURES or no War Measures, Daniel had to rent a

house for himself and his family, due in Ottawa in January. He had been posted to Ottawa, and War Measures Day One was his first day on the job. Mrs. Peabody from the Rockies and Appalachian real estate company told him, "I've just the house for you. It's on Seaforth Avenue in the Glebe. The Honourable Donald Daring, the roads minister in the Quebec government, owns the place."

The house was wonderful — three floors, four bathrooms, five bedrooms, finished basement, all for $350 a month, the lease to run for eighteen months. "I'll take the place, Mrs. Peabody," said Daniel.

"Fine! Come and sign the papers this afternoon."

Later that day, on his way to the realty office, Daniel read in the Montreal *Gazette* the names of the prominent people on whom the FLQ had murderous designs. On the list was the Hon. Donald Daring, now about to be Daniel's landlord.

In the office of Rockies and Appalachian Realty, Mrs. Peabody had the lease ready. Daniel signed it, but Mrs. Peabody then presented him with another piece of paper. It read: "If any untoward harm, imperilling situation, or exceptional circumstance should befall the lessor, his wife or any of his family, then the lessee agrees to vacate 247 Seaforth Avenue in thirty days." If I sign this, thought Daniel, all I've really got is a thirty-day lease. But if I object I'll be known as Shtarker the ghoul, who refused to vacate his house to the landlord's survivors if his landlord was maybe kidnapped or murdered. Daniel signed the addendum. Mrs. Peabody congratulated Daniel. Daniel was her first successful piece of business since War Measures had been declared. Daniel was now the proud proprietor of a thirty-room mansion on a thirty-day basis.

ON THE NIGHT of October 16, 1970, Daniel was spending his time with one of his all-time loved ones — Louis Descaré, the bartender at the National Press Club on Wellington Street. It was late on a Friday night. Louis, his wife, Annabelle, and Daniel were watching the late movie. Since you know that Jews don't or can't drink, or if they drink can't hold their liquor, you will be pleased to learn that Daniel had consumed a dozen doubles that night and was pissed to the eyeballs.

"Louis, another double," said Daniel.

"No, you're pissed and you should go home," said Louis.

"One for the road, then."

"No, the bar is closed."

"Okay, give me an orange juice. Make it a double."

Louis went to get it just as Daniel heard Annabelle shout, "Oh, my God, come quick! Mr. Laporte has been murdered. His body was found in a trunk."

Annabelle was right. The goddamned FLQ was crazy. The bastards should all be strung up, thought Daniel. At the same moment he had another thought: he had to sober up — quick. There was a TV camera in the Centre Block of the House of Commons and the CBC would start broadcasting soon. Soon, too, the Canadian people would wake up, and want to know what the CBC had to say.

Louis and Annabelle washed Daniel's face and soaked his head in ice-cold water. Coherence returned rapidly, and the soldier of the CBC was ready for duty again. "Go get those bastards," said Louis. Daniel, saluting, strode out the door. At the House of Commons the CBC camera was on and Ron Collister was interviewing John Diefenbaker. Collister was glad to see Daniel, the second CBC reporter on the scene, and Daniel immediately hustled off to Jean Marchand's office to see how that powerful Quebec minister was taking the murder. When the door briefly opened, Daniel saw Gérard Pelletier, Jean-Pierre Goyer, and Marchand himself. Marchand was weeping openly.

Daniel picked up a bit of news from John Turner and went back to report. The mood was grim but there were comic moments. Denny Dogood, executive assistant to Robert Stanfield, leader of the opposition, arrived and handed Daniel a press release describing Stanfield's grief at Laporte's death. Denny said Stanfield was sleeping, and wanted Daniel to read the press release on the air. Daniel laughed. "Look, Denny, your nemesis Diefenbaker has been here for an hour. David Lewis from the NDP has just joined him. If anyone finds out your boss slept through the night of Laporte's murder, Stanfield will get two votes — yours and his. If *The Toronto Star* finds out about it, tomorrow's headline will read: 'Stanfield Sleeps As Laporte Garrotted.' Get Stanfield dressed and get him here fast." Denny ran to fetch Stanfield. Daniel returned to his duties.

In the next two days, journalists from all over the world poured into sleepy little Ottawa. The outsiders found the FLQ crisis hard to cover, mainly because the Trudeau government — eager to get its message out in Canada — favoured Canadian reporters and broadcasters over their American and British equivalents.

Early in the crisis Daniel received a message from Knowlton Nash, chief of TV News and Public Affairs, who wanted Daniel to interview, for half an hour each, the two living former prime ministers, Lester B. Pearson and John Diefenbaker. "Have them reassure the nation — you know what I mean, Daniel?" Daniel knew a propaganda interview when he heard about one, but it meant an hour of prime time in which he could shine.

Daniel arranged the interviews so that Pearson and Diefenbaker — who hated each other — wouldn't meet: separate makeup rooms, separate doors of entry, a quick exit from the set after the first interview was done. The arrangements took up the morning, and at noon Shtarker headed for the Press Club. It was jumping. For once Ottawa had the hottest story in the world. Why not jump for joy?

After a few doubles Daniel returned to the Centre Block. There he saw a line of foreign American crews and reporters hoping to catch a glimpse of Trudeau before Question Period. Standing in the crowd, sensibly dressed and sensible looking, was someone Daniel recognized: Robert McNeill, a Canadian by birth, then with BBC "Panorama," and later co-host of the McNeill-Lehrer PBS program. Shtarker liked McNeill's work.

Looking at him, empty-handed and ignored by the Trudeau press people, Daniel suddenly decided to act. "You're Robert McNeill, the Canadian expatriate, are you not?"

"Yes, I am," said McNeill.

"You don't know me — my name is Daniel Shtarker. Some

Canadians say I'm a national institution, others say I should be put in one. If you don't mind my saying so, I think you've got dick-all today, Mr. McNeill. You'll be babbling like a brook on BBC tonight because you've been unable to get anybody here in Canada to talk to you. Now me, I'm just your old-fashioned Good Samaritan. How would you and the BBC like to interview two former prime ministers?"

"Very, very much," said McNeill.

"Good," said Daniel, "I like to hear the sound of begging." McNeill and Shtarker both laughed. "I'll talk to both of them. I'm sure they'll do it," said Daniel. "I have the studio for three hours. I'll do each one for a half hour. Then after each one, you put your tape on and you do your interview. Okay?"

"Okay," said McNeill.

"See you at the CBC Lanark studios at 8:00 p.m. sharp."

"I'll be ready," said McNeill.

THE DIEFENBAKER house, when Daniel went there to pick him up, was an armed camp. Dief was on the FLQ hit list. There were ten soldiers on his roof and two at his front door. There was a platoon at the ready in jeeps parked on his front lawn. Inside the house, Diefenbaker had his own soldier bodyguard.

Dief and Shtarker sat in the back of a cab on the way to the studio. Up front, behind the driver, was a young soldier with an automatic assault rifle. When the cab turned into a cul-de-sac by mistake, the young soldier pushed the barrel of the gun into the driver's head. "No, no, he's not FLQ," said Diefenbaker. "He's just another Ottawa driver!" The soldier lowered his assault rifle and the cab went on to the CBC.

Shtarker's interview with Diefenbaker was a classic mix of humour and stroking, and did indeed reassure the nation. McNeill's interview with Diefenbaker was a bit bizarre — Diefenbaker tried to teach this damn Yankee a few Canadian tricks, and McNeill barely survived. Pearson went smoothly for Shtarker, and McNeill — finding a fellow intellectual at last — blossomed under Pearson's warmth.

As Shtarker and McNeill were cleaned up in the makeup room,

McNeill asked Shtarker, "Now that this is all over, what do you want from me, really want from me — you know what I mean?"

"I know what you mean. I'm not sure what I want from you now, but you owe me a favour. Someday I'll call it in. If you don't deliver, who knows, I may have your kneecaps broken." McNeill laughed a bit nervously. "Maybe it's all a parable, Mr. McNeill — you know, the McLuhan version of the Good Samaritan story. Maybe it was electric impulses in me that made me do this. But do we have a deal, Mr. McNeill?" Daniel asked.

"We have a deal," McNeill replied.

They shook hands and departed.

SITTING IN HIS STUDY, after the reading at the Belfast Loyalist fair, Daniel knew exactly what had to be done. He began to write a letter.

Dear Mr. McNeill: You may not remember me, but I remember you standing in the House of Commons during the October Crisis. You had no access to anyone when a guy with a big, big nose came up to you and acted like a Good Samaritan. He lined up two former prime ministers for you. In return, you agreed you owed me, Daniel Shtarker, a big favour. Now I'm calling in my favour. I'm a thirty-year veteran of television, so the directions I'm about to give will be simple.

I want you, for one day only, to scrap your usual format. I want you to open "The McNeill-Lehrer Newshour" one day on a close-up of my book, *Scorpions for Sale*. I then want you to pull back to a wide shot of the studio. In the middle of the studio will be me reading one of the stories. That should take about fifteen minutes. Then I want you to run an eight-minute video bio of myself that I happen to have on hand. That should lead naturally into a panel discussion of my book featuring Northrop Frye, Leslie Fiedler, and Adrienne Clarkson. Then, perhaps, a studio interview between you and me will round out the program.

Finally, that reference I made about kneecapping you if you didn't grant me my favour — I, of course, was only joking. I wouldn't know a Mafia member if I fell over one and have always thought Frank Sinatra, at worst, was a member of the B'nai B'rith.

Yours sincerely . . .

Daniel checked over his letter and sent it off. Returning to his study, he sat down at the phone. "Hello, Guillamo, is that you? Good! I might have a small collection problem I'm sure you can solve."

Postscript

D aniel Shtarker: At last, a chance to get out from the shadow of that master puppeteer, Zolf. He's been dangling me from his strings since this voyage started, and I'm seasick. I have never before been manipulated by a paranoiac egomaniac like Zolf. He's so thin-skinned that if you say, "Excuse me, I have to blow my nose," he at once blows his. The thing that drives me crazy is his obsession about Jews. Do you really believe that a rabbi would beat his son half to death? Is that kind of stuff good for the Jews, I ask you? Do you think it's fair to imply that other people are anti-Semitic when Zolf himself is probably a Jewish anti-Semite?

Larry Zolf: Wait a minute, Shtarker! I love my people! They're funny, smart, endearing.

Shtarker: Endearing, eh! Then why don't you write nice things about the Jews?

Zolf: What do you want me to do — write a fun piece about how wonderful the Reichmanns are? That's been done already, and look what happened!

Shtarker: No excuses, please! You berate rabbis, Jewish war heroes, Jewish women, outstanding Jewish leaders like Sam Bronfman! Let's face it, you're ambivalent about your own people!

Zolf: Who isn't ambivalent about the Jews? Jewishness breeds ambivalence! Why only ten commandments? Why not twenty? Why only one Wailing Wall where surely four are needed?

Shtarker: What about your slurs against the CBC? The CBC has nurtured and protected you for more than twenty-five years! Where's the gratitude? The Fernand Dubois you portray is some kind of monster! Are you really making fun of Pierre Juneau?

Zolf: Hold on! I can get rid of you by just trashing this whole manuscript right now. It might be fun to beat the critics to the punch. It might be nice to be an author of a nonexistent book. As for the CBC, I worship the ground Pierre Juneau, Denis Harvey, Trina McQueen, and Darce Fardy walk on. It is not an employment question but just plain admiration that adds Mark Starowicz, Ivan Fecan, Mike Lavoie, and Louise Lore to that list. The CBC encouraged me in all my writing and put their full resources behind me. The CBC is my life, so get off my back, you pushy little Jew!

Shtarker: Pushy little Jew, eh? You're at it again, Zolf. Ass kissing is not going to help you. Remember, no one is indispensable at the CBC. But let me pick another bone with you! Did you thank your wife and Julia Walden of the CBC? Did you thank the Boys at the Hop and Grape upon whom you foisted your stuff all the time — I just list Richard, Stanley, Frank, and Gordo. Did you thank Peter Worthington for the military advice he gave you? No. Did you thank Bruce Powe for his encouragement? Not a chance! How about Jack Hutchison, TSN, for his expert sports advice? Negative. What about Ben Keyfitz, former executive director of the Canadian Jewish Congress, who howled with laughter at your stories? Did you thank him? How about Vivian Rakoff, the world-famous psychiatrist who listened patiently to all your stories? Him too you forgot!

Zolf: I would have, given half a chance, if you hadn't been such a blabbermouth, Shtarker. I truly thank all the people you've mentioned. I would also like to thank my gifted lawyer, Michael Levine. And I wish to add thanks to Gloria Smith for the prodigious amount of typing that needed to be done. Now let me also add Jeanine Locke, Terry Filgate, George Robertson, F. M. Morrison, Paul Wright, Susan Teskey, and Brian Vallee of the CBC, who read my stories and urged me on.

Shtarker: What a laugh! You drove your CBC colleagues nuts, thrusting your stories at them in elevators, in their offices when

they were busy at work, on locations where they were filming —
shall I go on?

Zolf: Okay. I'm a bit insecure. Wouldn't you be? Critics criticize
me for writing about Jews or the CBC when that's all I really know
anything about. Canadian politics is only a hobby for me. Isn't
there anything in this book you really like, Shtarker?

Shtarker: Need some stroking do you, Zolf? Forget it. You've
abused, traduced, and compromised me and the Jewish people!
You've robbed me of my soul! You better find someone else to
manipulate in your next book!

Zolf: One at a time, Shtarker! One at a time! You're already being
remaindered at $3.99. If I had to live off you, I'd starve to death.
Thank God for the CBC! Mulroney tells me the CBC has got at
least twenty-five more years to go. That should enable me to
punch in my pension. As for you, Shtarker, I'm done with you.
Good riddance. You'll never darken my pages again!

Shtarker: Want to bet? Without me, you're nothing, Zolf — just
a motor-mouth in search of words to spew. I'll be seeing you again
soon!

Zolf: I know — and the thought is killing me.

Shtarker: You're a blowhard, Zolf — you always have been!

Zolf: Ladies and gentlemen, that's the last word Daniel Shtarker
will utter in this book, *Scorpions for Sale*, $26.95 at your nearest
bookstore.